ALSO BY VALERIE MARTIN

Set in Motion
Alexandra
A Recent Martyr
The Consolation of Nature
Mary Reilly
The Great Divorce

Italian Fever

Valerie Martin

Italian Fever

a novel

Alfred A. Knopf NEW YORK

1999

This Is a Borzoi Book
Published by Alfred A. Knopf, Inc.

All rights reserved under International and Pan-American Copyright Conventions. Published in the United States by Alfred A. Knopf, Inc., New York, and simultaneously in Canada by Random House of Canada Limited, Toronto. Distributed by Random House, Inc., New York.

www.randomhouse.com

Knopf, Borzoi Books, and the colophon are registered trademarks of Random House, Inc.

Library of Congress Cataloging-in-Publication Data
Martin, Valerie.
Italian fever : a novel / Valerie Martin. — 1st ed.
p.   cm.
ISBN 0-375-40542-9
I. Title.
PS3563.A7295I83   1999
813'.54—dc21   98-31824
CIP

Manufactured in the United States of America
Published July 1, 1999
Second Printing, September 1999

For Antonella Centaro and Sergio Perroni,
generous Italian friends
who resemble no one in this book

"Let her go to Italy!" he cried. "Let her
meddle with what she doesn't understand!"

—E. M. FORSTER
Where Angels Fear to Tread

Italian Fever

*D*V SAT AT his writing table rubbing his tired, itching eyes with clenched fists. A pad of paper lay between his elbows; a capped pen rested upon it. A cube of ice floating in a tumbler of bourbon gave a startling crack. The cool night air moving softly through the open window lifted the edge of the paper, then let it fall again. DV cursed, added her name, gave up rubbing his eyes, and rested his chin in his palms, gazing wearily out at the blue-black sky.

Once nothing had been easier. Now, night after night he sat like this between his former allies, the paper and the bourbon, waiting for a sentence to come to him, but nothing came. He took up the glass dutifully and swallowed the bourbon without tasting it, but he could feel it, the delicate adjustment in his consciousness, the muddling of his reflexes, the easing of his pain. He was still holding the glass to his lips when he heard the distinctive and familiar sound of gravel crunching underfoot on the drive outside. Two steps, then a pause, then another step.

He was on his feet, on the staircase, stumbling but quick, across the living room to the front door, which he threw open easily, for it was not locked. The man was there at the end of the drive, looking back at the house. He carried a rifle propped against his shoulder, but his posture was relaxed, not stiff; there was nothing soldierly about him. DV stepped out past the trellis that shaded the doorway. He wanted to be seen. "Wait," he said. His own voice mocked him. The word was useless, of course. He searched his memory for the proper substitute. *"Aspetta,"* he added.

But the man had turned away and was disappearing from the feet up as he plunged down the slope into the olive grove. In a moment he would be gone. "Not this time, buddy," DV said, hurling himself out across the drive. He could see his quarry moving away, though it was dark and there was a mist rising from the damp earth beneath the trees. Again he called out, *"Aspetta!"* and gave what chase he could. He had drunk too much. He could feel the dulling effects of the alcohol in his movements, the increased potential for losing some elementary contest with gravity. The man paused, looked back, then went on, ever downward, through the silvery trees. "He wants me to follow him," DV muttered, stumbling against a tree root and righting himself with a grasp at a passing branch. The ground was leveling out. They had come in a wide semicircle, for just ahead was the long, low wall that hid the villa from view. The man hurried alongside this wall, then abruptly turned toward the road. DV knew where they were now; he could see the lights from the windows of his landlord's cottage. The gate to the villa was ahead, guarding the Cini mansion, where the others were even now, doubtless, brooding and plotting against him. As he hurried past the gate, he glanced through the iron filigree, but all was darkness beyond. The cypress-lined lane curved away into the mist, like something from a movie or a dream, at once alluring and menacing. The man with the rifle had crossed the road and struck out into a plowed field. DV followed his quarry, but his thoughts circled the figure of the Cini grandson, his world-weary smile as he flicked open his lighter, his unctuous "Allow me," the oily, confidential way he inclined his head over her shoulder as he brought the little flame down to light her cigarette. No, DV thought, as his shoes sank in the soft mud of the field, there was nothing like the Cini family in America. Thank God for that.

It was hard going in the field. To keep his shoes from becoming bogged in the mud, he had to keep moving, so he adopted a kind of high-stepping jog, which was tiring but effective. There was a low fence at the far side; he could see the man leaning his rifle against it, then squatting to squeeze between the cross poles. He looked back, taking up his rifle, and DV, floundering in the mud, had a sudden humiliating vision of himself as a helpless and amusing target. The man was wearing a soft old-fashioned hat with a wide brim, not at all the sort of headgear one expected to see in the countryside, and as he turned away, he touched the edge with his thumb in a gesture that looked like a greeting. Then he stepped down— there was evidently a sharp decline at the edge of the field— and, shouldering his rifle, continued on his way.

By the time DV got to the fence, the man was nearly out of sight. There was a dry dirt road on the other side. He clambered down to it eagerly and stood for a moment stomping the mud from his shoes. His exertions had left him warm and nearly sober. He was able to consider the question of whether it was wise to continue his pursuit. He didn't know the road;

there was no telling where he might end up, how difficult the return would be. But going back now meant struggling through the muddy field. If he went along the road, he might find an easier route. As if to confirm this hope, he saw the diminishing figure of the man turning off toward the right, back toward the villa. He broke into an uneven trot. It was a relief to run on the hard-packed roadbed. He had lost sight of the man but didn't doubt that he would come into view again around the bend just ahead. But when he got there, to his surprise, the road forked and the man was nowhere in sight. DV stopped, bemused and breathless, and stood looking this way and that through the steam of his own breath upon the cool night air. One road led uphill, curving back the way he had come; the other went down, disappearing into a patch of low bushes and trees. He peered into the darkness, detecting some motion, a flash of white, which must surely be the man with the rifle. As he hurried along this low road, it crossed his mind, in some distant, half-conscious, inaccessible way, that if the man had been wearing anything white, he would have noticed it before now. The road narrowed steadily until the bushes on either side caught at the cuffs of his pants, but he pressed on. Soon there was only a thin path, so encroached upon by the surrounding vegetation that he was forced to look down to find his way. The ground was going up now; the path twisted, first right, then left, until he was not certain in which direction he was headed. There was no sign of the man with the rifle. DV lumbered on, but he was moving slowly. As he stumbled over a tree root, his fatigue and frustration surfaced in a string of low curses. He stopped again, looking behind, then ahead. Did he really have to turn back, retrace his steps and struggle across the wretched field again? The air was heavy; gradually, he became aware of a sickish odor, something more pungent than decaying vegetation. He would go a little farther, he decided; then, if the path continued impracticable, he would go back.

As he reached this decision, he heard the sharp crack of gunfire off to his right. His first impulse, which was to throw himself facedown on the ground, gave way to anger, and he veered toward the sound, his head lowered, his shoulders hunched forward, as if he expected to tackle his opponent. He charged a few yards through the underbrush, then came to a halt, finding himself in a wide, empty clearing. He turned around slowly, listening, trying to gauge the dimensions of the space, which was difficult in the darkness. Overhead he could see a spray of stars, very bright, for there was no artificial light to dim the heavens. The smell, fetid and sickening, was stronger. He covered his nose with his hand. Whatever it was, it was nearby. Suppose, he thought, it was a dead body, another American perhaps, lured out here, as he had been, by the man with the rifle, and murdered, as he would be if he didn't give up the chase.

Then, as he stood in the clearing, a terrible confusion came over him and he understood that he was lost. He couldn't remember where he had come in, and the vegetation was as closed all around as a room with no door. He went to the spot where he thought he might have entered, but there was no evidence that it was the right one; there were no broken leaves or branches and he couldn't see the ground well enough to make out anything like a footprint. The unpleasant smell made him anxious; it seemed to be rolling over him in waves. His stomach turned and his throat contracted. What was he doing out here? How had he come to this insalubrious pass? He covered his nose with his hand again and stood, head lowered, listening to the dense silence of the woods. Surely if he could only manage to walk straight in any direction, he would eventually come to some road. This was Italy, after all. It wasn't some uncharted wilderness. He scanned the heavens for something to navigate by, but the truth was, he knew nothing about the stars, nor was the moon anywhere to be seen. At least if he kept walking, he could eventually escape the gagging smell. He pushed at the foliage, which gave way easily enough, and took a few steps. As quickly as the way opened before him, it closed behind. He went on—there was nothing else to do—though the way grew more difficult and the rancid air invaded his nose and mouth and burned his eyes. Again he took up a slow jog, trying not to notice the disproportionate increase in his heart rate. He was going steadily downhill, he could feel it, and this seemed comforting for some reason, perhaps because it indicated some discernible direction. Then, through a break in the trees, he saw something promising, a low hill covered with scrub and at the top a whitewashed building, perhaps the outbuilding of a farm. There would be more difficulty ahead; he would have to explain somehow who he was and where he wanted to be, but if he just kept repeating "Villa Cini," surely he could get someone to lead him that far. A wave of optimism buoyed him up and spurred him on. He picked up speed.

Then several things happened at once. He emerged into a narrow, open area where the decline was suddenly very steep. The fetid smell rose up around him like a swarm of furious insects, so that even as he lost his footing, flailing his arms to regain his balance, his stomach contracted violently, causing him to pitch forward, stumbling and vomiting, first to his knees, then, as the ground slipped away beneath him, head over heels. His brain buzzed with activity, every system becoming alert, but he was completely at the whim of gravity, dragged relentlessly down, while terror pumped out such a flood of adrenaline that his senses were suddenly, excruciatingly acute and time came to a standstill. He saw the slick sole of his own shoe go by and thought wistfully of the running shoes in his wardrobe at the house. His fall was generating a shower of dirt and gravel, which stung his cheeks and choked him. His chin was wet. Was it blood or vomit? One arm was trapped behind him, causing the muscles in his bad shoulder to tear painfully. He would be sore for weeks. If he could only get his legs under him long enough to lie flat, he might be able to stop this endless hurtling downhill. His head and chest came up into the air. He saw something just ahead, something white, jutting out of the soil, and he heard the word *concrete* as clearly as if someone had pronounced it next to his ear. It had not, he thought, been a good idea to come to Italy. She was gone, and now this. He said her name. He heard a sharp pop, not gunfire, but something much worse, very close, and then, in the last moment, he knew he was entirely free of the earth and that the all-engulfing blackness he was entering had nothing to do with anything outside his own shattered skull.

Chapter 1

"OH, FOR GOD'S SAKE," Lucy exclaimed. "It's a ghost story." She dropped the page she was reading onto the smaller of the two stacks that filled every inch of the available space on her cluttered desk. This manuscript, the first half of DV's latest novel, had arrived from Italy the day before. The package was tattered and stained, the postmark a month old. Why had DV shipped it by sea mail? In preparation for the labor of transcribing it onto the computer, Lucy had passed the morning reading it, experiencing, as she always did when confronted by her employer's contributions to the world of letters, a steady elevation of blood pressure and an involuntary clenching of the jaw that made her face ache. The page she took up next was as covered over with scratches, lines, and mysterious explosions of ink as an aerial photograph of a war zone. Why, she wondered, did it take such an effort for DV to write so poorly?

Under different names, in different settings, the narrators

of DV's novels were all the same man: a self-absorbed, pretentious bore, always involved in a tragic but passionate relationship with a neurotic, artistic, beautiful woman, always caught up in some far-fetched rescue adventure, dipping occasionally into the dark underworld of thugs and hired murderers, or rising to the empyrean abodes, the glittering palaces of the wealthy and the elite. The whole absurd mess was glazed over with a sticky treacle of trite homilies and tributes by the narrator to himself for being so strong and wise and brave when everyone around him was scarcely able to get out of bed. He was usually a writer or a journalist; sometimes he traveled. When he traveled, he was always recovering from an emotional crisis and he was always alone. This time, his name was Malcolm Manx, described by himself in the early pages as "an American writer of some reputation." Devastated by the breakup of a passionate but tragic marriage, he has secluded himself in a villa in Tuscany, where he hopes to find peace, inspiration, and a renewed interest in life.

Lucy placed her frog paperweight carefully on the pages and stalked off to the kitchen. To read on, she would need a cup of herbal tea, a glass of water, and two aspirin. The book was awful. DV's books were always awful, but what made this one worse than the others was the introduction of a new element, which was bound to boost sales: There was a ghost in the villa. DV had gone gothic. It wasn't enough that the unsuspecting Italians must succumb to the bold and original charms of the devastated American writer; now he was haranguing the dead as well.

The ghost was the restless spirit of a dead Resistance fighter, a partisan, ambushed by fascist forces in the yard of his own estate. This dead warrior, mirabile dictu, shared with Malcolm Manx both a staunch love of liberty and an ancestor from the rugged Basque country. The presence of such a soul mate, a comrade, stomping through the family olive groves in search of peace and old-world wisdom had so excited the murdered partisan that he got right out of his grave, and now he was wandering around pointing at things, always in the dead of night, when everyone was asleep, everyone but Malcolm Manx, who was up and struggling with the big, hard questions of life and art.

For reasons Lucy usually tried not to think about, DV's books sold well. A few had been made into movies, and DV was encouraged by everyone around him to write more. Reviews were rare, however, and seldom favorable, which galled him, but he had learned to take satisfaction in the size of his bank account.

Through eight years and five novels, Lucy Stark had worked for DV. He never asked her what she thought of his books and she never told him. She was, in his phrase, "the assistant," or sometimes, more accurately, "the office." She kept track of everything, made sure he didn't see the worst reviews, kept his ex-wives at bay, handled his mail, supervised the flow in and out of large sums of money, and transcribed every word of his wretched prose from the tattered, indecipherable pages he sent her to the computer he had never learned to use.

In the early years, she had tried to straighten out some of his worst sentences; she had balked when a mixed metaphor strained to include a fourth incongruent element, but those days were gone. DV had complained to his editor, Stanton Cutler, who had called Lucy and explained, politely but firmly, that she must restrain her no doubt rightful enthusiasm. "Just think of it as a draft," he suggested.

Armed with her tea, dosed with painkillers, Lucy returned

to her desk and took up the page that had driven her from the room.

A dark and brooding figure beckoned him eerily on the moon-lit drive, and Malcolm felt his burning blood turn to ice in his veins.

"Jesus," Lucy said.

The phone rang. She dropped the page, reached over the lamp, caught the teacup in the cuff of her sweater, and watched in horror as the tea spilled out across the manuscript. Bringing the receiver to her ear with one hand, she lifted the soaking page with the other and tried to funnel the hot liquid into the wastebasket. The tea poured out across the carpet.

"Lucy Stark, please?" a woman's voice inquired.

"This is she."

"American embassy in Rome calling. Please hold."

And in the next moment, as she knelt beside her desk, blotting at the tea stains with a page of newsprint hastily torn from last week's book review, a hostile, disembodied male voice came on the line and gave her the astonishing news that DV was dead.

Chapter 2

"H E FELL DOWN a well."

"This is terrible." Jean McKay, DV's agent, was the first person Lucy informed of his unexpected demise. "How could a grown man fall down a well?"

"I don't know," Lucy replied. "The embassy man didn't tell me much. He seemed annoyed with DV for dying. He wouldn't even say when it happened; he just said, 'It wasn't yesterday.' And he didn't seem to know anything about Catherine. Where is Catherine? Why didn't she call?"

"It's mysterious," Jean observed.

"It *is* mysterious," Lucy agreed.

"DV would have liked that. He always wanted to be mysterious."

The women divided up the necessary business. Jean agreed to return the call to Italy, to call DV's lawyer and his editor.

Lucy would contact his accountant and his ex-wives. Then they would talk again and decide what was to be done.

It took Lucy the rest of the morning to finish these calls. She switched from tea to coffee and returned to her desk, where DV's ghost novel lay before her, still damp from the tea accident, its pages curling at the edges, mutely accusing. Was it possible? Wasn't it thicker than it had been before she received the call from the embassy?

It doesn't matter if it is, she thought. She would not now transfer even one word onto the computer; what would be the point? It wasn't finished and now it never would be. DV's ghost story would live in no other memory than her own. She tried to work up some feeling about this. It bothered her that no one she had spoken to so far had expressed anything more serious than vexation at the news of DV's untimely death. The wives had been particularly unfeeling.

Poor DV. Jean was right; he had wanted to be mysterious, but he never was. He was as transparent as a shallow pool. There were ripples now and then on the surface, caused by how thoroughly he failed to know his own limitations, his own lack of depth. In her opinion, the move to Italy had been one of those ripples, and now it had cost him everything. What had possessed him to make such a flamboyant, impractical move?

The phone startled her from her reverie. Jean had talked with the embassy official and, through an interpreter, the landlord and even the coroner, who wanted to ship DV's body home. "No one wants that," Lucy said. "It would be too macabre."

"I know," Jean agreed. "So someone has to go over there and get him buried. I can't. I can't leave right now. I'll arrange a memorial service here."

"Did you find out anything about Catherine?"

"She's gone." Jean paused. Lucy could hear her sipping something, coffee, no doubt. "The landlord was vague about that. He didn't know when she left, but he said he thought DV had been living alone there for some time."

"Really?" Lucy tried to picture DV alone, wandering about the vast and gloomy villa he described in the manuscript, an ancient stone mansion complete with tapestries, family por-traits, and a sinister family chapel in which the decadent aris-tocrats were routinely christened and from which they were carried out in their coffins. She couldn't picture it.

"Do any of the wives want to go?" Jean asked.

"No. They just want to know what's going to happen to the money."

"Can you go?"

She had been to Italy once, when she was still in college, a monthlong backpack and train trip with two friends from school. The trio had resisted the pinches and leers of gorgeous Italian men from Naples to Trieste, it was as hot as an oven, and they were so poor, they lived on pizza slices and little sand-wiches and slept in tiny, sparsely furnished rooms, with the bath down the hall. In the churches, piazzas, and museums of Venice, Florence, Rome, and Naples, Lucy sought the fabulous treasures she had studied, and each time she found one, she marveled anew at the inadequacy of reproductions to give even a hint of the power of the originals. Art in its home, she thought, at ease in its natural habitat. It was like encountering the tiger, seen previously stalking nervously behind iron bars at a zoo, sleeping peacefully in its own lair. At the end of the trip, the three friends had splurged on a big trattoria meal in Rome, then staggered full and tipsy out into the broiling streets, blinded by tears at the thought of going home.

"Yes," she said. "I can go."

So it was agreed. She was to leave that very night. Jean promised to have an interpreter meet her in Rome and drive her up to the villa in Ugolino. She called the neighbor with whom she had a reciprocal cat-care arrangement, canceled a lunch date, and made a new message for the answering machine.

Later, when she was packing, Lucy considered the questions she found most difficult to answer. Why had DV stayed on after Catherine left? And why had he never mentioned her departure? He had communicated with Lucy by express mail, sending lists and terse instructions; there was rarely a personal note. If he was anxious or unhappy, he hadn't bothered, or hadn't wanted, to let her know. But if Catherine had left him, he must have been more alone than he had ever been in his life: alone in his villa with his ghost.

And even the ghost, she speculated, couldn't have been much in the way of company: DV had never learned more than ten words of Italian.

LUCY HARDLY SLEPT on the plane. It was crowded, noisy; the food was terrible, the usual. Some passengers were resigned; others never would be. She tried to concentrate on her book, *The Art of Ecstasy: Teresa, Bernini, and Crashaw*, but after a brief perusal of the excellent photographs of Bernini's *St. Teresa*, her thoughts began to wander and she gave herself over to following them. She thought about DV and about DV's writing. The fact that there would be no more novels meant she was out of a job, though it would take a month or two to get everything cleared away. This didn't concern her, as she felt certain she could find another job; the years with

DV had provided her with many contacts and she knew how to do a great many useful things. She was enormously, inappropriately relieved that his unfinished book would not see the light of print, for it represented a departure she found troubling.

Everyone knew DV's novels were thinly disguised accounts of his own life; that was what he meant by the word *realism*. He was fond of admitting this in interviews, as if the paucity of his imagination made the books more valuable. Of course, anyone who knew DV even slightly knew he exaggerated some things absurdly, particularly the invariable physical attractiveness of his narrators. These were always big, strong men with large appetites, big ideas. DV was not five feet five. He was not strong, was often ill, and had so thoroughly destroyed his digestive tract with bourbon that he subsisted on a bland diet of boiled meat and rice. He did have a large, rather handsome head, which was displayed to great advantage on the back covers of his novels. His dark hair and brows were thick, his nose strong and straight, his mouth shapely, and he had lively, soulful brown eyes. He had a big laugh he used when he needed attention and couldn't get it any other way. The laugh was heard mostly in public, at readings and dinners, and especially during interviews, when he used it to cover embarrassing pauses.

He had been married three times, never for long. In his mind, the wives were all insane and he had done his best to rescue them from themselves, but it was hopeless; in spite of his passionate attachment to each of them, in the end he had had to save himself. He had not been able to save a large part of his income, however, which went out in alimony and child-support checks every month. In Lucy's view, the wives were interchangeable, stupid, mean-spirited women who had spotted him as an easy mark. He had two children by two wives, a boy of ten and a girl of twelve. These, presumably, would inherit his estate.

Lucy had met Catherine Bultman on a few occasions and once they had chatted briefly about Caravaggio, Catherine's favorite painter. No one could figure out how DV had talked her into his life or what she saw in him. What he saw in her was obvious. She was beautiful, talented, intelligent, and eminently sane. She had refused to marry him, and the move to Italy was part of a plan he had to get her to change her mind. She had studied painting in Florence and spoke Italian fluently. DV promised her a studio of her own. He would write; she would paint—it would be a perfect artist's paradise.

The first two chapters of the ghost novel were all about life at the villa, how the shattered American writer endeared himself to the gentle country people who worked for him, how the neighboring aristocrats delighted in inviting him for long, elegant dinners, after which he walked back alone through the groves of olives and the lane of cypress trees that sheltered the drive to his villa. On one of these walks, while brooding over the tempestuous affair he was having with a beautiful artist, he first saw the ghost.

One thing that was odd, Lucy thought, was that Malcolm Manx's description of the affair was particularly painful and bitter. It was the closest thing to a description of real human suffering DV had ever written. It wasn't good, by any means; his rendering of their lovemaking was the usual clot of hyperbole, but there was a scene in which, after a violent quarrel, the beautiful artist, perfectly sane and utterly cold, closes the door on the American writer, leaving him undecided whether to go to the window and watch her drive away or remain with his forehead pressed against the door—this, Lucy had been forced to admit, was different from anything DV had written before. It was straightforward, sad, and touchingly rendered.

Was it possible that before DV fell down the well he had actually experienced the torture of love and loss, the overturning of everything, the 3:00 a.m. confrontation with the soul in which the ordinary, self-serving lies fail to disguise the unbearable truth, that through one's own folly the beloved has been lost and that without the beloved there is no light, there is no life?

It seemed unlikely.

The hours dragged by. She skipped the movie and tried to sleep, but the large man snoring next to her made it impossible. The air supply dwindled and the constant cough of the woman two rows ahead guaranteed the passengers the opportunity to contract something virulent and debilitating. The attendants fanned out carrying coffeepots and hard rolls, and the edges of the closed window shades began to glow dimly. They had flown through the night into the morning. Lucy opened her shade and looked out into the pale light of the upper atmosphere. Soon the plane would begin its descent over France, then a brief turn over the Mediterranean and down into Italy. In spite of the sad nature of her mission, she felt a keen rush of excitement.

In the early chapters of the ghost novel, DV always referred to Italy as "she." It was a convention Lucy despised. Italy was always revealing her treasures, turning her smiling face upon the visitor, spreading her table with the rich tapestry of her harvest, pouring out her hospitality, guarding her secrets, taunting her admirers with hints at the dark knowledge of her endless, mysterious, sinister past. She was a mother, a kind sister, a priestess, a strumpet, a generous, good-natured, but avaricious whore. DV couldn't get enough of this sort of language. The thought made Lucy so irritable, she decided to distract herself by queuing up for the bathroom.

Italy. La Bell'Italia. The smiling faces of her sun-loving people. It was guidebook talk. By the time Lucy got back to her seat, the plane was crossing her polluted, ineffable coast. Somewhere down there DV lay, out of this world now, but soon to be back in it; only this time, he wouldn't be writing about the experience. His pen had been silenced by the rich, romantic soil of Italy. Now he would lie mute forever—how it would have charmed him—tucked away deep in her ancient, all-encompassing heart.

HE WAS STANDING at the front of the eager crowd, resting the small cardboard rectangle with her name scratched lightly upon it against the rail that separated those arriving from those receiving. Unlike his neighbors, he was not scanning the passengers hopefully; in fact, he was not even looking in their direction. He was entirely absorbed by a spot he had discovered on the sleeve of his elegant jacket. He brushed at it with his thumb, frowning fiercely, his brow furrowed in concentration. Lucy approached the rail and stopped in front of him. Gradually, reluctantly, he became aware of her presence and looked up at her coldly. "That's me," she said, pointing to the sign.

"Signora Stark," he said without enthusiasm. He pronounced it "Staak." He gestured toward the opening at the end of the rail. "Go that way," he said. "I will meet you there."

Lucy turned her cart back into the crowd, pleased to have a few moments to recover from the unsettling combination of his icy manner and his extraordinary good looks. He was not a big man, but he was bulky and strong, of the bullish physical type Lucy classified as "stevedore," and which she always found attractive. He had the wonderful tan skin and thick black hair one associates with the country she was now entering, but his eyes were a light, clear green, quite startling to look into, like finding a wolf's eyes in a shepherd dog's face. His expression was gloomy, humorless, and bored. She judged him to be in his early forties, several years older than she was, at any rate. Chauffering American women around was clearly not what he wanted to be doing with his time. Lucy wondered how much he knew about her mission.

She cleared the rails and fell into step alongside him. "I am Massimo Compitelli," he informed her, chivalrously taking over her luggage cart. "I will be driving you to Ugolino."

"Will you be staying with me there?"

He cast her a quick appraising look. "I will stay with you until you are finished with the authorities."

"Good," she said. "That's a relief. How far is it?"

"A drive of perhaps three hours."

She glanced at her watch. It would be well past lunchtime when they arrived. The coffee and roll she had eaten had left her light-headed and nauseated. She didn't want to identify the remains of DV on an empty, rebellious stomach. "Could I get something to eat along the way, Signor Compitelli?" she said. "Just a sandwich would do."

They had arrived at the elevator to the parking lot. He gave her a long, steady, curious look, which she ducked by fiddling with her purse latch. Just what sort of creature is this, his survey seemed to ask, this foreigner I am to be responsible for? Lucy looked up, smiling weakly. "I'm very tired," she said.

He continued his scrutiny, his lips slightly pursed with thought. "Yes," he said as the elevator door snapped open, disgorging a surprising number of people and luggage carts. "I know a place not far from here where we can stop." She followed him into the narrow elevator. A few other travelers pushed in behind and she was pressed against the back wall between two carts. He turned to her as they began their ascent to the parking lot. "Please call me Massimo," he said.

Good, Lucy thought, sagging against the wall. He has made up his mind to befriend me.

Chapter 3

*D*v's books had not done particularly well in Italy, although three of them had been translated and published there—the two that had been made into films and another, his last book, which was sold abroad on the strength of a movie deal that never came off. Massimo Compitelli worked for the Italian publisher, though Lucy was not able to determine in what capacity. He didn't seem to be an editor. He did freelance work of some kind; it sounded a bit like agenting. Perhaps he was a scout. She questioned him about this over a grilled eggplant sandwich at the gleaming bar he took her to just on the outskirts of Rome, but his answers were cryptic. He was visibly appalled by her insistence on drinking a cappuccino with her food, but too polite to say anything. She tried changing the subject. "So you live in Rome?" she said.

"Yes."

"And your family lives here as well?"

He forced a little puff of indignation through his chiseled nostrils. "My family has been in Rome for a thousand years."

Ancestor snobbery, Lucy thought. The food, the excellent coffee, the sun that was warming the stones on the raised step where their table perched precariously, the fatigue of the journey, and the archetypal behavior of her companion combined to make her giddy. "Any popes?" she asked.

"What?"

"In your family. Any popes?"

He regarded her with suspicion. Was she making fun of his family? "Actually, yes," he said. "There was one, a long time ago. A very short time, he was pope."

"Was he a good pope?"

"No." He took a cigarette from a pack in his pocket and began feeling about for his lighter. "A very bad pope. He was murdered, I think."

Lucy finished her coffee, excused herself, and went off in search of the bathroom, leaving Massimo to stretch out his legs into the sunlight, clearly content to enjoy his cigarette alone. When she returned, he rose languidly, flicking the cigarette stub into the street. They got back into the car.

Since leaving the airport, they had been on congested highways, careening through ugly suburbs, but now, suddenly, they were in the countryside, the gently undulating cultivated vineyards, the olive groves, the stands of cypress and umbrella pines, the steep, jutting hills capped with ancient walled towns that have for centuries charmed even the most jaded, travel-weary eye. If the beauty of the scene hadn't taken her breath away, the speed at which they hurtled through it surely would have. However, Lucy noticed, Massimo wasn't passing anyone. Indeed, they were occasionally roared down upon and left behind. Massimo appeared perfectly calm. She put her seat back and gave herself over to dreamy contemplation of the landscape and the unexpectedness of finding herself in it. She felt a throb of gratitude to DV for dying here.

"You are married, Signora Stark?" Massimo asked.

Her head followed her eyes as she shifted them in his direction. He was studying the road ahead. "No," she said. "I was. But not anymore." He nodded. They both noted the quick inspection she gave to the wide gold band on his right ring finger.

"You can sleep a little now, if you like," he said.

"Thanks. I think I will," she said. And she did.

TUSCANY IS STUDDED with beautiful little towns, each justly famous for something, be it the perfection of its piazza, the charm of its bell tower, the unusual frescoes in its church, the refreshing air of its hilltop setting, the view from its ancient walls, or the incomparable *bistecca* served at the restaurant, formerly a monastery, a castle, or a farmhouse, which can be reached by a short drive along a picturesque lake, a cypress-lined avenue, or a vineyard. Ugolino is not one of these. "Before yesterday, I never hear of this town," Massimo commented as he turned down a rough narrow road between two fields of dry plowed dirt. "How did your friend find it?"

"He wanted something quiet," Lucy said.

"Something quiet," Massimo snorted. "The grave is quiet." Then, after a moment in which the cruel irony of his remark became apparent to them both, he said, "Please excuse me. I have spoken without thinking."

"No. It's all right. What you say is true."

The road diverged at the end of two fields. One fork was paved, leading uphill toward a line of cypress; the other, dirt, ran downhill between more dried clods of earth. Massimo swerved onto the latter, raising a cloud of dust in the cool afternoon air. The sky was a deep, almost alarming blue and it stretched ahead of them like something solid; it seemed they might smash into it at every moment. DV died in this autumn light, Lucy thought. Did he fall into the well under a sky as bright and serene as this one? They came to a sign—UGOLINO, 2 KM—and after that a few ugly modern apartment buildings perched at the edge of the road; then the road widened. They passed a bar where a few men sat at two plastic tables. After that, their way was lined on both sides with stone dwellings, the shutters open to the light, clothes dripping from lines stretched between the windows, the occasional flower box, an old woman leaning out on one side, upbraiding a sullen-looking boy on a bicycle who moved reluctantly out of their path as they passed. Then, abruptly, they entered the treeless, dusty piazza of Ugolino with its cluster of public amusements and services: a bar, an *alimentari,* the doorway shielded from bugs by strips of faded multicolored plastic, the town hall and police station, with CARABINIERI printed neatly in large black letters on the white plaster over the door. As Massimo pulled up, this door opened and two young men in uniform came out, talking animatedly. Massimo got out of the car and Lucy followed. The two policemen, absorbed in their conversation, which was punctuated by shouts of laughter, ignored them and strolled away in the direction of the bar.

"We will go in here," Massimo said. "They are expecting you."

They entered a long, low-ceilinged whitewashed room with a counter across one end, beyond which a few desks and straight-backed chairs were scattered haphazardly. Each desk sported a typewriter of classic design: Like the ones in fifties film noir, Lucy thought. The room was dim; the only light came in at two long windows on one side.

It was also completely empty of humanity. Massimo looked about pointedly for a few moments, as if he expected to scare someone into view by the penetration of his eye beams, but he, too, was soon forced to admit that no one was there.

"Perhaps they've gone to lunch," Lucy suggested.

He glanced at his watch. "Lunch," he said impatiently. "It is four-thirty."

"Well. I guess we'll have to wait."

"I have no time for waiting," he exclaimed, and went back through the door. Lucy followed and stood watching as he charged down the street—there was no sidewalk—to the bar. I am fortunate to have Massimo, she thought. She looked up and down; the town was eerily silent. As there were no trees, there wasn't even the occasional twittering bird in residence. After a few moments, the bar door flew open and the two policemen came out into the bright street, followed by a gesticulating Massimo. He herded them toward her; they were clearly unwilling, eager to run astray. When they got closer, she saw that they were really just boys, perhaps eighteen or nineteen, and that they were torn between their inexperience and their conviction that the perfectly tailored and pressed uniforms they wore gave them all the authority in the world. One sauntered past Lucy, hardly giving her a glance; the other followed, responding to Massimo with raised voice. His hand made little chops at the air near his face. As he passed, he delivered his closing remark with a quick thrust of an open palm, nearly striking her. She ducked; Massimo cast her a look of horror. Somehow, all four shoved back through the door. "These are idiots," Massimo said blandly as he pursued the two young men through the gate in the counter. One began taking files out of drawers, then carefully putting them back in. The other threw himself onto a chair with exaggerated huffiness, took up a pen, and began turning it over and over in his hand.

"What are they doing?" she asked.

"They are pretending that Americans fall into wells every day here," Massimo said.

"Will they let me see my friend? Is he here?"

Massimo burst into a long stream of Italian, which the young men interrupted almost at once and in unison. Gradually, the volume went up, each striving to make himself heard over the others. Then abruptly, the conversation ended. Massimo turned to her. "They say you cannot see him." He paused. Lucy detected a flicker of concern. He was uncertain how best to proceed. "There has been an autopsy." He lingered over the last word, got the stress wrong, on the second syllable. "It would not be a good thing for you to see him."

"But I have to identify him," she protested. "I have to be sure it *is* him."

He studied her momentarily, looking for signs of hysteria. "Signora Stark," he said, his voice controlled, conciliatory. "Your friend has been identified by his landlord and by his passport. There is no doubt that it is he. An autopsy is . . . It will not be good for you to see him."

"Because I wouldn't recognize him," Lucy said.

"I am afraid you would not."

"Can't they show me something? Isn't there some proof beyond someone's word?"

Massimo addressed the young man at the file drawer, who had, apparently, found the one he was looking for. There was a brief ceremony, the passing of the file from policeman to interpreter to American. A sensation of dread made Lucy turn away from the men. She took the file to the counter and opened it.

It was DV, she knew at once, but for a moment she tried to tell herself there was some mistake. How could the self-satisfied, confident, brash, excitable man she had known be reduced to this wizened and grimacing mask of fear? His upper lip was pulled back from his teeth in a way she had never seen it in life, and his forehead was furrowed over his open, sightless eyes. His thick hair was plastered flat against his skull, flecked with leaves and dirt. Just at the hairline, there was a dark gash, the skin puckered and bruised around it. There were three photographs, two of his face and one of his whole body stretched out flat on a table, still dressed, but without his shoes. She recognized the sweater he was wearing, though it was torn and stained—his favorite blue cashmere.

Lucy fought down a wave of nausea so powerful, it made her grasp the counter and groan. She had always referred to DV as "my employer." She thought of him sometimes as "the scribbler," or "the Marrying Man," but the word that presented itself then as she looked at this awful proof of his death was *friend*. My poor friend, she thought, and tears overflowed her eyes.

Instantly, the three haughty and quarrelsome men were transformed into a team of comforting grandmothers. "The signora is crying," she understood Massimo to say, followed by a few terse orders she couldn't follow. A chair materialized next to her, a clean white handkerchief was pressed into her hand, and a glass of mineral water was poured out from a bottle and offered to her with soft, encouraging words. She sat down gratefully on the chair, dried her eyes with the handkerchief, accepted and drank the cool water. "It *is* my friend," she gasped, before a fresh torrent of tears overtook her. "I'm sorry," she added between sobs.

"But signora," Massimo assured her. "You must not apologize. This is a great shock." The young policemen exchanged subdued phrases she took to be further sympathy. One hovered over her; the other spirited the empty glass away. She cried for a few minutes while the men waited patiently. They didn't seem to mind. Then she stopped. "I'm all right now," she told Massimo, folding the handkerchief and making a few last dabs at her eyes. "What do I have to do?"

Massimo spoke softly to the young policeman who was returning the photographs to the file. "You must sign some papers," he said. "Then, if you wish to bury your friend here . . ."

"I do," she said.

"We will arrange for a place—how do you say . . ."

"A plot," she said.

"A plot," he echoed uncertainly. "You will want the services of a priest?"

"No. DV was not religious."

"There will be no ceremony?" He looked distressed.

"They're having a ceremony in the States," she said. "His friends and his family."

His distress turned to puzzlement. "I see," he said.

Who would go to DV's memorial service? His editor, his agent, various people who made money from his books, maybe one or two of the wives, the ones with kids, maybe not. His parents were dead, and he was not on speaking terms with his brother. A few acquaintances might show up, other writers, as friendless, ultimately, as he was. More tears welled up at these thoughts. "Can I hold on to your handkerchief for a while?" Lucy said, getting up.

"Of course," Massimo replied.

"Thanks," she said. "Let's get on with it."

The funeral business in Italy is not the profitable, professional operation it is in the United States. The vigil is generally held in the deceased's home, and the interment is accomplished without the services of a funeral director. Ugolino was so small, Lucy was able to make the arrangements for DV's burial right there in the police station. There was some difficulty about money because the police were not equipped to take credit cards, and a check drawn on an American bank was useless to them. She explained to Massimo that she could get a wire transfer from DV's bank that night and would be able to have the cash in lire the next day.

"But how can you take money from his bank when he cannot sign for it?" Massimo asked.

"I know all the right codes," she said.

Massimo's light eyes darkened at this allusion to the recondite world of American technology. He said a few words to the policemen, who assured him that the burial could go forward the moment the money was in their hands. To this end, the grave digger was summoned. He arrived so quickly, Lucy assumed he, too, had been in the bar. He was a gnarled and twisted old fellow, garrulous and odoriferous, like something out of Shakespeare. Whenever he spoke, Massimo seemed to draw himself more tightly into his coat, his handsome features knit in an expression of deep revulsion. After a great deal of talk, it was decided that Lucy must see and approve the plot.

"What about a coffin?" she asked. "Don't I have to choose one?"

"This is provided," Massimo said curtly.

So after shaking hands all round and agreeing that DV would be laid to rest the evening of the following day, Mas-

simo, Lucy, and the grave digger walked out to the little cemetery that was to be the future home of the famous American
writer. The sun was going down and it was much cooler; there
was a gusty wet wind that made Lucy button her jacket as they
walked along. The cemetery was a simple, pleasant spot at the
end of a dirt road, surrounded by a concrete wall that rose
toward the back because the ground wasn't level. There were
four cypress trees, one at each corner. The graves were marked
with headstones or small urns; many had glass insets covering
photos of the deceased, who smiled benignly, eternally, upon
those who came to mourn. There were plastic flowers, some in
vases, some just strewn over the graves. The plots were lined in
concrete; they were, in fact, sunken concrete boxes filled with
dirt. The old grave digger, who had never stopped talking from
the moment he had first appeared, pointed from one grave to
another, rattling on, presumably about the occupants. He
stopped at one, the only one with fresh flowers on it, and after
a few sentences fell suddenly quiet. "This is a young woman,"
Massimo told Lucy, "who committed suicide a few months
ago."

"How awful," she said.

The old man, who stood with his head slightly bowed, his
dirt-stained hands clutching at each other over his heavy
thighs, raised his eyes to hers and flashed a lewd toothless grin.
Then he hurled a mass of language at Massimo. She detected
the word *straniera,* and *la signora.* He's talking about me,
Lucy thought. "What did he say?" she asked.

"It is difficult to understand this man," Massimo replied.
"He is very stupid and has not enough teeth."

DV's plot was at the back, on the high ground. She didn't
particularly want to linger over it; it was like the others. Massimo seemed to sense her reluctance, for after a moment he

interrupted the grave digger's endless monologue and led her away. The old man followed them to the gate, then took up a shovel he had left there and turned back, still muttering, addressing the captive audience under the soil of his grim domain.

The Roman and his American charge walked back down the road without speaking. Lucy was feeling low, cast down by the business at hand and fatigued from lack of sleep. She wanted a shower, a glass of wine, a plate of food—she didn't care what—then a long sleep. She didn't know what she would find at DV's villa, where it had been arranged that she would stay, and she was anxious about being left there. When they got into the car, Massimo took out a sheet of directions and studied it silently.

"Is the villa very far?" she asked.

"No," he said. "Only a few minutes. The *casa colonica* is just beyond that. We are to pick up the keys at the owner's, which is across the road from the villa."

This information arrived in her consciousness with a demoralizing though not unexpected thud, like the news that an incorrigible relative has been arrested again. "What's a *casa colonica*?"

"It is the house—how do you say?—the farmhouse where you will be staying."

"I thought I was staying in the villa?"

"No, that is not what is indicated here. Your friend had rented the farmhouse, and I am to take you there."

"That's odd," she said. "He called it a villa."

"These people call everything a villa. They call a converted cow barn a villa. It is the *agriturismo*. It is disgusting."

"I see," Lucy said, though she didn't. "Well, it will be fine with me, if it has a hot shower."

Massimo folded his instructions carefully and put them in his inside pocket. "It is cooler here than in the city," he said. "I will make sure these people have turned on the heat for you."

"Where will you stay?" she asked.

"I will stay in Sansepolcro. I have a cousin there. I will come again tomorrow to take you to the town."

"Thank God," she said gratefully, sinking back into the comfortable seat. "Thank God for you, Massimo."

He gave her a tight smile, then turned his attention to starting the car. Though it was not particularly cool, he pushed the heat up full blast as they whirled around the tiny piazza and up the hill to DV's last official residence on earth.

Chapter 4

ASSIMO'S NEXT STOP was a small stone house surrounded by a low wire-and-brick-fenced yard in which several chickens wandered about listlessly. He went to the door, vowing to extract the keys without involving Lucy, but the old couple and their son, who had been awaiting her arrival with a great deal on their minds, insisted that she be brought in, seated at the kitchen table with a glass of *vin santo* and a hard *biscotto,* and addressed in respectful tones on the subject of Signor Vandam's tragic end. Massimo translated the gist of their remarks; he couldn't be bothered with the details, so that a battery of sentences directed by the old lady at Massimo, her husband, the ceiling (Lucy took this to include an interested deity), and finally Lucy came to her through his medium simply as "expressions of sympathy."

She dredged out her all-purpose *"Grazie, molto gentile,"* to the delight of the group, who greeted it as clear evidence that she understood perfectly and began all talking at once at an escalated speed and volume. She smiled weakly, raising her hands in a gesture of self-defense, and Massimo cut in with some remark that seemed to calm the excitement. He probably told them I'm a stupid American and can't understand a thing, Lucy thought, biting nervously at her cookie, which resisted her effort as if made of stone.

"You must put that in the wine," Massimo advised her, demonstrating the proper method with his own.

"Could you tell them that I am very tired," Lucy said, "and would like to go to the house as soon as possible?"

"They are being gracious," he admonished her. "This is a compliment to you. It would be impolite to seem in a hurry to leave." Then he turned his attention to the son, whose opinion he solicited on some question, possibly, Lucy hoped, the heat in the farmhouse. The old lady proffered the cut-glass decanter, for Lucy's glass was empty. All the others, she noticed, were still full. *"Volentieri,"* she said, holding out her glass. Massimo flashed her a quick frown, which she refuted by mouthing "Why not?" His disapproval relaxed into something indulgent, amused curiosity, perhaps, or simply amazement. He concluded his various conversations, for he seemed capable of keeping two or three going at once, while she tossed back the sweet wine. To her relief, the son produced a ring weighty with keys and handed them to Massimo. The old lady pressed the bottle on Lucy again. "No," she said. "Thank you. Very kind." Massimo rose, saying the right thing to each person, shaking hands all around. Lucy said only *"Grazie,"* over and over, holding out her hand as he had done and passing along behind him to the door. In a few moments, they were out in the dark yard with the chickens. She stumbled on the uneven rocky ground and Massimo caught her by the elbow, steering her to the car. He pointed to a low stone wall across the road, which ran a long way ahead of them, so far that Lucy could not see where it ended; it was swallowed up at some point by the blackness of the night. Still wielding her by the elbow, he turned her in the direction of an elaborate iron gate closed and bolted between two posts with battered statuary on top: Animals, Lucy thought, maybe lions. "Back there is the villa," Massimo said, pointing between the twin lines of cypress. Lucy nodded, gazing at the wall with interest. The top, she noted, was lined with a pale stone that had broken off in places, leaving gaps overrun by eager vines. Massimo climbed into the car and Lucy followed. "Who lives there?" she asked.

"The family name is Cini. This is a very old family," he said. "The house you are going to belonged to them until a few years ago. Signor Panatella, who is a bank clerk, bought it from them. It was in bad repair. He restored it and now he rents it out to foreigners."

"So DV wasn't connected to the villa in any way."

"No, though he may have visited there. The Cini family would naturally take an interest in the property."

"I see," she said.

"Signor Panatella found it very strange, what your friend did."

"You mean falling down a well? It is strange."

"No. Not that. We did not speak of that. He said the house is divided into two apartments. Your friend rented both of them because he didn't wish anyone else to be near him."

"Except Catherine," she said.

"What?"

"He was with a woman, at least he was when he first came. Her name is Catherine Bultman."

"No," Massimo said. "Signor Panatella did not mention this."

They had been driving along the villa wall, which curved off gracefully to the left. Just beyond, they came to a long, narrow rocky road, little more than a path, which ran up a hill and through an olive grove. The pale gray leaves of the olive trees vibrated in the breeze and seemed to shimmer in the dim moonlight. "At least there really are olive trees," Lucy said as Massimo, grinding through the gears in search of one low enough for the challenge, turned onto the path and began an arduous ascent.

"Why would there not be olive trees?" he asked. He pronounced olive *oh leave*.

"Because DV said there were, and so far, it looks like almost everything he said was a lie."

"Why would he lie about such things?"

"He lied about everything," Lucy said sadly. "He always did. He made it all up as he went."

"This is not a way to have a friend."

"We weren't really friends, you know," Lucy admitted. "He was my boss."

Massimo cast her an interrogative look as he came to a halt in a space next to a red Ford at the end of the drive. "That must be DV's rental car," Lucy remarked. The house loomed up suddenly, thrown into relief by the headlights. It wasn't a villa, Lucy thought, but it was impressive.

"Here we are," Massimo said, switching off the engine. "This is the house."

SHE AWOKE with a start, for a harsh voice had spoken her name. She lay still, looking out into the unfamiliar room, recalling where it was, why she was in it. The morning sun poured through the uncurtained window, making a golden pool on the terra-cotta floor, and another shaft of creamy light fell across the bedside table, picking out the pale embroidered roses on the pillowcase next to her cheek. She reached through the brightness for her travel clock, which she had set the night before when she climbed into the unfamiliar bed, so exhausted that she feared she might sleep through the next day, right through DV's funeral.

The clock reassured her. It was only ten; plenty of time. She stretched, yawned, then curled back under the quilt. Why did her joints ache so, as if she had taken too-vigorous exercise? The room was chilly; she didn't look forward to putting her bare feet on the cold tiles. Her suitcase lay open on the floor near the door, a door, she recalled, that led to the sparkling tiled bathroom, where she had already taken an adequate though not luxurious shower; the water pressure was laughable, but the water was hot.

Massimo had managed everything the night before. He had carried in her bags and lit the temperamental-looking gas burner. He had even talked on the phone with Jean McKay to arrange having the money wired directly to his bank in Rome. He went over the apartment with Lucy, peering into closets, opening cabinets, approving the renovation, which he described as "meticulous and in good taste."

"Your English is very good," Lucy told him, receiving for her compliment his dismissive shrug.

Best of all was the cold supper and full pitcher of red wine that they found under a cloth-covered cage on the kitchen table. This had been left for her, Massimo explained, by Signora Panatella. Lucy looked it all over hungrily; there was cheese, bread, a few thick slices of roast pork, and a dish of something green, shiny with oil and flecked with bits of toasted garlic—was it spinach? *"Cicoria,"* Massimo said. To her relief, he declined her invitation to share this simple meal. It was too early for him, he explained; he planned to dine with his cousin in Sansepolcro. He gave her the keys, received her thanks again and again as he shook her hand at the door. He seemed distracted, eager to get away. Lucy watched him walk briskly down the gravel driveway to his car. Then, distracted herself by the thought of roast pork, she locked the door and went straight to the table.

After she had eaten and drunk a few glasses of the wine, she walked about the apartment, which was heavy on tile and open beams and low on comfortable furniture. It was designed for vacationers, everything shiny, practical, and as inexpensive as possible. But the bed was a good, old, solid piece and the mattress was hard. It was a sunny house, or would be when the sun came up. All the old windows had been replaced by new insulated casement windows with brushed brass handles and locks. On an impulse, she opened one and leaned out into the chilly, black, utterly silent night, a silence so deep and intense, it felt tangible, forbidding. Overhead, the stars glittered icily. In the distance she could see a ridge of black cypress, like tall sentries along the crest of a gray hill, and beyond that more hills, which faded in the distance like a line of black watercolor paint touched with a wet brush. Over these hills St. Francis had walked, begging and preaching from town to town, and later Giotto had come, followed by a train of his assistants, and his pots and jars of colors, winding his way to Assisi to immortalize the story of the saint. Or perhaps it wasn't Giotto, but Cavallini; the final word on the frescoes in Assisi was not in. Lucy closed the window, chilled, elated, and went off to try the shower.

Now, recalling that beautiful view, she gave up trying to sleep, threw back the covers, and sat up on the side of the bed. There was bread left in the kitchen and she had seen a coffeepot; surely there was some coffee, as well. As her feet touched the cold tile, she gave a soft cry of surprise. Then she remembered the voice she had heard, harsh, angry, close to her ear, saying her name. It had waked her in terror and she heard it again in her memory, for she had known at once who was calling her, impatiently, out of her dreams.

It was DV.

Chapter 5

*T*HE PHONE RANG four times before Lucy discovered it mounted inconveniently between the refrigerator and the doorjamb in the kitchen. A familiar deep voice answered her hesitant "Hello."

"Signora Stark," Massimo said. "This is Massimo calling."

"Good morning," she said. "How are you?"

He was very well. However, he was calling to tell her that the funeral was being pushed ahead to allow for the arrival of Stanton Cutler, DV's editor, who had left New York last night and was flying to Florence. He had requested that the service, such as it was, be delayed for him. DV's editor at the publishing house in Milan had also decided to drive down and would be joining them in Ugolino. Unless there were further complications, which was certainly possible, Massimo would arrive at the farmhouse at four. He hoped she had slept well and would be ready at that time.

"Very well," she said. "I'll be ready."

Stanton Cutler, she thought as she hung up—or *Cotler*, as Massimo had pronounced it. It would be something to see him towering over the locals in Ugolino. He and the police would all be wearing Armani jackets, but apart from that, they would have little in common. Cutler was a New Yorker to his toenails, accustomed to going first class, at top speed, without obstructions or regrets. He was a powerful, much-sought-after figure in the hectic world of publishing, reputed to possess a refined and cultivated sensibility coupled with a sure instinct for just how much intelligence the masses would tolerate. Tall, affable, charming, well-educated, and well-heeled, he fascinated Lucy because she could not understand how a man of such clear superiority could have committed so much of his time, energy, and intelligence to the interminable, tiresome productions of a writer as overmastered by his own language as DV. Cutler had made, for his company and himself, quite a fortune out of that peculiar willingness and was the person in the world best situated to feel a sincere pang of sadness at the thought that there would be no future additions to the Vandam canon. It was right that he should make the effort to stand at DV's graveside and say something respectful and encouraging to the assembled mourners, no matter how few and how disinterested they might be. Lucy went off to examine her wardrobe. With Stanton Cutler at the scene, it would be a real funeral, not the poor travesty she had envisioned. How badly wrinkled was her black silk suit? Was there such a thing as an iron in the farmhouse?

By one o'clock, she was unpacked and the suit was relaxing in the steam-filled bathroom, where she had enjoyed a second hot shower. She put on her most comfortable clothes and wandered through the rooms, toweling her hair. She could hear birds twittering in the trees outside; otherwise, it was quiet, the air still and bright. The famous light, she thought, examining her hand in a shaft of it that outlined a table's edge in the sitting room. There were a few magazines in the stand next to an uncomfortable plastic chair, two in German, three in Italian. Presumably, the Panatella family had straightened up after DV's death. There was little evidence that anyone had been living here. Where, for example, were DV's clothes?

Then it occurred to her that this was not the apartment DV had used. There were two, and this one, made up of the sitting room, bedroom, and kitchen, was probably the smaller. She dropped the towel off in the bathroom and went to the kitchen, where Massimo had left the keys. There were six on the ring, some new, others old, worn smooth and dark with years of service. Surely no one would object to her sorting through DV's possessions; sooner or later, it was a task that must fall to her.

The kitchen door led out to a small stone terrace. She had hardly noticed it the night before. There were big pots of trailing geraniums all around and a wrought-iron table with two matching chairs stacked under the eave of the house. To one side, stone steps led down to the drive. Lucy followed these to the open space where Massimo had parked the car. From there, she could see the whole house.

It was a beautiful old building in a picturesque setting, tucked into the slope of a low hill amid scattered cypress and stands of pine trees. The stone was ocher-colored and the shutters were black; there was a trellis over the main entrance, laden with crimson bougainvillea. The delicate flowers quivered in the light breeze as if they were breathing. The apartments were cleverly designed to have separate entrances; each had its own terrace. The one she had slept in occupied the part of the house that jutted out over a rise in the land, which gave more privacy, for there was no way to get to it save up the stone steps.

Jangling her keys as she walked, she went to the trellised door. It had two locks, one new, one old, and after a few tries, she succeeded in turning them both. She stepped into a long whitewashed room. There was one exposed beam—a tree trunk, really—that ran the length of the room. The furniture was spare: a couch with a checked cloth slipcover, two chairs exactly like those in her sitting room, a portable butler's table. These were gathered around a big fireplace strewn with ashes and bits of burned wood. A pair of iron fire tongs and a poker lay half in the soot, half on the brick hearth. The room was divided by a wide stone staircase with an iron rail that appeared to hang in the air unsupported. Lucy stood just inside the door, thinking of Goldilocks and the Three Bears. She would look around, but not long enough to break anything. She crossed the room quickly and hurried up the stairs.

Three doors faced the upper landing. One stood open, revealing a lavish bathroom covered floor to ceiling with startling emerald green tile. Lucy tried the closed door nearest her and looked inside. Then she opened it all the way and went in, for she had found what she was looking for. Against the far wall was a wide pine bookcase crammed with books, the contents of the thirty boxes DV had shipped at enormous expense, and next to it, pushed up flush to a window, was a long trestle table on which various notebooks and papers were arranged in orderly stacks. At one end was DV's old manual Royal typewriter. Beneath a second window, there stood a narrow iron bed and a nightstand, on which she noticed two folded pieces of paper. She examined these first. One was a page of numbers; the other was a grocery list written in DV's spidery handwriting. Even composing a list had posed a challenge to DV,

Lucy observed. He had scratched out the word *milk*, then written *milk* in again next to it.

She went to the table and opened the leather calendar book, which she recognized at once; it was the one DV had always carried with him. He had made no entries in the six months he had been in Italy. "Busy social schedule," Lucy said as she flipped through the empty pages. She turned to various stacks of paper. One was the original of the manuscript DV had sent her. Another appeared to be the continuation of that manuscript. *Ghosts* was scrawled across the top page. She read the first sentence. *Malcolm steered the powerful Porsche expertly through the sinuous curves of the winding Tuscan road.* There were also empty notebooks; folders crammed with credit-card receipts, insurance papers, and miscellaneous mail; unopened packs of typing paper; a drinking glass full of pens and pencils—all very orderly, which was unlike DV. She looked around the room for some other evidence, but there was nothing, so she went out to try the other room.

This was a bedroom, neatly made up, with the furniture in a line against one wall: a wardrobe, a nightstand, a double bed, all of the same yellowish wood and decorated with the same design of carved fruit. Beneath the wardrobe was a row of expensive shoes she recognized as DV's. She opened the double doors, startling herself momentarily with her own reflection in the mirror affixed to the inside. The wardrobe was full of DV's clothes. Sweaters, coats, and pants hung on one side; socks, T-shirts, and underwear were folded carefully on the shelves running down the other side. The sight of his folded underwear struck her as unaccountably sad. She had never, she realized, wondered what sort of underwear DV wore. Now she knew: He preferred briefs to boxers; he liked pastel colors.

She was about to close the wardrobe when her eye caught something partially covered by the suit coats hanging above it. It was a drawing pad, the inexpensive newsprint kind artists use for pencil sketching. Lucy eased it out carefully and opened the pasteboard cover.

A man's naked figure filled the page, though the drawing was so skillful that the impression of size, of fullness, was created by a great economy of line. His hair stood out wildly on end, his eyes were black holes, and his mouth was stretched in a grimace of pain. The cause of his agonized expression was evident; his torso had been flayed from the neck to the abdomen. As if to display the full extent of his suffering, his hands gripped the flesh and held it open, exposing the bony white cage of his ribs, beneath which could be discerned the black knot of his heart. The drawing was frightening—it had been designed to shock—but what horrified Lucy most was the man's tortured face, which was, in spite of the stylization, the sockets for eyes, and the strangely equine quality of the visibly grinding teeth, perfectly recognizable: It was DV.

Lucy carried the sketch pad to the bed, turned on the nightstand lamp, for the room was shuttered and the light was dim, and stood gazing at the drawing for several moments. So Catherine had been here. Was this nightmarish vision her parting gift to DV? Lucy flipped through the other pages, but the pad was otherwise unused. She reached out to turn off the lamp, but before she did, on an impulse, she opened the nightstand drawer.

An envelope lay inside, nothing else. She took it out and turned it over; there was no address, no stamp. As she extracted and unfolded the two pages inside, she noted several things at once: that there was no date, that the handwriting was bold—it looked masculine—that it was written in Italian, and that it was addressed with something warmer than the ordinary greeting. *"Carissima, amatissima Caterina."* She turned to the signature, *"Ti abbraccio, tesoro mio, Antonio."*

Lucy had seen Catherine and DV together on only a few occasions, but she had seen enough to conclude that in Catherine DV had found a nature more passionate and a will far stronger than his own. She had been persuaded—how, Lucy couldn't imagine—to accept his attentions for a time. He deferred to her. He wanted to change his life for her. Being with a "real" artist, he told Lucy, in a rare moment of candor, changed everything. He felt he was breathing a new, richer, more oxygenated air. He was exhilarated, breathless; he believed himself to be in love.

As Lucy looked from the letter to the drawing, a prickly sensation moved along her spine. DV's eyeless terror seemed to leap out from the page, to clutch at her, drawing her in. "What went on here, DV?" she said.

The shiver was followed by a bolt to the heart, for there was suddenly the sound of heavy footsteps moving quickly up the stairs. Before she could move, the old woman who had plied her with *vin santo* the evening before stood in the doorway, her features set in an habitually obsequious expression that did not entirely conceal the deeper and equally habitual suspicion in her eyes. Lucy dropped the letter back into the drawer, then hastily closed the drawing pad while the old woman poured out a stream of language. *"Non ho capito,"* Lucy said, closing the drawer and moving toward her. *"Mi dispiace."*

The signora began again at a faster clip, but this time Lucy picked out the word *pranzo* and gathered that she was to follow her to the food she had prepared. They went back down the stairs together, out into the bright sunlit drive, Signora Panatella rattling on all the way. Her car, a vehicle that looked as unpredictable and temperamental as Lucy suspected its owner of being, was parked in the drive, the driver's door left wide open. So she had driven up, noticed, with what must be excellent eyesight, the door Lucy had left slightly ajar, and come straight in to find out what she was up to. Now she went ahead to her car, reached across the driver's seat, and brought out a basket, from which issued an aroma so tantalizing that Lucy's only thought was to get closer to it. *"Signora,"* she said, taking the basket, *"grazie tante. Molto gentile,* you are so kind." The bottom was warm; the old woman instructed her to keep one hand beneath it. Then, dismissing her repeated thanks with fluttery hand gestures and various phrases in which the word *niente* figured strongly, she climbed back into her battered automobile, started the engine, and drove off down the drive, leaving Lucy clutching her basket and blinking nervously in the bright afternoon sun. She felt chastised, yet curiously grateful, like a child who has been reprimanded and sent to her room, but with no harsh words and, at the end, an unexpected treat pressed into her guilty hand to ease the humiliation of the righteous judgment against her.

DV's FUNERAL WAS a simple business, performed without benefit of clergy and attended by mourners who were, for the most part, only distantly acquainted with the deceased.

The mourners had all gathered at the piazza in Ugolino and, after the necessary introductions, had walked together out to the cemetery, where the coffin was already in place, balanced on a lattice of thin boards and a net of ropes over a deep, dark hole. Lucy was impressed by the number of locals who had turned out, dressed appropriately in black, to accompany the American writer to his grave. All three of the Pana-

tellas were there, as well as the entire Cini family (The artisto-
crats, Lucy thought; DV would have appreciated that): the
grandmother, a tiny white-haired, sharp-nosed, black-eyed
lady brandishing a carved walking stick; her son, whom Lucy
guessed to be seventy, though a very hale and sturdy seventy,
unencumbered by feebleness or fat, and with a great shock of
white hair that must have been a daily trial to the third Cini
family member; his son, the heir, a gentleman in his forties,
nattily dressed but seedy in spite of it. He wore his graying hair
slicked back, which made it look darker, but it started farther
from his temples than his father's did and he had clearly
combed it with close attention to the necessity for coverage at
the crown.

Paolo Braggio, DV's editor from Milan, who had greeted
Massimo with an enthusiastic hug and pumped Lucy's hand
gleefully, as if he had been waiting to meet her for many years,
though she was certain he had no idea who she was or why she
was there, was easily distracted from actually finding out anything about her by the arrival of Stanton Cutler, who really did
seem to know him. Signor Braggio was a short, dense, fierce
personage with fiery eyes and sudden manners, and as Lucy
watched him embracing Cutler's elegant waist, she thought
the two looked as if they had been created to demonstrate the
full range of human variety. Stanton Cutler's languid gaze flut-
tered over the gathering as he divested himself of his fellow
editor, settling on Lucy with a bemused shrug. What was to be
done about Italians? his expression seemed to say. One had
simply to endure them.

They set out, walking in pairs. Lucy fell in naturally with
her fellow countryman. "This is awfully sad," he said. "And so
sudden."

"I'm relieved you've come," she replied. "I'm afraid the

arrangements are a bit slapdash. It seemed important not to let him lie around in somebody's refrigerator here."

"Perfectly right," Stanton agreed. "You can take your time clearing things up once he's buried. You've done an excellent job. It can't have been easy."

"Actually, Massimo did it," she said. "I just signed things so he could get the money wired to pay for it."

"And you'll stay on a bit, at the villa?"

Lucy smiled ruefully. "It's not a villa. It's a farmhouse."

"Um." Stanton looked ahead at the party of Italians toiling up the hill ahead of them, for they had fallen behind. "Look at that amazing old woman," he said. "She must be a hundred, and she has outstripped everyone."

"There is a villa," Lucy continued. "It's hers, actually. DV wasn't in it."

Stanton gave her a sympathetic smile. He had been DV's editor for nearly twenty years and understood better than anyone the essentially cavalier nature of his author's relationship with reality. "Have you had any time to look through his papers?"

"Only a little," she said. "There doesn't seem to be much."

Stanton's blue eyes opened wide. "But you did find the last half of the manuscript?"

"No," she said. "Was he finished with it?"

"Well, I'm assuming he was. It was due in a week or so. DV was never late with a manuscript. He always needed the money."

"That's true," Lucy agreed. "But I got the first half the day before he died, and he never told me he was finished. There may be some kind of rough draft in the house. I'll have to look."

"Perhaps I can look with you," Stanton suggested. "If there's time, once we're finished here."

For here they were, at the gates of the cemetery, where the

unhygienic grave digger stood waving them in as if greeting guests at his dining room door. They wound their way through the less recently dead and arranged themselves around the coffin.

Lucy stood at the head of the grave, or perhaps it was the foot—she had no way of knowing which end of the plain coffin was which—between Massimo and Stanton Cutler, feeling ill. It occurred to her that she had felt steadily worse since her arrival. Her throat was sore, her joints ached, and she was uncomfortable and hot, though the air was delightfully cool and fragrant. The scent of fresh-cut hay drifted over the cemetery wall from the fields just beyond.

Paolo Braggio was to speak, translated by Massimo; then Stanton Cutler would follow. Lucy had declined the opportunity to comment on her employer's life and death. Someone, probably Stanton, had managed to get a few large flower arrangements sent out, one of which nearly covered the lid of the coffin. Two more stood on wire frames at the far end. They were grandiose, elaborate, expensive bouquets; the local florist must have hung up the phone with a shout of joy when the order came in.

Paolo Braggio began to speak, slowly and sonorously, pausing at the end of each sentence for Massimo to translate. This was a sad occasion, he observed, though he did not appear to be cast down; rather, he radiated life, good health, energy. He was a man who loved to speak and always had something to say; his tongue never failed him. Lucy observed the other mourners, buoyed by his self-confidence, listening attentively. Even the ancient Signora Cini, whose keen eyes never seemed to rest, looked him up and down with satisfaction. Massimo was more animated than Lucy had seen him before; his translations were exact. He paused now and then to choose the precise English word. His light eyes flashed when they met hers, as if to rivet her wandering attention. Braggio was going on about the relationship between American and Italian letters, the excitement of being, as he was, in a position to create an exchange of ideas between two important cultures, the one embodying the wisdom of the past, the other the hope of the future. DV, he believed, had been drawn to Italy, to this landscape, at this time, as American writers had been drawn before—here he named a few—and would be again.

One of the names was Henry James, which he and Massimo both pronounced as one word: *Enrijahmbs*. The absurdity of this sound coupled with the outrage of mentioning the great chronicler of American innocence and experience in the same breath with DV made Lucy smile. She cast her eyes down, struggling to suppress her amusement. Summoning seriousness, she forced herself to concentrate on the coffin and to remember that its contents had once been her employer.

And this worked; she was instantly sober, so much so that she noticed once again that she felt ill. Signor Braggio droned on, but she was no longer listening.

There would be no talk of faith at this burial, no hints about the afterlife or reminders of the promises made to us by one who was rumored to have conquered the limitless kingdom of death. DV's view—and in this, Lucy was for once in agreement with him—had been that all notions of an afterlife were wishful thinking. It would be so satisfying, so reassuring if the end of our busy lives were the beginning of something else. Nature herself seemed to make the case for death and resurrection; the seasons declared it, and so did the endless cycle of days and nights. To be, as DV was now, a rubble of bone and sinew, senseless and inanimate, DV's form emptied of the conscious force that had been DV, this was an imponderable mystery, cruel, bitter, insupportable. That we must all be empty bodies, Lucy thought, envisioning the mortal mess inside the coffin, and never see the beautiful world again—no, anything was preferable to that.

Anything but hell.

Perhaps just down this road, Dante had stumbled upon his guided tour of the infernal regions, where the shades of the eternally damned raised their agonized howls to make vain inquiry after the living. There was a gate to hell, she recalled, somewhere in Tuscany.

Paolo Braggio concluded his remarks with the fervent hope that DV's countrymen would make the pilgrimage to this peaceful valley, this simple village, this humble grave, which had called DV, unbeknownst to him, from across the ocean.

He made it sound as if DV had been lucky to fall down the well, Lucy thought. The group was quiet. She stared coldly at Signor Braggio, but he was looking down, keeping a respectful silence, which was clearly difficult for him, until Stanton Cutler should feel moved to speak.

Stanton was gazing up beyond the grave at a cypress tree swaying slightly at its top in the pleasant breeze. He looked relaxed but alert, his habitual manner. He worked in a world full of hysterics and blowhards, but they never seemed to astonish or offend him. How does he manage it? Lucy wondered. Does his height liberate him from earthly concerns? He looked down upon Paolo Braggio, who was chafing visibly under the silence as he knotted his hands and cleared his throat, craning his neck up over his collar as if to escape an impending fist. Stanton began to speak. His voice was softer than the Italian's, but it carried beautifully and he spoke slowly, allowing pauses for Massimo's translation. DV had been his friend, he explained; they had worked together for many years, and he would feel the loss. He spoke of DV's generosity and his energy. Lucy noticed he said nothing about his writing. He said DV had loved Italy and admired the Italian people for these same qualities. Lucy thought this was stretching the truth, but not much. DV did love wherever he was and always thought the best of people, the best being his conviction that they admired and trusted him. Perhaps his way was not so bad, though it was almost criminally naïve. This insight was the closest thing to an explanation for the popularity of his novels that Lucy had ever come across. She looked around the grave at the faces of the mourners. Wasn't it just as well to assume their impenetrable expressions masked only good intentions, agreeable sentiments? The Panatella family kept their eyes on Massimo, who directed his translation to them. The parents were a stolid pair, dressed in faded black, their faces lined by work in all weather. Their hands, rough and reddened from service, hung limply at their sides. Their son, Lucio, looked respectable, a serious bourgeois who had doubtless exceeded his parents' wildest hopes and directed their lives now with the same passionate interest they had once lavished on him. Facing them, across the grave, the Cini family occupied a different kind of air; they seemed to exhale it and breathe it in again: the air of the landed aristocrat. Lucy's effort to imagine a docile interior landscape behind these countenances, so studied in arrogance, so vestigially haughty, met with more resistance. No, she concluded. They had not been charmed by DV. They had not been charmed by anything for several centuries. The old man had the bearing and regard of a raptor. The son studied Stanton Cutler with a tired smile; he looked decadent and as full of guile as a snake. Stanton concluded his remarks, thanking the assembled strangers who had gathered to bury another stranger in their midst. The Italians turned to one another, speaking softly. The grave digger and a dark, foul-smelling young man who must have been his son began to push and pull at the planks holding the casket over the grave. The assembly dispersed, ambling back through the cemetery to the town. They could hear the rough exchanges, the creaking and sliding of boards as the coffin was lowered skillfully into the earth.

At the gate, Stanton and Massimo paused and shook hands with the others. First came the Panatella family, who murmured condolences, which Massimo didn't bother to translate. Paolo Braggio said quite a bit, but the gist of it was that he was on his way back to Milan and would see Stanton in only a few weeks when they would meet in Frankfurt for the annual book fair. As he ran on, the Cinis stood quietly behind him, waiting their turn. The son, who was near Lucy, exchanged a few words with his father; then, to her surprise, he addressed her in heavily accented English. "Are you the agent of this unfortunate writer?"

"No," she said. "I'm his assistant."

"You help him to write?" His eyebrows shot up in dismay.

"No," Lucy said. The inappropriateness of the present tense grated on her. "I kept track of his business interests—his mail, for example. And I transcribed his novels onto the computer."

Signor Cini smiled weakly, closing his eyes for a moment as if he'd been subjected to an unexpected obscenity. "Ah, yes," he said. "The computer."

His father interrupted at this point with some gruff questioning, which his son answered snappishly with what Lucy took to be the equivalent of "Shut up." Paolo Braggio had released Stanton's hand at last and the Cinis moved forward. Lucy was left in the awkward position of facing the scion and his mother, who eyed her warily, unwilling to speak. The son turned toward her, including her in an invitation to dinner at the villa. "We would be so happy if you would join us," he concluded. Massimo, who seemed to think this a fine idea, said to Stanton, "I can drive you back to Florence afterward. There will be less traffic, and I am staying the night there, as well."

It was agreed. Massimo, Stanton, and Lucy would return to the farmhouse, then go on to the villa at nine, which was the Cinis' dinner hour. There was more handshaking, forced smiles, polite exchanges. They walked out through the gate and back down the dusty road to the piazza. The old couple led the way, followed by Stanton and Massimo, then Lucy and the man she had begun to think of as "son of Cini."

"I'm afraid in all these introductions your name has become lost to me," he said as they walked along.

"It's Lucy," she said. "Lucy Stark."

"Lucy," he repeated, trying it out, but it felt wrong to him. "Will you mind if I call you Lucia?"

"Not at all," she said.

"Santa Lucia." He hummed the familiar musical phrase.

"She is always shown carrying her eyes on a plate," Lucy pointed out.

"You are a student of the saints." He had a way of making statements that were really questions.

"A little," she said.

They had arrived at the parked cars. His father and grandmother had already climbed into the backseat, where they waited, looking peevish. Their heir and driver rolled his eyes at Lucy, indicating the tiresomeness of his obligations. She put out her hand, which he took limply. "Until later, Signor Cini," she said. "I look forward to it."

"Lucia," he said, fastening his shifty eyes on hers for the first time in their brief acquaintance. "You must call me Antonio."

Chapter 6

AS LUCY STOOD in the doorway to the Cini family's dining room, contemplating the expression of boredom and intolerance knit into the lineaments of her host, it occurred to her that beautiful objects do not have an ennobling effect upon the souls of those who possess them. She could, she thought, amuse herself for several hours just in examining the contents of the massive breakfront against which Antonio Cini leaned his aristocratic behind. She recalled St. Teresa of Avila's comparison of heaven to the Duchess of Alba's drawing room, where the saint had seen so many things of beauty, such an abundance of silver, gold, precious stones, intricately worked, elaborate tapestries, silks, satins, such colors, textures, and dazzling contrasts of light and dark that she had come away unable to describe any single object, though she was certain the experience had been divine. Massimo, who was not in the least overawed, brushed past her, his hand extended in greeting, which provoked Antonio to bestir himself and advance with studied diffidence upon his guests. Lucy looked back over her shoulder into the entrance-way, a long, cool, high-ceilinged area, entirely bare but for two life-size statues of naked, though modestly posed, young wo-men flanking an enormous baroquely framed design of the Cini family tree, where Stanton Cutler ambled toward her in his easy, affable way. He made a wry grimace of alarm at the overbearing genealogy. Signora Panatella, who had greeted them at the door with much obsequious bowing and mutter-ing, shuffled along behind him, her eyes inspecting the marble floor minutely and critically, as if she expected to find evidence of unusual wear.

Massimo and Antonio had begun a conversation, which, as Stanton and Lucy joined them, modulated into English. They had been speaking of the farmhouse and of the *agriturismo,* a subject, Lucy observed, that agitated her Roman friend. Like the Cinis, he explained, his own family had sold portions of their holdings to former tenants and retainers, thereby upset-ting relationships of long standing that had been beneficial to all concerned. His cousin, Deodato Tacchino, in Sansepolcro, for example, in order to pay taxes as well as the enormous expense of maintaining the ancient villa, had sold off five hun-dred olive trees and an outbuilding formerly used only to shel-ter lemon trees in the winter. The buyer, a farmer who was now also a partner in an unsightly supermarket, had claimed that he wanted to renovate the building for his parents. This couple resided in a miserable hovel on a busy road near the supermarket. But once the repairs were done (and they were extensive, expensive, and of the highest quality), the parents persuaded their son that it would be better to rent out the house to the hordes of German tourists that swarmed over the hills almost year-round now, seeking refuge from their own uncongenial political, social, and physical climates. This plan was an immediate success; the little house was brimming with foreigners throughout the year. There was even a waiting list, and the deutsche marks flowed in without pause. The aging parents looked after the property, which was really nothing more than a hotel now, supplying fresh linens, cooking occasionally, and attending to the various problems of the invaders, who were notoriously difficult to please. The old woman was too frugal to buy a new washing machine, so now, in her retirement, she did laundry from dawn until dark, cooked and cleaned for two households. She worked harder than she ever had in her life. Her family was made miserable, but, of course, this was progress. Why would it be expected to improve the lives of those foolish enough to pursue it?

Lucy listened to this story with interest, though her attention was divided between Massimo, who spun out the details artfully, and Antonio, who received it all with a blank, wondering expression, as if he were listening to a description of life on a distant planet. At the conclusion, she laughed politely, as did Stanton Cutler—it was, after all, a story with strong ironic elements—but Antonio Cini only looked at them all bemusedly. He didn't get the point, his expression suggested, but he didn't care. The laughter dissipated quickly and a nervous silence fell over the group. It is going to be a long evening, Lucy thought. She hoped she could be seated next to her fellow American. During the conversation, Signora Panatella had shuffled past them into the kitchen, leaving the door open. The sound of pots and crockery being rattled about, and a delicious aroma of roasting poultry and herbs issued from within—that much, at least, was promising.

"May I offer you something to drink?" Antonio said at last. "Wine or an *aperitivo*? We have many things Americans like, I think. We have gin and whiskey and beer. There isn't much ice. Americans are very fond of ice, isn't that correct?"

Stanton and Lucy chose red wine, which Antonio poured out from an unlabeled bottle he designated as "our own." Massimo wanted nothing but an ashtray. Antonio poured something red into a crystal glass and gestured to a set of carved double doors at the end of the room. "Let us sit out on the loggia," he suggested. "Unless you think it is too cool."

To Lucy's surprise, Massimo, who had been complaining of being cold all afternoon, consented with the same alacrity he had shown for the idea of this dinner party, an idea that obliged him to drive nearly two hours down winding country roads at some hour after midnight. Antonio threw open the heavy doors and the chilly air poured in. Lucy followed the others out onto the wide stone balcony. It was a lovely though uncomfortable arrangement. The only seats were of wrought iron, gathered around a table that was unsteady on the cracked flagstones of the floor. She pulled her cashmere shawl close about her, congratulating herself on having thought to pack it, and took the chair Antonio indicated. He leaned against the cold stones of the outer wall, framed by an open semicircle, beyond which the glitter of stars and the cries of night birds announced the natural world.

Lucy had recognized the house at once: It was Malcolm Manx's villa. The entry foyer, with its twin statues, the dour portraits brooding over the dining room, the enormous dark wooden table, the sideboard where Antonio had poured their drinks, and now this, the loggia, from which Malcolm Manx first spied the ghost of the dead partisan. DV had exaggerated everything, of course. In his novel it was all massive, ancient, crumbling, and evil, whereas in reality it was more dreary than sinister, and though the rooms were very large and the walls undoubtedly remarkably thick, it bore the crude prints of many centuries of modernizations and had been altered through some curious vicissitudes of judgment and taste. The light fixtures in the loggia, for example, small, bare, flame-shaped bulbs gleaming on the ends of exposed electrical cord at the upper corners of the room, were neither practical nor aesthetically pleasing. The ceiling, dimly illuminated thereby, was frescoed with a delicate, lighthearted scene including dancing ladies holding garlands aloft and, at the center, a trompe l'oeil cupola opening into an eternally blue sky. Lucy leaned back in her chair to examine this marvel while Stanton introduced the subject of DV's funeral, which he thanked Antonio for attending. "Did you know him very well?" he asked.

"Hardly at all," Antonio replied.

Lucy, bending forward to release the tension caused by craning her neck at the ceiling, said, "He was here, though."

"I beg your pardon?" Antonio said.

Lucy glanced at Stanton Cutler, who returned her look attentively. "He was in this house," she continued. "It's in his book."

Antonio moved slightly. Perhaps he only straightened his spine or squared his shoulders toward his visitors; it was a subtle motion and completed in an instant, but they all felt it. It was, Lucy decided later, a declaration of the commencement of hostilities. "He has written a book about my house?" he said.

"He started one, but he didn't finish it. At least we don't know if he finished it. Stanton thinks he may have, but we can't find the last half."

"It may be in the mail," Stanton suggested. This was his hopeful theory.

"It may be," Lucy agreed. "I've seen only the first part. But it takes place here, no doubt about it. This room is in it." She looked appreciatively about her. "Is there a chapel?"

"There is," Antonio said. "But I am certain your friend was never in it. The only entrance is through my father's apartments."

"Most large villas have chapels," Massimo observed, stamping out his cigarette stub in the ashtray he held in his lap. "Perhaps he saw one somewhere else."

"I trust there are no members of my family in this story," Antonio said. It was one of his combination question/statements, which, Lucy observed, were a salient feature of his conversational method.

"I don't think so," she replied. "Unless you have a ghost who walks on the driveway late at night."

Massimo snorted. He was in the process of lighting his next cigarette and the sudden exhalation blew the flame off course. Lucy noted creases of amusement at the corners of his eyes as he jabbed the thin white column after the elusive flame. She smiled at him.

Antonio was not amused. "What sort of ghost?" he asked coldly.

"The ghost of a dead partisan," Lucy explained. "Of Basque extraction. Murdered in the driveway by Nazi forces during the war."

"I must ask you not to bring this up in front of my father."

Having drained his wineglass, Stanton Cutler leaned forward to set it on the table. "*Is* there a ghost?" he asked.

"Of course there is no ghost," Antonio chided him. He turned to Lucy. "But my uncle was killed during the war in much the way you describe. He was not of Basque extraction, however. I don't know how your friend heard about this sad moment of my family's history, but it would upset my father to learn that a foreigner has made"—he paused, searching for the most forceful representation of his feeling—"a mockery of it in a work of doubtful quality. My uncle was my father's brother. They were very close."

"Of course," Lucy agreed. "We won't speak of it." She glanced at Stanton, wondering if he would make some defense of DV's novel, but his attention was engaged by a burst of activity in the dining room. Antonio came away from the wall. "Here is my father," he said. "We will go in."

Signor Cini had entered from a dark hall, followed by his ancient mother, who was muttering at him irritably. He ignored her, making straight for the table, where he took what was evidently his customary seat. From the kitchen, Signora Panatella appeared, accompanied by a woman who might have been her twin, carrying two large plastic bottles of water. The loggia party filed in, headed by Antonio, who directed them to their chairs. Lucy was placed between Massimo and the grandmother, Stanton across the table with the old man, and Antonio took the chair at the head of the table. The bustle of moving, of greeting the elder Cinis, of taking seats while the glasses were filled with wine and water and the first in a series of large platters appeared from the kitchen served to dispel the torpid, mildly threatening atmosphere that had settled over the company on the porch. To Lucy's relief, Signora Panatella, assenting to a terse command from Signora Cini, crossed the room and pulled closed the doors to the loggia. For several minutes, the diners were all occupied with passing various platters and bowls back and forth and piling food onto their plates. Lucy, who had eaten very little during the day, was now aware of three conflicting sensations: extreme fatigue, aching hunger, and an undercurrent of nausea. She helped herself to the bowl of white beans, a round of toast spread with liver paste, a slice of prosciutto, and a few olives, taking each dish from Massimo and sending it on to Antonio, who served out his grandmother's scanty portions. The old woman riveted her fierce eyes to her plate. She terrifies her food into submission, Lucy thought, an idea that made her smile. Her eyes met Antonio's. He was watching her over a basket of bread he was passing her way. His mouth was pursed, his eyebrows had a slight interrogative lift, but his eyes were cold, devoid of amusement or interest. Lucy sent the bread along to Massimo and swallowed half a glass of the excellent wine.

"I hope you won't think me rude, Lucia," Antonio said, "if I ask you how long you are planning to stay with us."

"Not at all," she replied. "Only I'm not sure I can give you a satisfactory answer. There's a little business to be cleared up. I have to arrange to ship Signor Vandam's books back, return his car, organize the papers he left. Once that's done, I may stay on for the pleasure of it. I believe the lease runs until the end of the month."

"Signor Panatella is naturally anxious to know," Antonio continued. "He has, as you say"—here he lifted his chin to include Massimo in his purview—"a waiting list."

The commencement of the second course, hard on the first, Lucy thought, distracted her host from his line of questioning. There were so many dishes that a third recruit, a flashing-eyed, voluptuous young woman, her thick black hair only partially controlled by a strip of red ribbon, joined Signora Panatella and her twin in transporting the food to the table. Lucy noted that old Signor Cini came briefly to life at the sight of the young woman. He sat up straight in his chair and, when she was near him, put his hand out to touch any part of her he could reach. She laughed as his fingers closed on her forearm and she leaned provocatively over him to set the dish on the table. He lifted his head, breathing in her fragrance, which was apparently so intoxicating that he lost himself in it, for his eyes closed, his fingers loosened on her arm, and she slipped away. In a moment, the table was laden with dishes, plate after plate, and the diners began again the business of moving them about. The various appetizing aromas rose over the table, mixed with the soft exclamations of pleasure that escaped the guests as they tasted the first bites. Lucy inquired about a dish of stewed meat even as she chewed a bite of it, for she knew it was no animal she had ever tasted before. "*Cinghiale*," Antonio said, and Massimo added, "Wild boar. It is a dish special to this region."

"It is a pest special to this region," Antonio corrected. "They come in the night and damage the vines; even the trees are not safe from them."

"Fortunately, they are also delicious," Stanton Cutler put in. He was attempting with only a modicum of success to make a space for a serving of spinach on his overcharged plate. His cheeks were flushed, his eyes lively. He probably hasn't eaten since lunch, Lucy thought, if then, and he has a big frame to feed. Signor Cini, she noted, had not heaped his plate, though he had taken advantage of the variety available, whereas his son, so inferior to him in robustness and muscle tone, had served himself only one quail, which he was divesting of its meager flesh with the speed and skill of a surgeon.

"I wonder what business there is to be cleared up," he inquired, addressing his question to the dismantled carcass on his plate.

"I gather there will be some questions from the embassy," Lucy said. "Forms to fill out, that sort of thing. And I've a few questions myself I wouldn't mind resolving."

"Certainly there is no anxiety about the manner of his death."

"Not really," she replied.

"It does sound so odd," Stanton put in. "Was the well on this property?"

"No," Antonio said.

Lucy sawed the wing from a joint of chicken. The Cini silver, she observed, was weighty, venerable, and sharp. "What I want to know," she said, "is what happened to Catherine Bultman."

At the mention of this name, Antonio and his father exchanged a look so charged, Lucy was reminded of a silent movie. It would be too ridiculous if in the next moment Antonio denied any knowledge of Catherine's existence. The old man fixed her briefly with his predatory eyes, then returned his attention to his plate.

"She was here a very short time," Antonio said. "I gathered that she was not happy. We are too isolated here. She was bored perhaps, and she went away."

"Do you know where she went?"

"I hardly know *when* she went. Our family spends the month of April at our house in Firenze. It is the only bearable season there now; the city has become impossible. Signora Bultman was still here when we left. When we came back, she was gone."

Massimo agreed with Antonio that Florence, once an easy, comfortable, fascinating city, had become progressively unlivable. Even old Florentine families of his acquaintance abandoned it each year for longer and longer stays in the *campagna*. It was the same in Rome: the traffic, the tourist buses, the unbreathable air. Roman youths had taken to wearing surgical masks while riding their *motorini* through the poisonous atmosphere.

Lucy watched Antonio as he gathered the last fragments of quail onto his fork. She recalled the salutation of the letter,

"*Carissima, amatissima Caterina.*" He was lying, of course. He knew exactly when Catherine had left, and why as well. He probably knew where she was. Her stomach turned so forcefully, she covered her mouth with her hand, for she had had an unexpected thought: Suppose Catherine is dead?

But that was ridiculous. Why was she jumping to such a wild conclusion? What Antonio had said was probably true— Catherine had gotten bored and left. And if he had been sending her love letters, it wasn't surprising that he became somewhat ruffled and defensive at the mention of her name.

Massimo had finished speaking, but Antonio did not take up the subject of urban blight. He seemed determined to view all his guests' efforts at conversation with incredulity. He allowed a pause just sufficient to make it clear that Massimo's remarks did not, after all, apply, before he turned to Stanton Cutler and asked him if he wouldn't like another serving of *cinghiale.* Lucy pushed her food around disconsolately; she had served herself too much. As the meal dragged on, she felt more and more uncomfortable. The nausea she had been fighting all day asserted itself as a primary sensation, not to be ignored. She experienced a few stabs of pain in her lower abdomen that she couldn't classify; was it the digestive or the reproductive system? Her joints ached and her head had begun to throb. Massimo was speaking again, this time to Stanton Cutler, who was willing to take up any subject. She listened absently; they were talking about a young Italian writer Paolo Braggio was pushing. Did Stanton think his last book would appeal to an American audience?

Lucy's mind wandered. She thought of what she would do on the morrow. Massimo would be gone; she had a number of phone calls to make. She would look for DV's car keys. Perhaps they were in one of his coat pockets.

But her first priority would be sleep. She was so weary that, if only her stomach would calm down, she could sleep for days. She reminded herself to have someone, Massimo or Antonio, tell Signora Panatella she wouldn't require further food deliveries. She wanted to spend the day alone, uninterrupted, and she already had enough food to last several days.

Antonio Cini entered the conversation briefly with the observation that the only novel worth reading in the last hundred years was Giuseppe Tomasi di Lampedusa's *Il Gattopardo*. Lucy took a sip of wine, which provoked another surge of nausea. To take her mind off her discomfiture, she observed her dinner companions. Stanton Cutler spoke about the difficulties of publishing foreign books in that most provincial of countries, the United States. Massimo appeared to listen, but he could barely restrain himself from interrupting; his lips moved slightly, so intent was he on his own response. On her other side, Signora Cini had finished eating and resumed mumbling, addressing only her grandson. He looked down at her, his impatience and disdain animating every line of his face. He said a few short words, which the old lady ignored. Lucy watched him until he felt her eyes on him and looked up. She was thinking that he was a liar and this thought so absorbed her that she did not redirect her gaze, as she normally would have. He was one of those men—she had known a few; DV had been one—who lie routinely, about everything, often for no reason apart from a total disregard for the practical value of the truth. If he were caught in a lie, she thought, he wouldn't care; he would simply move on to the next one.

He seemed to be reading her thoughts and to be content for the moment to meet the fascinated horror of her gaze with the nerveless arrogance of his own. He did not so much look at her as present for her inspection his perfect indifference to the conclusions published in her eyes. It was like staring at a cat, and, as usual, the cat won the contest. She broke the spell and turned away, only dimly aware that Massimo had spoken to her. "I beg your pardon?" she said.

By the time the coffee and after-dinner drinks were served, Lucy's only hope was that she would be able to get back to the farmhouse without vomiting. She tried a swallow of *amaro*, reputed to have a salutory effect on the digestion, but knew at once that her condition was beyond such a homely remedy. The conversation had continued, never fluid, but in fits and starts, and she had tried to follow it. This effort had only served to intensify the throbbing pain in her head. However, some matters were resolved. Signora Panatella came to the table with what was agreed to be the last basket of food, and Massimo promised to return from Florence in two days to help her with various final arrangements. As the party rose from the table, the elder Cinis bid them good night and disappeared into the dark hall from whence they had come.

Antonio escorted his guests all the way to the car. The cool air revived Lucy, and she was able to make coherent expressions of gratitude and to receive Antonio's offers of further assistance should she find herself "troubled" in any way. The brief, bumpy car ride up the hill was a difficult trial, but she managed it, and she climbed out onto the farmhouse drive, feeling a combination of relief and urgency. Off they went, Massimo and Stanton Cutler, waving and smiling, apparently delighted at the prospect of the long drive they had yet ahead of them. Lucy foraged in her bag for the keys as she hurried up the steps. On the terrace, she did not stop to note the clear sky, the bright stars, the fresh, invigorating air. She opened the door hurriedly, pushing it closed with her hip, deposited her purse and the basket on the kitchen table, and ran for the bathroom.

Chapter 7

LUCY HAD RETURNED from the dinner party just after midnight. By 3:00 a.m., she felt reasonably certain that no morsel of food she had eaten in the last forty-eight hours was still in her body. The evacuation was violent, thorough, and enervating, accompanied by alternating waves of sweating and chills. Whatever it was, she assured herself, was surely gone. She staggered toward the bed, awed and humbled by the powerful machinery of the body, which, indifferent to the will, unaffected by the abstract flights of the imagination, proclaimed its dominion in implacable terms: Without me, you are nothing.

She would sleep, she thought, weak, empty, weary to the bones, for a hundred years. But no sooner was she under the thin quilt than she began to shiver uncontrollably. She could hear the involuntary chattering of her teeth; it reminded her, pointlessly, of the rapping of woodpeckers she had often heard in the woods near her home in Concord when she was a child.

"This is ridiculous," she said, climbing out of bed and hurrying across the cold floor to the drawer where she had put her warmer clothes. There wasn't much. Fortunately, recalling the likelihood of tile floors in Italy, she had packed one pair of her warmest wool socks. She put these on first, then added a long-sleeved cotton shirt and her hooded sweatshirt, took off her short pajama bottoms, pulled on a pair of cotton leggings, then put the shorts back on top. She looked around the room briefly for another blanket, but there was nothing. Her socks slipped smoothly across the tiles. She skated to the bed and got back under the quilt. By pulling the hood forward and the quilt up, she created a low tent that she could warm with her own breath. She curled her legs in tightly, still cold and a little dizzy from her excursion. A few scenes from the dinner party came back to her. Was she right in thinking that Massimo had some regard for Antonio Cini, that he had exerted himself to make a good impression? She thought of Antonio's damp, limp hand, which he had offered her in parting, along with his lubricious smile and the soft repetition of her name. "Dear Lucia," he had called her. The recollection gave her yet another chill. She adjusted the pillow, gave a final tug at the quilt. The impressive silence of the house bore down upon her, welcome and sedative, silent as thought. Silence is the sound thought makes, she observed; then, trying to make some sense of this meaningless proposition, she drifted away into sleep.

But not for long. Within an hour, she was awake, burning with fever. She threw off the quilt and the sweatshirt and lay flat on her back, looking out into the dark confusedly. Where was she, what bed was this, and why was it on fire? She could hear dogs barking distantly; it seemed important to listen to them. They weren't moving, she concluded. They were standing in one place, barking and barking. "They must be tied up," she said. Gradually, specific recollections appeared, but they were disorderly and some were inappropriate. She was in Italy; that much was certain. This was DV's rented house. He was dead. She had been ill, and now was weak and had a fever. This much was useful, but why did she recall, in detail and with bitterness, an argument she had once had with her husband about money? She moved her lips. Her mouth was so parched, her palate throbbed. I'll drink some water, take some medicine, she thought brightly, fumbling for the lamp switch. The dim light illuminated an unfamiliar room, but she recognized the bathroom door. She was so hot, she felt she might be giving off light, and she was giddy, possessed of a wild, foolish optimism. Gingerly, she swung her legs over the side of the bed and slid down into a sitting position on the floor. The floor was much too slippery, she concluded, and she was too unsteady on her feet. To get to the bathroom, she would have to take off the socks. For a few moments, she didn't move. The floor was cool and reassuringly hard. This was not, she felt confident, a dream, though some elements, the reddish glow around the edge of her vision, the unearthly stillness of the room—the dogs had stopped barking—the desultory command she had of her own musculature, were suspiciously unlike ordinary reality. Her stomach felt hollow and petulant. It was some kind of flu. Food poisoning wouldn't cause a fever. She would have to be careful not to dehydrate. She pulled off the socks, then, clinging to the bed rail, rose unsteadily to her feet. The bathroom was a long way away. Slowly, with the small, uncertain steps of the aged, she crossed the space and arrived at the welcome support of the sink. She flicked on the light, which was for some obscure reason sealed behind a sheet of heavy clear plastic, and stood looking dazedly at her own reflection in the mirror.

She looked bad. Her skin was pallid, it had a greenish tint, and her eyes were sunk in dark bruised-looking circles. She fumbled in her cosmetic bag and extracted a bottle of aspirin. Her packing had been hurried and she had forgotten the travel packets of medications for indigestion, diarrhea, colds, and allergies that she usually carried along. She drew a glass of water from the tap and shook out a few pills onto the counter top. "Aspirin it is," she said, tossing two back and following up quickly with the water. But her mouth was so dry, the tablets lodged at the back of her tongue, and the water failed to move them along. She gagged, then made herself cough, trying to force them free, but nothing worked. Choking, she tried more water. The water was alarmingly cold; she pictured a pool of it bubbling up from some deep subterranean spring. She could feel it pouring down her gullet and dropping like an icy water-fall into the empty, hypersensitive pit of her stomach. When the water hit bottom, her stomach contracted furiously. Clutching the sink with one hand and holding her hair back with the other, she vomited the clear liquid along with the undigested aspirin into the basin. This cataclysm left her so exhausted, she sat down wearily on the toilet seat. So much for aspirin, she thought. It might be best just to let the fever burn out whatever microbe it was after. If she took a glass of water and put it by the bed, when it was room temperature, she might be able to hold it down. She rested her forehead on the cool porcelain sink, working out this plan. She could stay in bed all day if necessary. No one was coming and she had no business that couldn't be postponed. She recalled seeing a jar of beef bouillon cubes in the kitchen cupboard; she could have that for a day, and there was also a box of herbal tea. But what herb was it? Mint? Was it fennel? Camomile? Her brain flagged at the rigor of this inquiry. She had looked at the box;

the answer was surely in her memory. But all she called up was a recollection of a favorite teacup she had at home. It had been her grandmother's, lilies of the valley, handpainted, with a handle in the shape of a vine.

Gradually, as she sat there in the glare of the bare bulbs arrayed around the bathroom mirror, she became aware of a sound, repeated, but at intervals, like fingernails scratching on plaster. How long had she been hearing it? She got up, stepped into the bedroom; it was coming from that direction. But then it stopped and she was arrested by the problem of how feeble and hot she was, how difficult it was to stand, even supported by the door frame. Mindless of all but the pressing need to lie down, she tottered out across the floor, gained the bed, and sank down on it, drawing her legs up after her with a groan. Dimly, she knew that the scratching sound had begun again; against her will, she understood that it was coming from the wall next to the bed. After that, there was the shock, dulled and diffused by fever, of the irresistible conclusion that on the other side of that wall was DV's former bedroom, the room where she had discovered the terrible drawing and the letters. *"Carissima, amatissima,"* she recalled, but the voice she heard saying these words was not that of the oily, overconfident heir to the Cini fortune. It was someone else, and it was so seductive, she yearned toward it. It spoke to her; she was the dearest, the most beloved, the *amatissima.* The words repeated themselves like warm caresses; they lulled her, and she gave in to them willingly and slept.

When she woke again, it was daylight, but the sky was so overcast that the room was gloomy and chilly. The travel clock informed her that she had slept until noon. She made a mental inventory of her condition, still feverish, but not the raging fire of the night. Her head throbbed, her joints ached, and her stomach felt truculent but empty—therefore not an imminent threat. She was weak, thirsty, and anxious. At length, she made up her mind to get up, brush her teeth, and try a cup of tea. She was content to be alone. She could groan and mutter as much as she liked, and she certainly had no desire to talk to any of the people who might be available to her. In the kitchen, she moved slowly, but it was satisfying to do what she could. The tea was fennel, the best thing for someone in her condition.

The food basket was still on the table where she had left it the night before. She busied herself in emptying it, eyeing the dishes warily as she transferred them to the refrigerator. They were leftovers from the dinner party, soggy and unappetizing, for the most part, but there were a few pieces of fruit, oranges and a beautiful golden pear that she set aside in a bowl. When she could eat again, these would be her first food. Then she sat down at the table with her teacup, drinking in small, discreet sips, so as not to cause any sudden disturbances within. She heard a spattering sound against the window, the start of a light rain. Once again, she considered the likelihood that DV's car keys were in one of his jacket pockets. That would have to wait. She was certainly not well enough to go out into the rain to the other apartment.

When she had swallowed half the tea, a steadily rising tide of nausea lifted her to her feet and sent her stumbling for the bathroom. She arrived in time to fall on her knees before the toilet, where, for many minutes, she was compelled to go through the violent involuntary spasms of dry retching. Her limbs trembled and her hair and face were soaked with perspiration when, at last, she managed to crawl across the floor and pull herself back into the bed.

She slept fitfully, waking again and again to the sound of

rain. As the afternoon wore on, she was aware that her temperature was going up and that she was disoriented and confused. She muttered various comments, nonsensical even to herself. Occasionally, she tried to get up, then fell back hopelessly. Her lips were chapped; she could not recall ever having been so thirsty. But when she did have a lucid thought, it was to the effect that she had best remain where she was. Eventually, the fever would break and she would open her eyes to a solid and recognizable present.

For she was lost in time. She was conversing with people who were lost to her, some to the past, some, like her grandmother, no longer to be found among the living. She rehashed the four-year argument that had been her marriage; she upbraided a landlord who had taken advantage of her when she was in school. The line between sleeping and waking fantasies was obscure, more and more difficult to trace. In the late afternoon, the rain stopped and she woke. A few horizontal shafts of light splayed across the floor like the fingers of a pale hand. Then, as she watched, neither sleeping nor fully awake, the fingers rushed up over the footboard of the bed and leapt into the air as two flames, one red, one blue. There was a rushing noise, like wind, and the hissing and crackling of a wood fire. She tried to lift herself, for she was frightened and wanted to escape, but her body was inert and unresponsive. The flames, she understood, were communicating with each other; they were deciding her fate. Would she live or die?

Later, it was dark. She woke again, soaked in sweat, and dragged her fingers through her hair; the fever was breaking. Now she would get better. But she was so weak, so empty, so thirsty, and hungry. How long ago had it been, that last meal? She reached out for the lamp switch, found the cord, felt along it for the plastic switch box. But something was wrong. The box had a toggle switch—surely she was not mistaken—but this box had a button. Still she pressed it. There was no light. Then, as her heart expanded so abruptly that she felt it as a blow to her rib cage, a hand closed over hers and another stripped the quilt from her shoulders. She shouted, "No!" flailing out into the darkness, but the hands were strong and pinned her back against the mattress. Now there was harsh breath over her face, fetid and hot. The hands held her tightly by her shoulders and shook her. Why was he so angry? She tried to hold her head still, but she was too weak. She could feel her chin repeatedly striking her breastbone. Her tongue got in the way of her teeth and she bit it hard; for a moment, everything was red. "Lucy," he said angrily, shaking her as if he intended to break her neck. All around, the silent room seemed to brood over her struggle; the darkness was an accomplice, a further agent of terror. She had recognized the voice, knew, in some powerless center of knowing, that what was happening could not be happening. "DV," she cried out. "Stop it."

At once he released her and she fell back a long way, for a long time, falling and falling through black space. Then she felt the give of the mattress, the compression of the soft material in the pillow. Feathers, she thought with relief. She opened her eyes and looked out into the empty darkness of the room. The rain had started again and far off she could hear a low roll of thunder. She passed her tongue over her lips, tasting blood.

The horror of the encounter clung to her in the darkness, and she to it, as to a friend. Why was he so angry? She concocted a paranoid narrative in which DV had been murdered and she had been poisoned. Soon she would join him in the dreary cemetery at the end of the dirt road in Ugolino, and no one would be able to do a thing about it. It would be a strange but not entirely unimaginable coincidence that she had come out to arrange one funeral and ended up the subject of another. She waved away the obvious problem of a motive; the Cinis were certainly dreadful enough to murder Americans just for the interest of the thing. Or perhaps they were annoyed with the Panatellas for turning the farmhouse into a hotel and had decided that if everyone who stayed there turned up dead, it would soon fail as a business venture. She sat up, fighting panic, turned on the lamp—it *was* a toggle switch—and pushed back the covers; she wanted most of all to be out of the bed. The light emphasized the absurdity of her imaginings and the cold floor gave her a jolt sufficient to turn her thoughts to practical considerations. One part of the dream, if it had been a dream, had been true. Her fever had broken and she was now damp and cold. She rummaged among the bedclothes for her sweatshirt, then, pulling it over her arms, stumbled off to the bathroom. No matter what the result, she would rinse the blood out of her mouth and brush her teeth.

She succeeded in this operation and determined that the blood was seeping from her gums and was not the result of an injury to her tongue. It was disquieting to have bleeding gums, but much less so than finding hard evidence of a supernatural encounter. She was alone, she was sick, but surely not dying, and DV was dead, but surely not murdered. She was ravenously hungry and cold. Her head was clearer than it had been in many hours. Whole sentences containing not only sense but grammar passed through her mind and she followed them with pleasure. Her stomach, though empty, felt calm. She tried a few swallows of water, careful not to gulp it down, though it was tempting to do so. "What good water," she said, setting the glass on the counter. A few moments passed without incident. She drank a little more, watching her reflection in the mirror, a pale, ill woman in a sweatshirt, drinking water. Her hair needed washing and her face looked haggard, but her eyes were clear. "I'm making a comeback here," she said. She would try the tea again, and if that went well, maybe a cup of bouillon.

Chapter 8

*L*UCY WAS NEVER ABLE to recollect, though she tried often enough, the sequence of thoughts that led to her decision to leave the apartment that evening. Doubtless she was overconfident, restless from being ill and cooped up in bed. She had drunk the tea, the bouillon, and even nibbled at a few crackers she found in the bread box, all with no ill effects. It had stopped raining. She had become obsessed by the problem of DV's missing car keys. She feared a relapse, which might make it impossible for her to look for them in the morning. Though she had no idea where she would drive, she felt trapped without access to the car.

So she pulled on her jeans and sneakers, took up the house keys, and went out onto the terrace. It was chilly, damp, and breezy. The air was alive with the odors of wet vegetation. The geraniums in their planter boxes stood tall on their turgid stems, presenting, like jewels on velvet, the drops their petals could not absorb. The sky promised more rain; the clouds were thick, black, moving like water on the upper air currents. Best to go now, she advised herself, before it starts up again.

She was careful on the steps, which were wet and slippery. The effort it took to get down them reminded her that she was still unsteady on her feet. It was equally difficult to negotiate the gravelly decline of the drive, but she achieved the second terrace without mishap. Beneath the dripping shelter of the bougainvillea arbor, she turned the locks and opened the door into the sparsely furnished sitting room. She closed the door firmly behind her—she didn't want to be surprised by unexpected visitors again—and deposited the heavy key ring on the table just inside. Then she crossed hurriedly to the staircase. She was thinking that there was another reason for her visit: She wanted to look at that letter again.

When she turned on the light in DV's bedroom, she recalled the scratching sound she had heard the night before. She leaned against the door frame, studying the blank plaster wall behind the bed. It was mice; an old house like this must be mouse heaven. That was why everything in the kitchen was in jars and tins. She went to the nightstand, opened the drawer, took up the letter, and shook it open. She read again the fervent address, then scanned the first paragraph for words she recognized. These were mostly adjectives, *sincero, appassionato, furioso,* combined with occasional nouns, *i tuoi occhi sereni, i tuoi capelli come un fuoco d'oro.* This last bit about hair like a golden fire was strong evidence on two counts: first, that this was in fact a love letter, and, second, that it was intended for Catherine Bultman, who, Lucy remembered, gazed out upon the world from beneath a cascade of thick blond curls of the type commonly referred to in romances as a "mane." Lucy turned the page over and looked at the closing. The handwriting was strong, the name *Antonio* so firmly pressed into the paper that she could fairly feel the pressure of the pen. She tried to picture Antonio Cini, fired with passion for his American neighbor, bent over some antique desk in his somber mansion, concluding his paean of praise and longing with this clear and resolute signature.

She couldn't picture it. He seemed to her too lifeless and, though he was certainly not thin or frail, too desiccated. Why would a woman as confident and energetic as Catherine Bultman give such a man, no matter what his lineage, a second glance?

But then, of course, she ran up against a problem, which was that Catherine had given DV, who had not even the recommendation of an impressive family tree, something presumably more penetrating than a second glance. If she had been willing to entertain DV's inelegant pursuit, might she not have responded to the effusive entreaties Lucy held in her hand?

It was hard to tell. Lucy had never been much courted, had never received compliments, written or spoken, on the serenity of her expression or the effect of her hair. Your hair, she thought, like straight brown hair; really, it was not surprising that she hadn't. She didn't think of herself as unattractive, when she thought about the question at all, which wasn't often, but she knew she was not likely to inspire the sort of ardor that resulted in secret letters, impulsive trysts, or imprudent promises. She was steady; that was what the occasional admirer had seen in her. She was clearheaded, reliable, and nice enough to look at. That was what her husband had been drawn to: a pleasant, friendly young woman, resourceful and competent, who could support him while he went through law school, which was exactly what she had done. This had meant working hard and not seeing much of him, a situation that she'd believed would be rectified once he finished school. And it did change, but not, as she had anticipated, for the better. She saw less and less of her more and more successful husband, who, she understood at last, was consumed by fear of failure, and by ambition, greed, and an insatiable appetite for attention, driven by these forces as if by furies, so that he had never a moment's rest or peace of mind. Their marriage had long been a battlefield. They fought about money. When he was in school, there was never enough of it. He was extravagant, preferred silk shirts to health insurance, refused to see the importance of paying bills on time. Then, when he was working and there was quite a lot of money, it still was never enough, and he resented every penny Lucy spent on herself.

She had applied for the job as DV's assistant without any definite plan in mind. DV was impressed by her; he saw what everyone saw: steadiness, competence. During the interview, he told her that his former assistant, who was leaving him to marry a Finn, was giving up her rent-controlled apartment in Brooklyn. Lucy came away with the offer of a good job at an adequate salary and the phone number of a promising lodging. Later that afternoon, as she stood in the sunny kitchen alcove of her future home, looking down over the quiet tree-lined street, she took what felt like the first deep breath since her marriage. And that was how she had come to prefer liberty to passion.

But now as she leaned against the bed, looking at the letter she could not comprehend, it occurred to her that what kept her from understanding it was not so much that it was written in a foreign language, but that it issued from a foreign universe, the universe of desire, passion, and obsession. If she had never received such a letter, wasn't that only the inevitable outcome of a condition that rendered her unable to imagine ever sending one? Didn't the woman who had received these effusions inhabit another plane of consciousness, a place of tempests and transports, where the postmen didn't drive ugly gray trucks but arrived trailing clouds and folding wings? No, Lucy thought, her conclusion was incorrect. She hadn't chosen liberty over passion. Passion had never been one of her options, nor was it ever likely to be.

This revelation left her weary and disgruntled. It was as if the letter offered her a glimpse at an intriguing dramatic scene, but she was allowed to see it only through a keyhole. She had to get down on her knees and peer through the door, knowing that she would mistake everything because of the limitation of her view. And the door was locked. It had always been locked.

She dropped the letter back in the drawer and, pushing Catherine's drawing pad aside, lay down across the bed and drifted into a light sleep.

She awoke with a start. Someone had fired a gun outside, nearby, near the drive. She sprang to her feet, staggered to DV's study, and leaned over his desk to look out the window. It was still dark. How long had she slept? The gravel of the drive reflected a little light; was it the moon between clouds or the dawn? And she was right: There, at the far edge, a man stood bent over his boots, and on the ground next to him she could make out the long metal shaft of a rifle.

"DV's ghost," she said, though there was nothing ghostlike about the man; he looked perfectly solid, preoccupied, as only the living could be, with the matter of his bootlaces. Surely in the ghost realm, petty annoyances like bootlaces and shirt cuffs ceased to be at issue.

Was it Antonio Cini? Lucy rapped at the glass, but he was too far away to hear her. He stood up, felt about in his pockets, and drew out a pack of cigarettes. Then, because she was hardly awake, confused by her illness and light-headed from lack of nourishment, she arrived at the unlikely conclusion that the man who now turned his back to the house to light his cigarette, inclining his head in a way she was sure she recognized, was Massimo.

"He came back early," she said, rushing headlong from the room, for all the world like a woman running to meet a lover, down the stairs, across the sitting room, and out the door. But no sooner had her feet touched the drive than three hard bits of reality came down upon her with the force of boulders clattering down a mountainside. First, the man, who was surely not Massimo, was nowhere to be seen. Second, the weather had changed for the worse; it was bitterly cold, gusty, and wet. An icy blast sent her cowering back under the arbor, where she discovered a third fact, the most alarming, the most irrevocably hard: The metallic click she had heard as she stepped off the terrace was the sound of the door, which was equipped with an automatic lock, blowing closed behind her.

"Oh no," she cried out, throwing herself against the unyielding wood. She twisted the knob, rattled the door in its frame, but to no avail. The keys were inside on the marble-topped table. "Oh no," she said again. She pressed her back against the door and slid down into a crouch, covering her face with her hands. Her forehead was hot; the fever was back. A few sudden sharp abdominal pains reminded her that her period was due; she had taken the last of the light blue pills in the cycle the night DV died. Her stomach, though largely empty, felt queasy again. She took her hand from her eyes and looked out into the dark night, too sick to feel afraid. The rush of adrenaline that had carried her boldly into her present predicament ebbed away and she found herself barely able to stand. But she would have to move; it was too cold to stay where she was. On the chance that the man was still near enough to hear her, she called out, "Is anyone there?" The words, querulous and weak, blew back at her, mocking her. They had not, she realized, carried beyond the arch over her head.

Surely there were choices; there were always one or two. She could try to get back up the steps to her apartment in the hope that, somehow, the door there was not locked. But she knew it was. And she knew there were no windows she could reach, and even if there were, they were all closed and locked. She could try to find the man, the cause of her trouble, who must have gone down into the olive grove at the end of the drive. The wind dealt her a rough slap at this presumptuous notion, and she huddled down against it. Then, as if to finalize the reprimand, the dim light of the moon was abruptly shut away behind a cloud and a soft whispering rain swept down from the hills behind the house. "Great," Lucy said.

If she had found the car keys, instead of mooning over Catherine's letter, then she could have driven to the Panatellas', roused them from their slumbers, and gotten another set of house keys. The rain intensified and a sudden gust of wind sent a cold sheet of it under the arbor. Lucy pressed herself against the door, taking it all on one side. The car was unlocked; of that much, she was certain. Even if she couldn't drive it, it would provide some shelter from the cold and rain. And wasn't it downhill all the way to the Panatellas'? If the rain let up, she might be able to coast down the hill. But she would have to do it backward; the car was facing the wrong way. It was a harebrained scheme, requiring more wit and physical coordination than she could presently call upon, but her imagination was enchanted by it, and lit upon it with a great buzzing intensity, like a bee entering the florid, ambrosial chambers of a Venus's flytrap. Just get to the car, she advised herself, and then see what happens.

It wasn't far, but it was far enough to get thoroughly

soaked if she didn't move quickly. She pulled herself to her feet, clinging to the doorknob. Could she run? She shook her head, trying to clear it, but all that did was hurt her eyes, which felt as if they were being struck from behind by hot pistons. The wind was fierce, rattling the thin wooden lattice of the arbor and forcing thick drops through the tight mesh of the foliage. She took a few steps to the edge of the terrace, hunching her shoulders forward, as if a supplicating posture might appease the increasing fury of the storm. The night was black now; she could scarcely see a foot in front of her face. But if she stayed on the drive, bearing always right toward the house, she reasoned that she could not miss the car. She pulled her sweatshirt hood up, tightening the laces at the neck to bring it down close over her face, and rushed out into the rain.

She had gone only a short way, perhaps ten yards, when her left foot lodged in a hole and she pitched facedown onto the gravel. She heard the soft pop as the ligaments in her ankle gave way to the strain, followed by a hard wrench of pain so intense that she howled as she fell. A cynical bystander in the jeering mob that had overrun the center stage of her consciousness informed her that she sounded like a whipped dog. The gravel bit into her hands; two pebbles flew up, stinging her cheek. At once she raised herself to her knees and tried to stand, but the ankle folded under her like wet cardboard and she came down again hard, this time on her arm. The rain poured over her, soaking into the thick cotton of her sweatshirt, adding weight. She rolled over onto her hands and knees and lifted her head, trying to see where she was. A shaft of lightning split the atmosphere and for a moment it was as bright as day and she saw everything—the house, the drive, even the back bumper of the car, which protruded beyond the house wall. The lightning was close. In the next moment, the world was black again and the deafening clap of thunder sent such a shout of alarm through her system that she fell off her hands and lay flat on the wet gravel. For a few moments, she didn't move. She could feel the rain penetrating to the bare flesh under her sweatshirt. It was cold; it ran down her back and pooled just under the waistband of her jeans. She was dimly aware that she was crying. *Just what we need, more water,* shouted the mob. "I can't make it," she said. "I'm too weak."

But she wasn't allowed to rest. Her stomach began twisting and contracting until she was forced to lift her upper body over one elbow, bracing herself with the other hand while she vomited a thin stream of liquid onto the wet stones. When this process was over, she let herself fall back, away from the disgusting sputum. She lay faceup, but not for long, for the rain was so furious, it poured into her eyes and nose, blinding and choking her. She rolled over, following the decline of the drive, and managed, after the first full turn, to come up on her hands and knees. Then, weeping and muttering, she began to crawl, making steady progress in spite of the elements and with such determination that even the jeering crowd in her head was silenced. As she turned the corner at the end of the house, she could see the gleam of the bumper. "Almost there," she said, and the crowd, fickle as crowds always are, turned from contempt to admiration and encouraged her with an Italian word—*coraggio*.

"*Coraggio,*" she said, pushing on.

But it was one thing to reach the car, another to get inside it. She pulled herself up by the door handle, balanced on one foot, and yanked the latch upward. Though she succeeded in releasing the mechanism, she hadn't the strength to pull the door open. The car was parked on an incline and she had chosen the door on the higher side. Once more, she observed, gravity was working against her. The wind buffeted her as she tried again. This time, the door opened a few inches, but as she tried to wedge some part of herself into the narrow space, it slipped closed again, catching her sleeve in the process. Struggling to free the sleeve, she lost her footing and slid down onto the soggy ground, her arm twisted up behind her. She was, she knew, well past the point of total exhaustion. Her body was sending distant, unreadable alarm signals, like coded messages. There was throbbing in her ankle and her head; her face was both burning from fever and cold from the icy rain. She held her free hand up to her face and determined that the pain she felt there was caused by a network of cuts and abrasions from the gravel she had crawled across. The rain drove over her; she offered it the wounded hand to wash. "Where am I?" she asked, and a voice she did not recognize responded, "Somewhere in Italy."

Her arm began to ache; a knot of pain issued from her shoulder joint. She struggled as well as she could, pulling this way and that, and, to her relief, the sleeve came free. This success encouraged her. She resolved to struggle on a little farther. With dull determination, she dropped forward onto her hands and knees and crawled around the back of the car to the other door. Gravity was her enemy; she understood that perfectly now, and she was on her guard. She knew that a door held shut against her on one side, would fly open and try to smash her down on the other. When she pulled herself up by the handle, this time she was careful to stand clear of the path the door would follow. And she was successful. The heavy door, like those magic doors that welcome princesses into the dark realms of mystery and romance, flew open before her. "Thank God," she cried out with the last ounce of her strength as she bid farewell to consciousness and collapsed across the narrow, dry backseat of DV's rented car.

Chapter 9

HEN LUCY OPENED her eyes again, a man she did not recognize was leaning over her. At once he began speaking in rapid Italian. Behind him, another man, his back to Lucy, stood shouting into a cellular telephone. It was Massimo. The strange man kept talking. Lucy closed her eyes, which was as effective as turning a radio dial; the man stopped talking. She tried to make out what Massimo was saying, but it was like trying to isolate a teaspoonful from a torrent of water. She gave it up, concentrating instead on figuring out where she was and how she had gotten there. Gradually, the memory of her struggle to reach the car surfaced, but it was confused and dim. She opened her hands and rubbed her palms against the smooth surface of the sheets. She was back in the apartment; this was the bed. Her hand brushed against her hip, which was covered only by the thin cotton of her pajamas. Someone had changed her clothes.

Massimo was repeating the word *no*, each time at a higher

decibel; then he concluded with the time-honored *"Basta, ci vediamo,"* and snapped the telephone closed, evidently much vexed. Lucy's hand had strayed over her hip and made the embarrassing discovery that someone had fitted a cumbersome sanitary pad inside her underpants. She kept her eyes tightly closed while a hot flush rose from her neck to her cheeks. Now Massimo and the stranger were talking animatedly. A word recurred between them, one Lucy recognized with a shudder: *ospedale.*

If they wanted to put her in the hospital, she must be seriously ill. She might die there, helpless, unable to make herself understood amid uncaring strangers. The doctors would be unsympathetic and cold, the nurses impatient. She opened her eyes again, this time looking out through a shimmering screen of tears. "Please don't take me to the *ospedale,*" she wailed.

The men, startled, turned their attention upon her. The tears welled over her eyes and streaked down her cheeks, and she was too weak to brush them away. "I don't think you should go," Massimo said. "That's what I'm telling this imposter."

"Tell him I'm feeling better," she suggested.

He pressed his lips together and raised his chin slightly in a gesture Lucy took to be promising. Then he plunged back into the argument with the stranger, who was, Lucy surmised, a doctor. For a while, the match was energetic and even, each boldly interrupting the other at steadily diminishing intervals, but gradually it became clear that Massimo had the upper hand. His volleys were sustained at greater length and higher volume, while the doctor relied heavily on shrugs, grimaces, and monosyllabic exclamations. A standoff was declared. The doctor left the room, huffy but resigned; Massimo turned to Lucy with the grim, self-satisfied expression of a victorious combatant. "He's going for his bag," he said. "He'll be back to ask you some questions and take your blood pressure, et cetera."

Lucy nodded, thinking how odd *et cetera* sounded in conversation. "What's wrong with me?" she asked.

"This fool would be the last to know," he replied. "He says if you take a turn for the worse, you will be worse, but if you become better, than you will certainly be better. I have told him, 'This is not information.'"

"I thought it might be food poisoning."

"It could be. He has also suggested *colera*."

"Cholera!" Lucy exclaimed. The doctor returned, his bag in hand, his stethoscope draped across his chest, proclaiming his status as a professional. He approached Lucy with an air of gravity and seriousness so transparently fake, it would not, she thought, have fooled a five-year-old child. He was a good-looking man with thick, straight black hair, dark expressive eyes, well dressed, and carefully groomed. As he took Lucy's wrist to check her pulse, she noticed that his fingernails were perfectly shaped and buffed. He began his examination. Massimo stood beside him, translating his questions and her reluctant answers, for the questions were of the most personal nature: How long had she vomited? Did she vomit blood? Was there diarrhea, as well? Had her period started on time? Was she taking any medication? Did she experience pain while urinating? Massimo was mercifully matter-of-fact and appeared more interested in rendering precise and accurate translations than in the content of the inquiry. The doctor asked her to sit up so that he might listen to her lungs. When she tried to comply, she found that she hadn't the strength to do it. Massimo fairly pushed the doctor out of his way, so ready was he to aid her. He lifted her by her shoulders and she leaned over his arm, taking the deep breaths the doctor requested while he pushed the cold stethoscope disk back and forth on her back. He muttered something Massimo didn't bother to translate; then he busied himself shaking down a thermometer he took from his breast pocket.

The revelation of her extreme debility had weakened the floodgate behind which a river of fresh tears roiled and swirled threateningly. Lucy struggled against it, but when, after he had lowered her gently down upon the pillows, Massimo laid his palm across her cheek and pushed back a straying lock of hair, she gave up the fight. Tears overflowed and, with them, a hard sob burst from her throat, so loud that the doctor looked up from his thermometer, his eyes still unfocused and his mouth set in his false professional frown. "I'm sorry," she said through her tears. The Italian equivalent appeared and she added, "*Mi dispiace.*"

Something that was not a smile but nevertheless a genuine expression of some feeling briefly animated the doctor's features. But it passed quickly. He stuck the thermometer between her lips and addressed to Massimo a lengthy summation of his findings. Massimo's reply was polite, controlled; having scored his point, he did not press his advantage. The doctor removed the thermometer, studied it seriously, and said, "No fever," pronouncing each of the three short syllables with care and evident pride. Then, exchanging pleasantries with Massimo, he pocketed his thermometer, closed up his bag, and the two men went out through the kitchen. Lucy took advantage of the few moments alone to dry her eyes and counsel herself into a calmer state of mind. She ran her fingers through her hair; it felt lank, in need of a wash. When she examined her hands, she found the fingernails jagged, lined with dirt, and her palms were crisscrossed with scratches. On the pads of each thumb, scabs had formed, surrounded by inflamed red skin with dirt caked in the creases. She remembered waking in the car. It was daylight and the rain had stopped, but she had been unable even to take off her sodden sweatshirt before darkness had closed in on her again. Then nothing, until now.

Massimo appeared in the doorway. She lifted her hand in greeting and asked, "Could I have some water?"

He disappeared, then reappeared in a few moments carrying a small glass. It won't be enough, she thought. She wanted a pitcherful. He pulled a chair up near the bed and handed her the glass, which she found remarkably heavy. "You must drink as much water as you can," he said. "You are dehydrated." He laid the stress charmingly on the penultimate syllable of the last word. "Later, a person will be coming from the hospital with—how do you say—a bag for injecting liquid."

"An IV," Lucy said.

"Ivy?" Massimo looked puzzled. "This is a plant."

"Just the letters—*I*, then *V*, for *intravenous*."

"Of course," he said. Then he was quiet, watching her steadily while she gulped down the water. She held the glass out to him. "Thanks," she said.

He shrugged. It was nothing. It is all and always nothing to him, she thought. He did as he pleased. He took the glass, held it loosely between his knees. A flicker of a smile played at the corners of his mouth, as if he was considering some matter that fascinated and charmed him. "How did you manage to become so ill in two days?" he asked.

"It was really something," she said.

"And why did you go outside?"

Good question, Lucy thought. She remembered leaving the apartment, looking at the letter, then running down the stairs. "It was the dead partisan," she said. Massimo gave her an uncomprehending look. "The ghost in DV's book," she added. "I saw him. I was following him. I thought he was you."

IN THE AFTERNOON, while the hospital technician, a short, jolly man who sat at Lucy's bedside, smiling benignly as the restorative fluid dripped into her arm, Massimo went away to make arrangements for conducting his various business affairs from the farmhouse. No sooner had he departed than Signora Panatella arrived, intoning what sounded like prayers as she unloaded provisions in the kitchen. Then, pouring out a litany of obeisances punctuated by sudden bursts of alarm, she came to Lucy's bedside. What a terrible thing it was, the poor Signora Stark, look at her, so weak, so ill, what a catastrophe. Lucy smiled weakly at these effusions; this much Italian she understood. The signora and the technician fell into a conversation that both seemed to find enormously interesting, until they were interrupted by a clatter in the kitchen. Her son, the signora announced, bringing in a folding bed—*un letto pieghevole*—for the Signor Compitelli, *che brava persona*. She hastened to help him set it up in the sitting room. Lucy lay quietly, drifting in and out of sleep until the technician removed the needle from her arm, packed up his apparatus, and bid her *"Arrivederla."* *"Domani,"* he promised, *"lei starà meglio, non abbia paura."*

"Don't be afraid," she repeated when he had gone and she was alone in the quiet house. But she was not afraid, not in the slightest. Like the spiny cactus that can survive for years waiting for the desert rains, her tissues had drunk in the electrolytic liquid greedily and she was refreshed and filled with optimism. She wanted to expend the new energy in some foolish, preposterous flowering. But when, longing for the sensual pleasure of a hot shower, she tried to get out of bed, she understood that her elation was premature. Her ankle would not support her weight. She might hobble across the room to the bathroom, but it was distinctly possible that she wouldn't be able to get back. If Massimo returned and found her lying on the bathroom floor, he might decide she would be better off in the hospital. No, she concluded, she would have to wait. She lay back down, allowing her thoughts to wander peacefully over the events of the last few days. In the soft, cool light of the quiet room, it was impossible to entertain suspicions, to imagine that anyone here wished her ill. On the contrary, the alacrity with which they had taken on the matter of her illness suggested a natural openness and generosity one hardly expected to find among strangers. Massimo, especially Massimo, who had so taken charge of everything and who was now willing to stop the busy progress of his life until she was well enough to take up hers; how would she ever repay such kindness? As she was considering this problem, she heard his step on the stairs. She didn't examine the possibility that the sudden racing sensation in her chest was something other than the pulse of convalescent gratitude, for he came immediately to her bedside. "You are awake," he said, stating the obvious, as was his habit.

"I'm feeling much better."

"Do you want anything?"

"If you would help me to the bathroom," she said. "I'd like to wash up a little."

"Can you walk? Shall I carry you?"

"Let's try walking." He helped her from the bed and she leaned on his arm, taking small, careful steps. It took all her concentration to cross the room. When they arrived at the door, she released him and, holding on to the door frame, stepped inside. "I'm fine," she said, for he looked doubtful.

"I will be here," he promised. She closed the door quietly behind her.

She went to the sink and spent a moment gazing at her face; it had been so long since she had seen it. There were a few scratches near her right temple, feathering down across her cheekbones, but otherwise she looked the same, tired, pale, and sick. She turned on the water and began washing the dirt from the cuts on her hands. She was by nature fastidious, and it pleased her to attend to her personal hygiene without supervision. She wanted to take a shower, but the simple business of washing her face and hands and brushing her teeth left her so tired, she gave up the idea. There was nothing resembling a washcloth in the place, so she stripped off her clothes and did what she could with a bar of soap and the bidet. She disposed of the disagreeable pad, substituting a tampon from the supply she had brought with her. This seemed an enormous, cheering improvement. Then she put her pajamas back on, stashed the underpants in the string bag she kept for laundry, and opened the door. Massimo had pulled up a wooden chair and was sitting there, waiting patiently for her.

"Thank you," she said.

He stood up without comment, offering his arm. He had undressed her, of course; she knew this. He had found her unconscious, delirious with fever, rain-soaked, filthy, bleeding, and he had somehow gotten her back into the apartment, changed her clothes, called the doctor. She imagined his struggles, his consternation and revulsion. She was torn between a desire to know the worst and a dread of hearing about it. She clung to his arm, concentrating on her shaky, pitiful little steps. The bed seemed a long way away. Eventually, she got there.

She slept and woke, but now she was in a world she recognized, without terror or confusion. Massimo brought her broth with egg cooked in it and sat by her while she spooned it down. "That was good," she said, handing him the empty bowl. "You are so kind to me."

"You must stop being grateful," he said, taking the bowl away. She slid back down among the pillows, trying to understand this demand, but she could make no sense of it. Dazed with gratitude, she was ambushed by a deep and dreamless sleep.

When she woke this time, she heard his voice from the kitchen speaking rapidly. The telephone agitates him, she thought, and that was as far as she got. Then he was sitting at the small table in her room, his back to her, working by lamplight, his various papers set out in stacks around him. The room, but for the insufficient light cast by the cheap lamp, was dark. He looked like a monk in some medieval cell, writing by candlelight. There was something of the hermit and the fanatic in his straight back and bowed head. She watched him without speaking and, watching him, drifted back into sleep.

It was morning and she awoke feeling excited. She could hear him moving about in the kitchen. After a few minutes, he looked in and, finding her awake, came to attend. "What can I bring you?" he said. "You must be very hungry."

"I am," she said. "But most of all I'd like to get out of this bed."

They agreed that she would try a trip to the kitchen, where he would prepare tea and bread for her. "It is too soon for coffee," he cautioned. She got to the table with very little help and sat dipping bits of bread into a cup of milky tea while he stood at the counter talking angrily into his portable phone. Who was he talking to? Was it his wife, his employer? His phone was always next to him, and whenever it rang, he looked at it with unconcealed rage. It contained his ordinary life, called him back, and this made him angry. Did that mean, she speculated, that he wanted to get away from his ordinary life?

He finished up abruptly and snapped the phone closed, looking down at her gloomily.

"Trouble?" she asked.

"Stupidity," he said.

"Is it difficult for you to stay away from Rome for so long?"

His frown deepened into irritation. "I do what I want," he said. "I am often away; it is my work."

"And am I your work now?"

He considered the question; it appeared to interest him. "You are too sick to walk across the room," he said. "How could I leave you?"

"That's true," she said.

"Do you want more food? More tea?"

"No," she said. "This was enough. What I'd like to do is wash my hair, but I don't think I can stand long enough to do it."

"I will put a chair by the sink," he said. "This is not a problem."

"I'm putting you to so much trouble."

He waved away her protest; it didn't interest him. He was already absorbed in the project. He took a chair from the table and carried it into the bathroom, then came back for her. "Are you ready?" he asked. She got up and, holding his arm only lightly, made her way with small hopping steps. In the bathroom, she went ahead of him and lowered herself into the chair. It was obvious at once that the back was too high and it would be impossible for her to get her head anywhere near the sink. "Try turning it sideways," she said, getting up. He agreed, shifted the chair, and she sat down again. By sliding her hips forward, she was able to rest her neck against the cool edge of the porcelain. "I'll need a pot," Massimo said. He went back to the kitchen, returning with a ceramic pitcher. "This will do," he said. He put a towel in her lap, took the plastic bottle of shampoo from the niche in the tub, and handed it to her. "Hold that," he said. Then he occupied himself with turning on the water, testing the temperature by holding his wrist in the stream.

"The water in this house gets really hot," Lucy warned.

"Do not fear," he replied. "I will not burn you."

"I'm not afraid," she said.

He filled the pitcher and poured the water, which was comfortably warm, slowly over her head. "How is that?" he asked. "Not too hot?"

"It's perfect," she said. He was so far behind her that she had to open her eyes as wide as she could to see him. "This is wonderful."

He looked down at her, his mouth fixed in the patient, indulgent near smile that seemed to express the full complexity of his feeling for her. Then his eyes shifted to the pitcher, which was full. He poured the water over her head again, smoothing her hair back from her forehead with his palm. She closed her eyes. "This is paradise," she said. He took the shampoo, squeezed a dab into his hand, and applied it to her hair, working up a lather with a gentle pressure that she found deeply soothing. She had expected him to make a poor job of it, to be awkward and impatient. "You do this so well," she said. "You could do it for a living." His fingers massaged her temples, rubbing smooth the last traces of anxiety.

"Did you think I would not know how to do it?" he asked.

"I thought you might be too rough," she said.

He took up the pitcher and began rinsing out the soap,

starting at the base of her skull and working up. "I am gentle," he said, "because you are so weak."

Lucy opened her eyes and looked back at him. He was raising the pitcher over her head. "Close your eyes," he said as the water streamed over her brow.

Afterward, when he bent over her toweling her hair, his lips brushed her cheek. She was not sure whether it was a kiss or an accident.

Chapter 10

LUCY WAS TO REMEMBER the days that followed with a combination of nostalgia and despair, as one recalls a vivid and erotic dream, a dream of bliss. She could not, no matter how often she might conjure it, bring back that particular sleep again. She was dependent on Massimo, whom she hardly knew, for everything, a condition that normally would have irked her, yet she was serene and contented. Though she was barely able to lift a spoon, if she had been asked how she was feeling, she would have responded, Never better. Perhaps, she speculated, she had simply needed a rest and her body had seized the opportunity to take it. She called Jean McKay, who assured her that DV's affairs could wait; there was some confusion about the will, and none of the wives wanted the books or the other odd bits that would have to be sold or shipped back. "Just get well," Jean said. "Charge everything and save your receipts."

One afternoon, Massimo asked her if she would care to sit

on the terrace. "It is warm," he said. "The sun is shining." She
was eager to leave the apartment, to recommence her ordinary
life, yet, as she stood in the doorway looking out at the blue
sky, the gentle slope of the green and golden fields, she felt
reluctant to enter the scene. Massimo fussed, arranging cush-
ions on the iron chair, laying out his supplies—an ashtray, his
cigarettes, and his telephone—on a plastic table he had pulled
into the sun. As soon as they were both seated and he had lit
his cigarette, the phone gave a shriek and he began another in
the never-ending series of arguments he was having with the
world. Lucy watched him bemusedly. She had eaten a few
slices of chicken and roasted potatoes at lunch, a meal that her
stomach accepted without protest, and she felt pleasantly full.
A sudden chatter of birds, followed by the crunch of gravel
under tires on the drive, announced the arrival of that which
she had no desire to receive—a visitor. Massimo had dismissed
Signora Panatella, whose cooking he pronounced too heavy
for his invalid, so presumably it was not this attentive lady.
Lucy listened as the engine was turned off, the car door
opened and closed. Massimo had turned away. He was gesturing to the hills with one hand while he pressed the phone to his
head with the other. His exasperated monologue poured forth
along the airwaves. She pulled herself up in her chair, straining
to see over the edge of the terrace, for the footsteps had arrived
at the stairs. In the next moment, the head, the shoulders, then
the entirety of Antonio Cini rose up into her view. "Ah, Lucia,"
he said as he approached. "What a surprise. Here you are, up
and about. You must be much improved."

"I am up," she said, "but not exactly about."

He held out his hand, which she took briefly, for it was so
cold and limp, it offered nothing in the way of greeting but
seemed, rather, to have been extended to inform her of his

acquaintance with and indifference to the ordinary forms of courtesy. Massimo, sensing motion at his back, turned and exchanged a similar handshake over Lucy's shoulder, followed by impatient gestures at the telephone, into which he continued his diatribe.

"He is always on the phone," Lucy observed.

"Then he has been neglecting you."

"No," she said. "Not at all. He has been wonderfully attentive. I'm in his debt now, I think, possibly forever."

Antonio smiled down on her, giving her the full benefit of his sickly and contemptuous address. "Forever," he said. "That must be a tiresome sensation."

Lucy looked back at Massimo. He had reached the conclusion of his call. His eyes rested upon her, then flicked past her to Antonio. She experienced a rush of affection for him, which, coupled with her visceral aversion to her interlocutor, left her edgy and defensive. "It is an obligation," she said, "that I look forward to discharging."

Massimo closed up his phone and greeted their guest in a genial stream of Italian, which Antonio returned affably enough, though he declined the questionable comfort of the iron chair offered him. "I will not stay," he protested, switching to English. "I came to inquire after our poor Lucia. Signora Panatella is anxious to hear of her improvement, but she doesn't wish to intrude, unless you have some need of her services. In which case . . ." He turned to Lucy. "I'm sure you can imagine her willingness."

Lucy smiled up at him, shading her eyes with her hand, for the sun was behind him. "That's very thoughtful of her," she said.

Massimo and Antonio exchanged a look that Lucy charac-

terized as sardonic. "Why does she bother you with this message?" Massimo said. "What does she want?"

Antonio shrugged. "She has never been able to accept the
idea that the entire house is rented to one tenant," he explained. "She understands that your unlucky friend leased it
that way, and that it makes no difference in her income, but
now he is gone, the lease is not in your name, Lucia, and, well,
she is an uneducated person, a peasant. For such a person,
there is something unsettling about owning an empty room."

Lucy pictured the conversation that had resulted in this
visit—the anxious, inexperienced, but avaricious up-from-
tenancy landowner soliciting the intercession and wisdom of
the great Cini dynasty, which had, after all, been keeping her
own family in line for centuries. Did she guess that her concerns were only another target for Antonio's universal scorn?

"What does she want to do?" Massimo sputtered. "Does
she want to fill the place with Germans?"

Antonio gave his most ghastly smile. "Oh, I suppose so,"
he said. "That is her vision of paradise."

"*Disgraziata!*" Massimo exclaimed.

Lucy leaned back in her chair, rubbing her eyes with her
thumb and index finger. "There's nothing she can do about it,"
she said. "I'll call the agency today and have someone explain
it to her."

"I believe someone has attempted this," Antonio replied,
looking glum.

"Well, they will have to try again," Lucy concluded.

Antonio shifted his weight from one foot to the other. He
never stood square, Lucy realized. He was always slouching or
leaning on something for support. "It's a pity that you should
be vexed by this trivial matter when you are so ill."

"It is an outrage," Massimo agreed.

Lucy said nothing while Antonio cast his moody eyes languidly from her to Massimo, who was stubbing out his cigarette, and back again, hemming them together inside the narrow, hot, distinctly lurid circumference of his presumptions.

"I'm not vexed," she protested. "The rent, which is exorbitant, by the way, is paid here until the end of the month. I know this, because I wrote the check myself. The house cannot be rented until then. Isn't Lucio Panatella a banker? Surely he knows this."

"Lucio is away this week. But when he comes back, I'm sure he will calm his mother's . . . perturbation."

Lucy chuckled. "What an amusing word," she said.

Antonio drew his eyebrows together and puckered his mouth in an expression of mock dismay. "It is not correct?" he asked.

"Very correct," she assured him. "Very precise."

"I am relieved," he announced. "And now I won't disturb you any longer. Lucia, I am pleased that you are feeling better. I hope before you leave you will find time to dine with us once more. And also you, Signor Compitelli, of course. You would be most welcome."

Lucy smiled, though the prospect of another stultifying evening at the Cinis' was so unappealing, she was not able even to mouth the proper formulas of gratitude. Massimo, however, was evidently charmed at the invitation. He got to his feet and advanced upon Antonio with sincere exclamations, half in English, expressing the great pleasure he and the signora would have in such an event. The two men shook hands, but not heartily; Antonio shrank visibly from Massimo's vitality. Then he made his way back down the stairs. Massimo stood looking after him, his head back, resting the backs of his hands on his hips. As they heard the car engine starting, he came to the table and resumed his seat.

"What a disagreeable man," Lucy said.

Massimo looked up sharply. "How can you say that? He has been most thoughtful."

"He's a liar," she said. "He lies about everything."

"That is ridiculous." Massimo tapped a cigarette out of the pack vehemently. "How could you know such a thing?"

Lucy studied him closely. His question was rhetorical; it did not even occur to him that she might have valid evidence for her charge. It annoyed her that he was so eager to take the part of the jaded aristocrat against that of the observant foreigner, and she was uncertain whether she wanted to share the secret of the letter. But if she didn't, he would assume that she was describing some intuition she had about Antonio, that she had confessed to a feeling rather than stated a fact. "He lied about Catherine Bultman," she said.

"How could you know this?" he repeated.

"He said he hardly knew her, when in fact he was in love with her. He wrote her a passionate love letter."

"You are still ill," Massimo said, getting up. "You are having delusions. It is time we went inside."

She waved him away. "I'm not having delusions. I saw the letter. Catherine left it in the other apartment. You can see it for yourself."

"You found someone's personal letter and you read it?" he exclaimed. "Lucy, this is too much."

"I have to go through DV's papers," she protested. "That's what I'm here for. And I didn't read it. I couldn't. It's in Italian. But it is a love letter—I could tell that much—and it's signed 'Antonio.'"

"How many people do you think are named Antonio in this country?" he said. "This is a common name. It proves nothing. Please, Lucy, you are overtired. We will go inside."

"You're not listening to me," she complained, but she didn't resist the assistance he offered her. He was right: She was not well enough even for this small excitement. Her heart was racing; she felt weepy and weary to her bones. As she rose, she dashed unwelcome tears from her eyes. "We're having our first argument," she mumbled.

Massimo passed his arm around her shoulder, holding her up as he steered her toward the door. "This is not an argument," he said. In the kitchen, he placed his cool palm against her cheek and for a moment she closed her eyes and rested against it. Gently, he raised her chin and she looked up into the clear icy green of his eyes. His expression was, as always, faintly amused, but wasn't there something else, something serious and intent? She couldn't be sure.

Perhaps he was right, she thought as her lips parted beneath the warm pressure of his kiss. Perhaps she was having delusions.

THAT KISS, that kiss. It would recur in her imagination with all its power and mystery intact whenever she read words like *voluptuous, passionate, sensuous,* for the rest of her life. Or so she thought as she lay quietly in her bed that evening, examining it with the care and precision of a jeweler setting a precious stone. In fact, she was convinced she had never had the slightest inkling of the real meaning of such words, especially the word *voluptuous,* which she sounded out softly, accompanied by a shiver of delight. *Surrender,* that was another one, often coupled with inappropriate adjectives like *sweet* in the writings of mawkish sentimentalists. There had been nothing sweet about it. She had nearly fainted. But she had struggled against the encroaching darkness, and the kiss had called her back, so slow, insistent, passionate yet controlled, with an element of tenderness that touched her to her core. She could not fall away from it; she would not.

She turned onto her side and pulled the pillow in close. Part of the beauty of it was there had been only the kiss, a brief and overpowering rapture (*rapture,* that was another word elucidated forever), and then he had released her without comment, escorted her the rest of the way to her bed, arranged her blankets and pillows, stroked her hair back from her temple in that gentle motherly way he had, and left her to rest.

And she had slept, although she didn't know for how long. Her room was dark. She was exhilarated, excited, but, most of all, she was hungry. She gave up her reverie and climbed out of bed, pleased to find herself more steady on her feet than she had been for days. She went out to find Massimo.

He was standing at the stove in the kitchen, stirring a pan of fragrant olives and tomatoes with one hand while he held the telephone to his ear with the other. When Lucy pulled out the chair from the table, she startled him. He turned around, looking angry, then, seeing her, he smiled, the anger vanishing. He said a few words into the phone. She understood *"Ora devo riattaccare"*—"I must hang up now." Then he closed the phone and laid it on the table, giving it a last impatient shove, as if he expected it to bite him. "You are up," he observed. "And walking about on your own."

"I'm cured," she said. She didn't add the hyperbolic corollary that sprang to her mind—I've been cured by your kiss—though she knew he might read it in her eyes if he cared to.

"Wonderful," he said, turning back to his pan. "Soon you will have no need of me."

Not so, she thought. Not soon. But she only said, "I'm starving."

He opened a pot lid on one burner, peered into an open pot on another. "You are having luck," he said. "This pasta is cooked."

"I THINK I've finally had enough sleep." Lucy poured herself another glass of wine from the pitcher. "I don't care if I never sleep again."

"That's too bad," Massimo said. He was standing at the sink, washing up the last of the dinner dishes. "Because it is nearly midnight."

"My clock is completely out of whack."

"Your clock is broken?"

"My biological clock. I'm wide-awake. I've become a night owl."

He put the last pot on the dish rack and turned to her, drying his hands on the dish towel. "You should be careful not to drink too much wine."

"You're right," she agreed. She took a decorous sip from the glass. "But the wine here is so good, how can I resist it?"

"Yes, I see," he said. "You are a hedonist. And it gets you into trouble."

Lucy smiled up at him, enjoying the absurdity of this new image of herself. "If you only knew how ridiculous that is," she said.

"Oh no," he disagreed. "I am an excellent judge of character."

She laughed. "Well, you haven't observed mine under ordinary circumstances. If you had, you would know that I am extremely practical, reliable, and incapable of doing anything . . ."

She paused. The word eluded her. What was it she was incapable of doing? Massimo was no help. He stood looking at her, his mouth set in the amused expression she found so provoking. "You always seem to be laughing at me," she said.

"I am not laughing. You are very charming," he observed.

Flustered, unused to compliments, Lucy could only look at her hands. Another swallow of wine seemed much the best option.

He moved from the sink, and when she had set the glass down again, he took it away. "You will make yourself sick again," he said.

"I feel fine," she protested. "My joints ache a little"—she stretched her arms up over her head—"and my ankle is shot, but other than that, I feel pretty good."

"Come and lie down on my bed," he suggested, "and I will give you a massage. I am very good at it."

"Are you?" Lucy said, opening her eyes wide. He nodded sagely. "Well, I can believe it. But I can't ask you to take any more trouble over me. You've done too much already."

"I do it for myself as much as for you," he replied. "It is my pleasure." He indicated the sitting room, where his narrow bed, neatly made, awaited.

"I know it," Lucy said. She got up, clinging to his arm as he helped her through the door. "But I don't understand it."

When she was stretched out on her stomach before him, she recalled the kiss—was it only a few hours ago?—and a nervous fluttering in her chest culminated in a hollow cough. He adjusted the pillow under her cheek and pulled her arms out to either side. "You must be perfectly relaxed and limp," he instructed her. The pillow smelled of him, a combination of cigarettes, a pleasant musky aftershave—she'd noticed the bottle in the bathroom and the name came to her, Toscana— the herbal shampoo he used—she'd seen that bottle, too—and through it all an undertone, heady and disturbing, that she identified simply as maleness. It had been awhile, she realized, since she had breathed in that particular essence. Since the divorce, she had had two largely unsatisfactory affairs, both resulting from friendships that would have been better left untested. What she felt about Massimo was different, entirely new: She was both wary and fascinated. She knew very little about him, and every bit of it boded ill for her peace of mind.

"I will begin with your feet," he announced. He took her left foot in his hands and pressed his thumbs firmly into the arch. In the next moment, a wave of release washed up into her calf so forcefully that she let out a soft groan of pleasure. "You see," he said. "This pain in your joints is caused by deposits of poison that have collected from your illness. Once they are dissolved, you will be free of pain and reenergized."

He switched to her right foot. She had no doubt that his medical theories were the equivalent of voodoo, but she couldn't be bothered to contradict him. He rolled her pajama leg up and began working on her calf. His fingers seemed to pry the long muscles away from the bones, and the resulting sensation, commingled of pain, pleasure, resistance, and submission, brought tears to her eyes.

He stopped. "You must take off these clothes," he said, pulling lightly at the waistband of her pajamas. "Take off everything but your underthings and I will bring a towel to cover you."

He went off to the bathroom. Lucy sat up and pulled off her pants. Apart from her underpants, she had on only a T-shirt, her preferred version of a pajama top, and a cotton sweater. She unbuttoned the sweater slowly, feeling awkward. He came back with the towel. She shrugged off the sweater and folded it carefully while he stood watching and waiting.

"It's too cold to take off my shirt," she said.

He shrugged. "Leave it on," he said. "I will work around it." He took the folded clothes and draped them over a chair while Lucy lay down again across the bed. Then he resumed the excruciating palpation of her right leg. "Are you embarrassed to take off your clothes in front of me?" he asked. His fingers had discovered an area of tension inside her knee, which he smoothed and prodded until she feared the whole joint might separate, and she groaned again. "Yes," she admitted.

"You should not be. Remember, I have seen you without your clothes before."

"That's what embarrasses me," she said. He worked up her thigh to the edge of her underpants, then back down again. She brought her hand to her mouth. Something was causing an increased flow of saliva; she felt a damp bit on the pillow beneath her mouth.

"Also, you know that I am married and have children, so I know many things"—he paused—"to do with the body."

"Thank you for reminding me," she said.

He pressed the heels of both hands into the small of her back and leaned into her with all his weight. Children, too, Lucy thought. How many? She pictured him in the midst of his family, a voluptuous, temperamental wife, pouting over a pot of boiling water while their mischievous daughter teased her spoiled, petulant younger brother, who glared at her with the icy, pale eyes he had inherited from his father. And if the fiery beauty knew her husband was massaging the legs of an American woman in a farmhouse in Tuscany, wouldn't she find a

way to pour that boiling water right over his head? No, Lucy
decided. Even though it was clear Massimo expected her to be
curious, she wasn't asking any questions about his family. She
closed her eyes and gave herself over to the pleasure of being
powerfully manipulated. After a few moments, he said, "Are
you falling asleep?"

"No, no," she assured him. "I'm wide-awake."

"Lift yourself up," he said, "so I can raise your shirt."

She did as he asked. An absurd shudder of embarrassment
came over her as the cloth came free of her breasts, causing her
to flop back down upon the bed gracelessly. Massimo spread
the towel over her, covering her from the waist down. "I'll have
to kneel over you to do your shoulders," he said. She felt the
bed give as he climbed upon it, planting a knee on either side
of her hips. Then he lowered himself so that he was sitting on
her buttocks. "I am not too heavy?" he asked.

"No," she said.

He walked his fingers up and down her spine, pausing here
and there to probe suspicious spots. Lucy looked out into the
dim-lit room dreamily. She thought of her apartment in
Brooklyn, her busy life there, which seemed so far away now,
so distant in both time and space, she could hardly remember
it. Then she imagined all the waves of the ocean, rising and
falling, silvered by moonlight on this side but there, perhaps,
still streaked with the deep red of the setting sun. And beneath
the waves all the vast array of sea creatures, bumping about in
the deep, never at rest because the sea, their atmosphere, was
never at rest, but always churning, treacherous, and difficult.
How vast it was, how mysterious. She had crossed it as if it
were a particularly wide thoroughfare, but now it was between
her and everything she knew and she could feel it out there,

pounding against the shore of this odd place where she had washed up, where she was as far from her proper element as a fish thrown ashore by a storm.

"What are you thinking?" Massimo said. He had lifted her left shoulder with one hand while he bore down upon her spine with the other. Her head drooped upon the pillow heavily, like a fruit grown too big for its vine.

"Of the ocean," she said.

He released her shoulder and dug his fingers in at either side of her neck. "Of what?"

"Of the Atlantic Ocean," she said. "Of how big it is and all the different fish in it."

He moved to the other shoulder. "What a strange woman you are, Lucy," he said.

"Am I? How am I strange?"

His hands came away from her neck. He raised himself from her back and in one motion brought himself beside her on the narrow bed. She had a momentary sensation of regret; the massage was over. But then he touched her cheek and rested his hand against her temple. "In such a way that I am wanting to make love to you."

She smiled. She thought of the care he had taken over washing her hair, the extraordinary kiss, which she knew could never be equaled, the sensual delights of the massage, so severe, yet tender, and now this simple declaration of desire, which her trembling limbs and suddenly racing heart told her she would return freely, without self-consciousness. She turned on her side to make more room for him. "This bed is so small," she said. "And it's not very sturdy."

He bent down over his ankles and began unfastening his shoes. "We will try very hard not to break it," he said.

Chapter 11

"THERE'S SOMETHING FISHY about the whole thing," Lucy said.

Massimo dropped the cover of the drawing pad over DV's agonized grimace. "Why would anyone keep such a memento as this?" he observed. "That is what is odd to me."

"It doesn't look like love," she agreed.

They had gone through DV's wardrobe, where, in the pocket of a favorite jacket, Lucy had found, as she had thought she might, the keys to the rented car. Then she had shown Massimo the drawing pad, which was still on the bed where she had left it when Signora Panatella surprised her; it seemed a long time ago now, though actually it had been barely a week. Before Massimo, she thought. Henceforth, a good many events would be classified for ease of recollection as "before" or "after" Massimo. He glanced at the half-open drawer where the envelope protruded, just as she had left it. "This is the letter you spoke of," he said.

Lucy leaned across him, lifting the envelope. "I wish I had a sample of Antonio Cini's handwriting," she said. "Maybe I can get him to write something down for me when we go over there tonight."

He stayed her hand with his. He didn't approve of her interest in the letter. He had a scruple she took to be part of his peculiar regard for the Cini name. "And if you were sure," he said, "that Signor Cini wrote this letter to your friend's mistress, what then, Lucy? What would that prove?"

"I don't know," she admitted. "It would prove he's lying. It would prove something happened here."

"What is it you think happened?"

This question touched something sensitive and tender, like a bruise. "I don't know," she complained. "I don't know. It's all a big mystery, isn't it, and it's written in Italian. I can't read this letter; I can't even read the police report. DV never told anyone Catherine had left him, but apparently she was here such a short time, the landlord doesn't even remember her. DV wasn't the sort of man who stays alone in some farmhouse"— she opened her hands, indicating the world at large—"in the middle of nowhere, and he certainly didn't take late-night walks on pitch-black roads just for the fun of it. He hated being outdoors; he had a horror of bugs. And where is this well he fell into? No one wants to talk about that. And where is Catherine Bultman? People don't just go up in smoke, Massimo."

"You are becoming upset," he observed.

"I am upset."

"You must calm down." He pushed the drawing pad aside. "Sit here on the bed."

She did as he suggested. He stood before her, holding her hands. "When I was sick," she said, "I had a dream. DV came to wake me up and he was angry. I've never seen him so angry."

She expected him to scoff at this confession, but he only looked at her steadily, as if she had said, at last, something that really interested him. "What did he say?" he asked.

"He didn't say anything. He just shook me."

He put his arm around her shoulder, and she rested her forehead against his chest. How odd he is, she thought. How completely unlike anyone I've ever known.

"Do you imagine he was murdered?" he asked.

"Not really. I'd just like a few straight answers, and they seem awfully hard to come by."

"But if you have no real suspicions, it is . . . so unnecessary to insist on such questions." He stroked her hair, pressing her forehead into his breastbone. "Why not just gather up all these things belonging to your friend, Lucy, and send them back to his family in America and—"

"And go home," she finished for him, her voice tremulous with frustration and self-pity. Was it possible that he only wanted to be rid of her?

He stepped back, holding her by the shoulders, bending down to look into her face. "And come to Roma with me," he said. "I have to go back tomorrow and I can't leave again for a week. I don't want to be away from you for so long. We have so little time left."

Rome, she thought. His family, his friends. Would he pass her off as a client? Perhaps they would meet only in her hotel room. However limited the opportunities, she reflected, she would be a fool not to take them. Later, she might be sick with regret, doubtless she would be, but it would not be regret for having missed this chance. This line of reasoning, so distinctly in the "after Massimo" mode, made her feel excited and reckless. She seemed to herself like a romantic film heroine, always ready—nay, eager—to cast her fate to the most vagrant of winds. She threw her arms about his neck, drawing him to her. "Yes," she said in a new, breathy voice direct from an imaginary film version of herself, "I'll go with you to Rome. I think I would go with you anywhere."

THIS PROMISE WAS NOT, Lucy knew at once, one she could be relied upon to keep, but making it gave her the necessary excuse to ignore the impropriety and impracticality of Massimo's plan. Everything about him that would normally have made her cautious—his enormous self-confidence, his clear preference for control over cooperation, his refusal to enter any but the most superficial conversation, the obvious duplicity of his relations with his wife, and therefore with all women, his peculiar lack of irony—combined in a mixture she found nonthreatening and oddly endearing. He seemed to think he was the only adult in a world of children and fools; he shouldered the burden of his incalculable responsibilities with an air of stoic resignation. His habitual smile was world-weary; she had not heard him laugh. He wasn't vain, for he did not concern himself with his image; rather, she thought, he entirely *was* his image. He saw himself complacently, and he was always seeing himself. He treated her like a child. She had become one of his dependents, and as such, he took a paternal interest and pride in her little accomplishments. He guarded her health, petted and fed her. He liked to see her eat everything on her plate. His interest in her was, she thought with amusement, entirely physical. No one had ever shown such an interest in her before.

And of course this all made him an extraordinarily exciting lover. His bulk, which had attracted her because it made him such an undeniable, solid presence, was revealed to be well toned and muscular. Though she admired his body, it was immediately obvious that she could not be more gratified by it than he was. All modesty was banished from their coupling because it was so evidently unnecessary. His body was a gift to her, and everything about hers interested him. He was determined to know everything that could be known about it. He reminded her of a man who has purchased an expensive and complicated new automobile; he wanted to maintain it perfectly in order to run it hard and fast. He found her responses gratifying; anything she did to please him seemed to please him inordinately. Afterward, when she lay stunned and satiated, she murmured, "How do you do that?" and he replied, "You do it, too, you know, Lucy."

She had the sense an erotic awakening brings to a young woman—younger than she was, she ruefully reflected—of the world being suddenly bigger, more various, more surprising and exciting than heretofore, but it did not escape her notice that for Massimo the world was much as it had ever been. She was breathless with excitement and amazement; he was as he always was. They both knew she was having an adventure that must come to an end when she returned to her old life in her own country. He was in his old life; he would never leave it.

They made love, and in the process, the drawing pad slid onto the floor, the cover flew open, and DV's image grimaced up at the ceiling. Then they made their plans.

Massimo would go down first; she would follow by train, for, he assured her, driving into Rome was "a madhouse," it was impossible to park, and she would have no need of a car while she was there. He knew of a hotel, small, near where he would be working, owned by a friend—hence inexpensive and personal. They would have to be discreet in public because of his family, but there was, he explained, no reason why he could not dine with her every day, at lunch or dinner, and he would arrange to spend at least one night of her visit in the hotel with her. As she listened, she couldn't help imagining the dismal situation his wife was so evidently accustomed to, figuring in her husband's plans as little more than an obstacle or an obligation. Lucy thought she could tell when he talked to her on the phone; there was a tone of self-righteous command, a greater frequency of the exclamation *"Non m'interessa,"* which he used to close or change the subject. A fair proportion of the world didn't interest Massimo, Lucy observed. It couldn't be long before she would herself fall into that ever-expanding category. But as he explained his plan for her, his hands moved over her body, sometimes gently, sometimes strong, but never rough or harsh, finding all the places that made her sigh and strain toward him.

He turned her onto her side, fitted her hips against his groin, and kissed her softly, repeatedly, along her shoulder and neck. As she moved against him, her head slipped over the edge of the mattress and she was looking down into DV's agonized face.

This was the bed DV had slept in with Catherine.

She pushed herself away from the edge, deeper into Massimo's embrace. But she could feel DV there, staring up from the floor, and lingering everywhere in the room, like a chill. He hadn't died here, but she did not doubt that he had suffered, and some residue of that suffering still coated every surface.

Go to Rome, she told herself. Forget DV. Get away from this house. Go spend a few days among the living.

Chapter 12

ITHIN THREE MINUTES of their entrance into his dining room, Antonio Cini, who constituted the first test of their discretion, surmised the new state of intimacy between Lucy and Massimo. He might have managed it sooner had he not been distracted by an argument he was carrying on with his father, which concluded when the old man broke away in a huff and stalked off to his dark hall without acknowledging the arrival of his guests. Antonio turned his attention upon them; his cold eyes raked over Lucy like a descending glacier, and she understood that something on her surface had altered since his last inspection and that he knew she and Massimo were now lovers. He took her hand and bent over her, placing light kisses on each cheek, murmuring her name like an insinuation. She noticed a fragrance—perhaps it was something he put on his hair—too sweet, and muddled by something acrid, perspiration, or just the odor of his flesh. The combination was sickening. She was reminded of the last time she had been in this dining room. None of the other guests had been ill that night; surely there had been nothing wrong with the food, but the memory of her illness and the oppressive closeness of Antonio combined to put a sudden check on her appetite. "So you are completely recovered," he said. "Thanks to the good efforts of this gentleman . . ." and he took Massimo's hand with something almost like enthusiasm. Lucy was struck again by the odd, archaic diction of his English. Where had he learned it?

The routine of the evening was much as it had been the first time. Antonio offered drinks and then suggested a sojourn on the loggia. It was a warm, clear evening, the air heavy with a lemony perfume. Lucy took her glass to the arch and leaned out over the thick stone sill, looking up at the stars dreamily, for in their progress from the dining room she had passed close to Massimo and he had brushed his fingers against her hip with an informed pressure that was unmistakably intentional. She didn't know if Antonio observed this sweet familiarity, but she decided that she didn't care, and not caring gave her an agreeable sense of bravado. The two men settled in the chairs behind her; she could hear them talking in a blend of English and Italian. Massimo was explaining his plan to return to Rome on the following day. Antonio showed no surprise at the news, nor did the addendum that Lucy would be spending a few days in the capital city as well provoke his habitual indifference to any exclamation beyond a polite expression of solicitude.

Lucy turned from the window. "I'm not going down with Massimo," she explained. "I have a few things to do here before I leave. I want to gather up some papers to mail from the post office in Sansepolcro. Then I thought I'd take the train from there. Do you think it would be safe to leave the car in the station for a few days?"

"I don't see why it would not," Antonio said. "But what car will you be taking?"

"The one at the house," she replied. "DV's rented car."

As if the mention of DV's name contained some silencing property, Antonio studied his *aperitivo* for a moment before answering, "I wonder if that car will even start."

"Why would it not start?" Massimo objected. "It is a new car."

"Oh, it probably will," Antonio agreed. "It's just that it hasn't been started in so long. Perhaps the battery will want recharging."

Lucy frowned. There was always some complication. "Surely DV used it now and then," she said.

"No. As a matter of fact, I know he didn't. He never went anywhere, you know, your friend. That car has not been moved in"—he did some mental calculations on his fingertips—"I would say it has been five months."

Lucy stared at him blankly, trying to incorporate this unexpected vision of DV as an expatriate recluse into the store of knowledge she already had about him. It wouldn't fit; it didn't make sense. "DV loved to drive," she said.

"Did he?" Antonio replied.

"It is of no importance," Massimo put in. "If the car is not running, I will send someone to start it up in the morning."

"Let me offer an alternate plan," Antonio said. "I have nothing to do and I would be happy to drive you, Lucia. The post office can be difficult; the workers there are without manners. I could be of help to you there, and, in addition, you would not have the worry of leaving the car at the station."

"You ankle is still so weak," Massimo reminded her. "It would be much better if you did not drive. I have never liked this idea."

"I couldn't inconvenience you," Lucy protested, though she could see that it was already decided between the two men and nothing she said would change that decision. She had been assigned to Antonio's care. The thought of half an hour alone in a car with him sent a needle of pain along the length of her spine, and she took a big gulp of red wine as an antidote.

"It is no inconvenience," Antonio assured her. "Nothing could please me more."

She smiled at this exaggeration of what she took to be his true feeling, which was, at best, idle curiosity. He is motivated by such weak and desultory forces, she thought. Even now, he was distracted from his disingenuous protest by the arrival of his father and grandmother, who appeared in the dining room trailing the cloud of disgruntlement that was the effluvia they exhaled. Lucy exchanged a look with Massimo, so brief that she couldn't read it, but it reassured her nonetheless. Antonio rose from his seat. "We will go in now," he directed. As Lucy passed in front of him, his fingers brushed her bare elbow. To her consternation, this contact, so accidental and surely innocent, made her flinch. Antonio marked her response. "Lucia," he said softly behind her, reprimanding her, and she felt the heat of blood flushing into her cheeks. The old man stood at the head of the table, fixing her with his raptor's eyes as she moved toward him. Behind her she could hear Massimo and Antonio exchanging what sounded like opinions. Why was the old man staring at her so fixedly? she wondered. He looked as if he wanted to tear her apart.

The gold and bronze of the sunflowers called up an unbearable memory—Lola in summer, long bronzed legs, full golden breasts, her golden mane loose and wild in the wind in a furious contest with the blazing sun.

Lucy sighed. It really was astounding how completely wrong DV got everything. First a comparison between a sunflower and a woman was just not appropriate. The colors were wrong; sunflower petals were not gold, nor were their centers bronze. It was as if he'd never seen one. Then there was the obvious leglessness of the plant, as well as the mathematical neatness of the petals about the center, the very opposite of the wild golden "mane" of the woman. Bad as it was, the sentence had caused DV some difficulty. He'd scratched out the word *hair* and, just to muddy things up and make the reader forget sunflowers and think of lions instead, he'd substituted the word *mane.* He'd inserted *loose and wild,* and changed *contest* to *competition,* then back to *contest.*

Poor man, Lucy thought. He had no gift at all, but because he made so much money, he was doomed to keep at it, year after year, page after page. Whenever he'd been interviewed, he'd talked about the sheer physical and mental torture of writing, how it took so much out of him, how he stumbled away from his desk like a fighter from the ring, bruised, battered, wondering where he would find the courage to go in for another round. Interviewers loved this sort of talk. They never thought to say, Well, if it is so inhumanly difficult, why not do something less arduous and possibly more fulfilling, something more suited to your abilities? Instead, they emitted sympathetic noises and wrote it all down. The artist suffers for his art—this was the accepted and ubiquitous party line subscribed to by the press.

But why, Lucy wondered, why exactly did they have to suffer so much? She didn't imagine that DV's difficulties, which were largely the result of a failure to master basic grammar and syntax, were comparable to the Olympian agonies of an artist like Michelangelo, or even to the stoic, brain-racked labors of Flaubert, or Henry James. No, DV was not an artist of that caliber. He was just a man who wrote books and shouldn't have. But even he suffered and even he imagined that it was in the service of the great god Art and that it was to be expected. If the Master was so cruel, so notoriously merciless and demanding, why enter his service? What was the charm of it?

Lucy pulled the chair out, sat down at the table, and gave her attention to the last writing DV had done before his death. There wasn't much of it. Malcolm Manx was still in the countryside, recovering from a love affair, but very soon things began to change. The Porsche modulated somehow into a rented Ford and Malcolm wasn't meeting anyone on his travels. He spoke to no one but the occasional shopkeeper, and no one was particularly nice to him or impressed by him. In fact, in a brief encounter with a gas station attendant, he was treated rudely and shortchanged of fifty thousand lire, but he was so intimidated and inept at the monetary system that he didn't realize it until much later. Then, although the money meant nothing to him, he felt angry and humiliated. His broken heart got worse instead of better; he realized that the woman, Lola, had left him not because she was neurotic, haunted by a nightmarish past, torn by her attachment to an old or even a new lover, but because she had found him boring. Everything reminded him of her. He stopped driving and started walking. The fields of giant sunflowers regarded him attentively as he passed. They're just plants, he told himself, but they were far from still. Their giant featureless faces rotated silently on their thick stalks, following the sun all day long. And, of course, like everything around him, they put him in mind of his lost love.

He was drinking a lot and not leaving the house. He fell on

the steps and banged his hip and shin. Then, abruptly, the voice changed. Malcolm was sitting at a desk, pouring out a glass of bourbon. He picked up his pen and wrote:

> I have lost the thread of this story. I thought I knew how it would end, but I was wrong. After you left—that was not in the plan, though it was in the story—after you left. After she left, he

That was it. After she left, he . . . Why had he stopped mid-sentence? Was he interrupted? Did the phone ring, or did someone knock at the door?

Or did he see someone through the window? The man with the rifle?

She looked out the window, across the drive to the place where she had seen the man. It was late afternoon, the sky was pale, the air cool, and there was a stillness in the scene that fascinated her. Nothing moved, not even the leaves on the trees, and there was not a sound to be heard. Massimo had gone to Rome, to the arms of his family, where he would be welcomed, fawned upon, served, where his wife would be impatient for the children to get to bed so that she could be alone with him. Oddly, this vision did not disturb her. In fact, she liked the thought of him there, comfortable and at ease among his own things in the city that was also, in a deep, familial way, his own. She was not, she knew, in any sense a threat to that world of his, and she assumed that he knew this. He had surprised her by telling her that he did not ordinarily "have affairs," because he hadn't the time or interest, didn't need such diversions, and he confessed that he had never made love to an American woman before.

"And what do you think of it?" she asked. "Is it different?"

They were lying in the big bed in DV's apartment. She had rested her head against his chest; their legs were casually entwined.

"Oh yes," he said. "Very different."

"In what way?" she persisted.

"In a way that is sweet," he said. "It is because you are so shy."

"Oh," she said. "I thought I was immodest and noisy."

He made a snorting sound—was it a laugh or difficulty in breathing? Then he changed the subject.

A small bird, some variety of sparrow, with a reddish stain across its breast and dark patches near its beak, had alighted on the windowsill and hopped right onto the desk. Lucy kept still. One so seldom sees a wild bird this close, she thought. The bird eyed her, tilting its head from side to side cautiously, then, satisfied that she was not dangerous, fell to picking at the edge of DV's notebook. Lucy's thoughts wandered back to Massimo, to his lovemaking, which so astonished her. Twice in the night, sleeping fitfully in what she thought of as DV's bed, she had waked to find his hands moving over her, and without speaking, in a state of dreamy arousal so complete and free of self-consciousness that the memory of it made her blush, she had encouraged his caresses. It was all so easy, this affair; it was like falling into a feather pillow. And the certainty that she must give it up soon gave it a poignancy that she could hardly bear, though she knew she would bear it when the time came. There was no particular reason to keep it a secret, but it irritated her that Antonio Cini had guessed something of it. And that was just it—he could only guess something, and that something was to him, no doubt, contemptible, or merely laughable. Wasn't this just what American women always did? They came to Italy to find lovers, and why shouldn't they be accommodated, since it was so easy, they were so willing, and then, of course, they went home and worked up their little adventure into a grand affair, something to curl up with on those long, cold, bitter American nights alone. She had read all this in his eyes. Surely he would find some subtle way to prod her about it on the ride to the train station tomorrow, just as she hoped to prod him about his pursuit of Catherine Bultman. It promised to be an unpleasant, though possibly rewarding, trip.

The bird had given up on the notebook and moved on to a pencil. It lifted the eraser in its beak, dropped it back to the table, then lifted it again. Each time it struck the wood, the pencil made a sharp rap, even and surprisingly loud, like the ticking of a clock. That was because, Lucy observed, the room was so quiet and still. The bird was maniacally occupied by this activity, as if it were practicing some important, necessary exercise. Bird calisthenics, she thought. She had not moved and did not move, so that her own stillness had become part of the room's furnishings, at least as far as the bird was concerned.

This was where DV had stayed in the last months of his life, alone, day after day, working on his poor novel. Perhaps he had been visited by this busybody sparrow before the bizarre accident that ended his life. That accident was another subject she intended to touch upon during the drive with Antonio. He was adept at avoiding it, or had been so far. But this time she would press him, and because they would be closed up in a car, he wouldn't be able to get away.

The bird had worked the pencil to the edge of the desk, where it slipped over the side and dropped to the floor. In the same moment, a queer, thin breeze ruffled the pages in the neat stacks of paper she had arranged across the desk. It was too much for the bird, which took off in a minitornado of feathers, out through the open window and off into the dull afternoon. The pencil rolled toward her feet; the floor wasn't level, she observed. The breeze brushed past her, cooling her cheeks and forehead. It was odd, like a current of cool water in a warm stream. It was odd, she thought again, this brief, specific chill, and then she felt a deeper cold that gripped her at the base of the spine and rushed up the length of her back, as palpable as a fingertip. The sensation in her scalp was unmistakable; the skin tightened, so that the hairs on her head, though they were not bristling like the fur on a cat's back, were, in some vestigial, cellular way, standing on end. If she moved even a finger, she knew the illusion that she was not alone would be dispelled, but she did not move. Instead, she listened intently. The breeze had dropped off as quickly as it had come up, and her ears strained into a void in which nothing save the listener breathed. Eventually, she heard her own heartbeat, which had steadily elevated. Whoever it was, whatever it was, was just behind her; she felt a gathered energy at her back exerting a barely perceptible pressure upon her, like the intangible, ineluctable press of eye beams. She was being watched.

Slowly, with an effort of will disproportionate to the difficulty of the action, she turned in place and looked back at the empty doorway, the bare landing, and beyond that to the open doorway of DV's bedroom. Then her eyes started from their sockets and her heart lurched in her chest like an engine thrown carelessly out of gear, for there was someone there looking back at her. Her hand flew up to contain a shout of alarm. She recognized her observer; it was her own reflection in the mirror on the open door of the wardrobe. But this discovery only intensified her terror and confusion, for she was sure, wasn't she, didn't she remember closing that door a few

hours ago, turning the key firmly in the latch? She was certain
she had not opened it again. She rushed out across the landing
and confronted her distraught, noticeably pale reflection. She
examined the wardrobe, which was as she had left it, empty
but for a few wire hangers. Next to it stood the suitcase she
had packed that morning, which contained DV's clothes,
shoes, everything that had been in the wardrobe. The suitcase
was open; the drawing pad lay across the top of the folded
clothes. She had been unsure what to do with it. She was
unsure what to do with everything, she concluded, closing the
wardrobe door. The latch was old. It must not have caught
properly and the bedroom floor, like all the floors in the house,
was uneven, so the door had opened on its own. The spell had
been broken by her brisk movement; she was her practical self
again. The isolation of this house and the omnipresence of DV
in it had played upon all that was suggestive in her. Or rather,
it was DV's omniabsence, the volume of the evidence that he
had been here but was no more.

It was only that the lock was old. As she turned the key, the
mechanism gave a sturdy resistance and she struggled with it
briefly, turning the key hard until she felt the lock had seated.
She gave the door handle a pull to make sure it was locked,
then went back into the study and looked over the boxes of
books she had spent the morning packing, the books no one
wanted, which would be so expensive to ship back to the
States, it hardly seemed worth it. Yet it would be a shame to
disperse them. It was one of the many curious ironies of DV's
personality that though he wrote trash, he seldom read it.
Lucy calmed herself with the problem of the books. If the
estate would pay for the shipping, perhaps she could buy them
cheaply herself.

But there was no telling what the estate would pay for, or

even, at this point, who the estate was. Jean McKay had approved Lucy's plan to go to Rome for a few days, asking only for whatever papers Lucy thought might interest her, and various records the accountants were after. Everything else was to stay at the farmhouse until she returned, a situation that would make Signora Panatella weep with frustration. Lucy had put it out that she was off to Rome on business for the deceased tenant, an excuse Antonio Cini had seen through as if she'd held up a pane of window glass, but which the Panatellas would probably accept. Americans were always moving about on business, and they were notoriously wasteful and extravagant in the process.

Why did it bother her, she wondered, what these people thought of her, since in a short time she would disappear from their lives, and they from hers, entirely, as if, like DV, she had fallen into a hole in the earth? She reached across the desk and pulled in the windows. She would sleep in the smaller apartment, where she was less likely to be visited by phantoms. In the morning, after the brief ordeal of an excursion with Antonio Cini, she would make her way to Rome and to Massimo. Though he had been gone only a few hours, she longed for him with a visceral ache she had never experienced before.

Chapter 13

AMONG THE MODERN MYTHS that had failed to excite Antonio Cini's devotion was the one that confers prestige upon the owner according to the size and power of his automobile. Or so Lucy concluded as she climbed into the narrow confines of the Cini car, an unimpressive pale blue steel box on wheels, with an engine that complained bitterly at the challenge of reversing on the mild incline of the farmhouse driveway. The interior was dusty, the plastic seats were covered with cheap black cloth covers printed over in a frightening array of pink dots, and the floor mats were gritty with gravel deposited by the shoes of previous passengers over what must have been a considerable period of time. Antonio did not fasten his seat belt, and Lucy, after a brief struggle with the recalcitrant strap on her side, which was so designed that it could not actually fit across anything resembling a human body, gave up and let it snap back into its preferred position against the door frame. The little car lurched down the driveway, rattling so hard she braced her-self by clutching the strap over her head and jamming her feet against the front panel of the floorboard. Antonio was entirely occupied with the wheel, the gearshift, and the clutch, so Lucy took the opportunity to observe him. For some reason, he had decided to make himself agreeable to her, and the effort subtly altered his appearance. She would not, she admitted, ever be able to say he was an attractive man. His body was too slack, his muscles lacked tone, and his skin was sallow. His mouth was a bilious purple, and he had the kind of heavy beard that always looks unshaven, though a red-rimmed nick near his chin and another close to his ear testified to a recent effort. His general aura of ill health, poor diet, and insufficient exercise was intensified by his taste in clothes, which ran to synthetic fibers and colors that clashed with his skin. Today, for exam-ple, he was wearing a light blue turtleneck shirt of a fabric that had an unnatural sheen to it and brown woolen pants with elastic insets at either side of the waistband to accommodate a vacillating girth. But his expression was more alert, less sour than she had seen before. He had arrived at her door exactly at the appointed time, bearing a gift that took her entirely by sur-prise, for it revealed both thoughtfulness and generosity, two qualities she had not expected to discover in his character. She glanced between the seats to where it lay across the floor, a sturdy but elegant walking stick, carved from a light golden wood, with a silver handle in the form of a leopard's head.

"Please, take this with you," he had said. "The streets of Rome can be difficult. They are all of small stones and the traf-fic is . . ." He touched his fingers to his forehead, indicating the impossibility of finding a word to describe the horror of the traffic. "And your ankle is still too weak, I think."

And, in fact, she had had these same thoughts and worried

about what she would do for support on those excursions when Massimo's arm was not available to her. She dreaded a reinjury, and her ankle, though much improved, was still not strong enough to walk for any length of time without a tight bandage.

"This is so kind," she said. "It is exactly what I need." She accepted the stick and examined the beautifully worked animal head with its protuberant brow and wide, vacant, shining eyes. It was old, a family heirloom perhaps. He might have pulled it from a rack of fellows equally wonderful, an afterthought on his way out the door. "Of course," she added, "I'll return it to you when I come back."

He shrugged. "Keep it as long as you need it," he said. Though it was certainly not gracious, Lucy found this remark sufficiently courteous, for it allowed her to return an object she considered too valuable to accept as a gift, without requiring him ever to demand that it be returned. She smiled at him and took a few steps back into the kitchen, leaning on the stick to demonstrate its usefulness. But he had lost interest already; the gesture was complete. He expressed surprise over the meagerness of her luggage.

They had reached the end of the driveway now, and the car settled onto the level road with a jolt and a shuddering at the seams, like an airplane touching down. Lucy readjusted herself, smoothing her skirt over her knees. She was thinking of how she might introduce the subject of DV when, to her surprise, Antonio did it for her.

"You have packed up your poor friend's possessions?" he said.

"I have," she replied. "Though I'm not sure yet where I'm sending them."

"Surely back to his family."

"He didn't have much in the way of family."

Antonio furrowed his brow, casting her a quick sidelong look of dismay.

"He was estranged from his former wives," she explained, "and his parents died some time ago."

"How unfortunate."

"I'm sending some of his papers to his agent," she added, indicating the thick envelope she had placed atop her small bag on the backseat. "Though there wasn't much to send."

"You did not find this unfinished book about my family?" They were rattling down the road that ran past his estate, and at the mention of "my family" he lifted his chin, indicating the stone wall behind which that entity was protected from interlopers and aliens.

"No," Lucy assured him. "He never finished it. It wasn't really about your family anyway. It was about DV. All his books were about himself."

"But my house was in it. My family history."

Lucy smiled at his evident anxiety. "You really have nothing to fear, Signor Cini. The book wasn't finished and will never be published."

"Please call me Antonio," he protested.

She nodded. She would never call him Antonio. "It's about DV alone in the farmhouse after Catherine leaves, about how much he misses her."

She studied his profile as she said the name Catherine and detected a hardening at the jawline, a flicker of the eyes. The name is painful to him, she thought. DV wasn't the only one pining for Catherine Bultman.

"And why, does he say in this story, did the woman leave?" He affected an amused nonchalance. Lucy considered a moment before giving her answer. She might say, Because of another man, just to see how he responded. But she settled, as was her habit, on the truth. "She leaves because she's bored with him."

Antonio's eyebrows shot up, while the corners of his mouth pulled down. It was an expression Massimo used, too; it reminded Lucy of him and she felt a pleasant twinge of desire. Soon. She would be with him soon.

"It is true," Antonio offered. "She was very bored here."

"Did she tell you that?"

They had reached the intersection with the paved road that would take them to the autostrada. Antonio brought the car to a full stop and leaned toward the windshield, looking up and down the empty roadway as if he expected a sudden explosion of enraged traffic. "She did not have to tell me," he said.

"Did you see much of her?"

He pulled out into the road, struggling with the gearshift and letting out the clutch so slowly that the engine nearly stalled. He was an awful driver; he drove like a teenage girl. Gradually, he worked his way up through the gears and settled into a cruising speed well below the limit. "Oh, yes," he said offhandedly. "I saw her now and then. Her Italian is very good, you know. She speaks very well, with almost no accent; I don't know where she learned it. Your friend spoke not at all. She did everything for him. When they went out in the car, she was always the driver. He was completely dependent on her." He paused, submitting this last observation with the formality of a lawyer presenting a bit of deeply incriminating evidence. "I knew, of course, that could not go on very long."

"But wasn't she painting? She came here to paint."

"Oh yes," he agreed. "I saw her about with her little water-color box."

The diminutive "little" moved Lucy to the defense of Catherine Bultman. "She is an excellent painter," she said.

Antonio gave her a quick, incredulous inspection. "I am no judge of such matters," he said. "The painters I admire have all been dead for five hundred years."

Lucy looked out the window at the beauty of the passing countryside. There was a vineyard rising on a gentle slope, and at the top a cypress-lined drive leading to a big ocher-colored farmhouse that glowed in the limpid morning light. The air was crisp, the foliage faded. Summer was over, but it would be awhile before the leaves turned. For now nature was merely exhausted from the heat of summer. Then, at an intersection, she saw a roadside altar, a brightly painted statue of Mary in a dark grotto made of small rocks, the whole thing set on a heavy pedestal with fresh flowers at the base. The road seemed familiar, and Lucy turned to look down it as they passed. There was a mown field, then a wall. Wasn't that gate she could just make out the one to the cemetery where DV was buried? "Is that the road to Ugolino?" she asked Antonio.

"Yes," he said. "You are observant."

"I recognized the gate. I want to go see the stone before I leave," she said. "Maybe I can plant something that will grow without much attention."

He said nothing, absorbed by maneuvering past a deep rut in the road. Then he cast her a brief, chilly look.

"Where is this well?" she said abruptly.

"I beg your pardon?" he said.

"The well. The one that DV fell into. Where is it? Can I see it?"

"I don't think you would want to see it," he responded. "There is nothing to see anymore anyway. It has been closed."

"They closed it up because it was so dangerous?"

"It was open only very briefly. Only a few hours, because it was being pumped. Then it was replaced and closed up."

"What was replaced?"

He frowned. "It is unpleasant to speak of such things."

"How could they pump out a well?" she insisted. "Aren't they all spring-fed around here?"

Now he gave her a look of real distress. "I fear there has been some misunderstanding," he said.

"He fell down a well, didn't he?"

"That is the English word for *pozzo*, I am correct?" he said. "It is a hole in the earth?"

"For water," she agreed. "Yes, that's right."

He released the wheel and pulled at the close neck of his sweater. "It is warm today," he said.

"So what's the misunderstanding?"

He swallowed, then, taking resolve, addressed her in the superior, emotionless voice of one whose interest in his topic is entirely academic. "Your friend did not fall into a well," he said. "That would be actually difficult to do, as they are normally raised and not very wide."

"That's what I thought."

"He fell into a *pozzo nero*. I am not sure how to say this in English."

"A black well?" she said.

"It is for the houses, because there are no pipes such as in the city, for the waste."

Lucy nodded as the grisly vision of DV's last moments materialized in her consciousness. "A septic tank," she said softly.

"What is the word?" he inquired.

"A septic tank," she said firmly. "It's for sewage."

"That must be it," he agreed. "It is not a term one learns."

"Jesus," she said.

"It had been cracked, the concrete, you understand."

"The tank," she said.

"Yes. It had to be replaced. But as often happens, once it was opened, the pumping equipment did not function properly, or perhaps it did not arrive. I don't remember. It belonged to the farm that joins Lucio Panatella's land. They had to give up because it was night, and they put up barricades around it, but somehow your friend managed to fall down the hill behind it, a very steep hill from a wooded area where it was not expected that anyone would be walking about late at night."

"And he fell into the tank."

He nodded. "Only partly. They found him early in the morning when they came to finish the work. He had struck his head on the concrete at the edge."

"What an ignominious end," she said.

"I am sorry to be the person to tell you."

"But why was he in the woods at night?"

"I did not see him often," Antonio said. They had come to the autostrada entrance. For a few moments, he was occupied in accelerating onto it. The car strained and whined, but there was little traffic and Antonio drifted into the far-right lane without difficulty. Lucy looked out at a field of sunflowers well past their bloom; the heavy dark heads hung facedown on the dry stalks, like an army of defeated soldiers. "He was drinking a good deal of alcohol," Antonio continued. "He didn't go out at all, as far as I know. He left lists for Signora Panatella, which I translated for her. On these lists, there was always whiskey. After some time, Lucio arranged to have it delivered to the house in boxes so his mother would not have to make the extra trip."

"He was a heavy drinker," Lucy said. "But he was social about it. He liked to drink with friends."

"He had no friends here," Antonio observed.

No, Lucy thought bitterly. You might have befriended him, but you were busy trying to steal his mistress. She looked away, out at the green and golden Tuscan hills, the brilliant, oddly assaultive blue of the sky pressing down upon them, everything poised and balanced with a postcard's glib perfection and something of its slickness. In centuries past, this scenery had served artists as a subtle, mysterious backdrop for the doings of imaginary heroes, or as an added dimension to portraits of the wealthy and the powerful. In the old paintings, it was often gray, shrouded in mist, and presumably, sometimes it still was. In the distance she could see, at the top of a hill, the sharp outlines of a town, its ancient wall still defending it, ready to draw into itself tomorrow if enemies would only arise.

"He never let on that anything was wrong," she said. "He didn't tell anyone Catherine was gone. We all assumed they were having a wonderful, romantic time here."

Antonio made no comment, though his expression was attentive. His eyes shifted from the road to his passenger, then back again. "He did not confide in you," he said.

"Well, I suppose he wouldn't have, even if he'd wanted to. He was my employer. We didn't really talk about his personal life."

Antonio nodded. "Of course," he said.

Lucy thought, Of course what? Of course I would know nothing about such things, having never been employed one minute of my life? She remained silent while her distrust of him billowed out in all directions, like a sail in a hurricane. He knew more than he was telling; she was sure of it. He was playing some absurd game, drawing her into it with his cryptic quasi-questions and his occasional hints at how much access he had to what went on in the farmhouse. Just to rile him, she said, "Maybe he really did see this ghost," and she knew at once she had succeeded, for he pursed up his face as if he'd bitten into something sour and replied in his most annoying and patronizing tone, "Lucia."

"Well, he didn't have much imagination," she insisted. "And he was writing a ghost story, which he'd never done before, so something must have given him the idea."

"It is a mystery to me how he learned this story of my family," Antonio admitted. He was so evidently perplexed, Lucy believed him.

"Maybe the ghost told him," she suggested.

"Surely you do not believe in phantasms," he protested.

She watched him closely. He told Catherine the story of the murdered partisan, she thought, and then Catherine told DV. "I didn't before I came here," she said.

"Oh. You have been converted."

"The night I got locked out, when I was sick," she said. "I went out because I saw a man on the drive looking at the house. A man with a rifle."

He gave a small puff of indignation. "This was no doubt Lucio Panatella hunting the boar that are so destructive of our property."

Lucy stared at him a moment. "Oh," she said. Massimo had dismissed the apparition of the man as the by-product of her illness, an hallucination or possibly a dream, and in truth, her memory of that night was sketchy at best. Though she had known there must be a simple explanation for what she thought she saw, she felt oddly disappointed by this one. It was so obvious. This was the country, not some cityscape where a man walking at night with a rifle was probably a murderer. He was a hunter, protecting his property and bringing home, literally in this case, the bacon. Lucy sat quietly, moodily contemplating the absurdity of her suspicions.

They had reached the outskirts of Sansepolcro, where the scenery changed abruptly from pastoral bliss to urban sprawl. Lucy noted a car dealership, a tile and building materials warehouse, and a garden-supply store flanked by plaster statues of gods, lions, saints, and enormous garlanded urns. Everything was cheap and ugly, the buildings thrown up by contractors without benefit of architects, constructed of concrete, steel, and glass. The Italians had evidently given up on the idea of architecture as art with as little struggle as the rest of the world. She looked back at Antonio, who seemed intent on driving through the ugliness without looking at it. This brief trip with him had certainly operated to dispel various mysteries, just as she had hoped it might. The ghost she had seen was Lucio Panatella out hunting, DV had fallen into a cesspool, and Catherine Bultman had not been spirited away, but had gone off in search of better adventures. She did not entirely believe this last bit. Antonio was not as disinterested as he pretended to be; she felt sure of that. He was too eager to dismiss Catherine, too impatient at any suggestion that she was an artist, a woman of substance and discrimination, as Lucy felt sure she must be, and his eagerness had an element of defensiveness in it that gave him away. She saw this because she knew about the letter.

"I found a drawing Catherine did of DV," she said. "It was hidden in the wardrobe."

He gave her his empty dead-fish look but said nothing.

"It was pretty shocking," she continued. "It was DV, but he was all cut open, in agony."

She caught the flicker of a smile at the corner of his mouth. "Doubtless he suffered on her account."

"Did she tell you she was angry with him?"

"You are so suspicious, Lucia. What is it you are suspicious of? Do you think something happened here in our little corner of the world, something out of the ordinary?"

"Maybe," she confessed. "Maybe I do."

"I assure you," he said, his voice heavy with boredom, "everything that happened here was ordinary."

They had come to the ancient wall of the town. Antonio turned along it, following its languid curve, then headed south toward the neat, serviceable train station with its double row of tracks running in and out. He pulled into a parking space and shut down the engine, which whimpered and shuddered into silence like a recalcitrant child being sent to bed. "Here we are," he said.

Lucy glanced back at the package atop her overnight bag. "I thought we were stopping at the post office?"

"I think there is no time," he said. "If you are not to miss your train. I have errands to do in the town, so I will mail it for you and you may reimburse me upon your return."

She glanced at her watch; he was right. Had he planned this all along, gauged the time of the trip to make it impossible for her to refuse his offer? "That's very kind of you," she said.

He opened his door, smiling agreeably. In fact, he seemed unduly pleased with himself. "I will go into the station with you to assist in buying your ticket."

Lucy got out, accepted the stick he held out to her, and hobbled along behind him into the busy, stuffy waiting room. At the counter, she stood beside him, grinning inanely while he conversed with the ticket agent, who seemed agitated by the business of issuing a one-way ticket. Lucy dug the requisite lire out of her wallet, said *"Grazie"* several times, and, at length, received the stiff cardboard ticket with the magical word *Roma* stamped in the space reserved for her destination. Her spirits lifted at the sight of it. Roma meant, among other pleasures, Massimo. Massimo's kisses, his embraces, the reassuring warmth of his skin next to hers, the curious thrill of her name on his lips, sounding exotic and romantic, as it never had before. She forgot all about Antonio Cini, though he escorted her down the tiled hallway to the platform where the train was being announced; they had arrived with only minutes to spare. Far away down the track she could see the engine growing larger and louder. The excitement of a train arriving, coming to carry her away, carry her to her lover, made her eyes damp and she felt her cheeks flushed with blood.

"I hope you will have a pleasant stay in Roma," Antonio said, and she thanked him distractedly, for the train was very close now. The other passengers all busied themselves hoisting up their bags, bidding farewells to their friends or families. She reached out for her own bag, which had a wide strap that Antonio helped her to settle onto her shoulder. Then, as the noise grew deafening and the passing cars ground to a halt before the platform, Antonio shouted to her one last, amazing bit of information. "If you want to see Caterina Bultman," he said, "you will find her in Roma." The doors snapped open and the exiting passengers struggled against the crush of those getting on. Lucy was swallowed up in the turmoil, pushed first one way, then another. "What?" she shouted back at Antonio. "What did you say?"

"In Via Margutta," he called out. "You will find her there."

"Via Margutta," Lucy said. But of course he could not hear her and she could no longer see him, for the crowd obscured her view, the doors had closed, and the train was already pulling away.

Chapter 14

SOME SAY HE IS putting his sword away, others that he is drawing it out."

They were standing on the Ponte Vittorio Emanuele, looking up at the forbidding crenellated walls of the Castel Sant' Angelo, which rises like a pale dune above the dark pines of the small park on its grounds. Massimo was referring to the presumed intention of the angel perched at the top, his wings extended, one hand raised before him, holding a downward-pointing sword, the other relaxed around the sheath at his hips. His head was bowed, yet even from this distance Lucy could make out the serene otherworldly smile, so unsuited to the drama of his pose. "He's putting it away," she said. "That's what the bishop saw. An angel sheathing his sword, and he knew the plague was over."

"Ah," Massimo said. "You know everything."

"I read it in an art book," she admitted. "Long ago. Maybe it wasn't a bishop. Maybe it was a cardinal. I'm not sure."

Above the castle, the intense blue of the sky deepened, the thin clouds shifted from light to steely gray, and the Tiber, which flowed sluggishly between the trash-strewn, dry, cracked dirt and patchy grass of its banks, took on a glistening sheen like oil. Massimo pointed to the platform opening out around the angel. "That is where Tosca jumped to her death."

"Yes," Lucy said. "Can we go up there?"

"It is possible to go. The view is very fine. But unfortunately, now it is closed."

Lucy laughed. It was already a joke; Rome, unfortunately, was closed. They had passed the morning in the uncomfortable bed at her hotel and by the time they'd gotten dressed and out on the street, it was afternoon and everything was closing for the *pausa*. They had walked through the narrow streets near the Pantheon, across the tourist hubbub of the Piazza Navona, along the quieter Via dei Coronari, where the antique dealers were busy pulling down the metal shades of their cluttered, fabulous shops, to the river. Lucy turned away from the castle and looked across the roaring fury of the bridge traffic to the other side. In the distance she could see the dome of St. Peter's and before it a more classical building—it looked like a Greek temple—set back among low trees near the riverbank. A tourist couple approaching stopped to snap each other's picture with the dome as a backdrop. Massimo took Lucy's arm and turned her back the way they had come. "We will have lunch near here," he said.

She leaned against his arm. Antonio Cini had been right: The uneven stones of the streets were torture for her. She picked her way among them carefully, but it was impossible to make much progress without putting constant stress on her ankle. She had not brought the walking stick. Massimo had noticed it at once and seemed annoyed by it; she wasn't sure

why. Was it because Antonio had offered it or because she had
accepted it? Was he jealous, or had she somehow offended his
sense of propriety? Perhaps he simply did not wish to be seen
with a woman so clearly disabled. Though he seldom disguised his displeasure, he was never willing to discuss it, or
even to own up to it. If she had said, What exactly is it about
my having this useful stick that bothers you? he would have
told her she was imagining things, that he was not in the least
bothered. She thought about this as they walked along the
Lungotevere while the cars and motor scooters roared around
them and a seagull swooped down toward the deceptive calm
of the river. She knew a few things about him now, though the
principal thing she knew was that he was closed to her.

Everything was different here, in his city, where his real life
was liable to pop up at any moment to claim him. She had
known some adjustment would be inevitable, and the moment
he had entered the cramped hotel room with its too-big furniture and too-busy wallpaper, she had felt the need of it, but she
was overcome with timidity and pretended nothing was amiss.
She chattered about the train trip and the wild taxi ride from
the station through the racket and beauty of the ancient city,
how immense and yet livable it was, for there were no tall
buildings to intimidate the pedestrian, and how magical and
marvelous it appeared in the crisp autumn light, especially
when they went careening through the old streets near the Pantheon, where her hotel was tucked away. He listened patiently,
but he was not much interested. His phone started shrieking
and he yanked it from his jacket pocket impatiently. *"Pronto,"*
he said, and then, for what seemed a long time, he stood before
her, his head inclined into the receiver, frowning and silent
while a woman's voice issued angrily and at considerable volume into the room. When she paused for breath, he jumped in,

speaking firmly and so slowly that Lucy understood most of it: "No, it is impossible. Tell him it is impossible. Nothing can be done about it. He must—" Then she missed the verb, he picked up speed, and she lost the gist of his reply. She sat on the bed, swinging her legs like a girl and taking note of the mixture of excitement, anxiety, and desire occasioned by his presence in the room. She felt vulnerable in a way she could not remember feeling before. She wanted to please him. When at last he closed up the phone, he jammed it under the mattress, to her delight, declaring he would not be interrupted again, and threw himself across the bed, pulling her with him. Then for some exhilarating time, there was no need to talk about anything.

But now, as he guided her into a narrow street off the Lungotevere and the fury of the traffic receded behind them, she was aware again of a subtle difference in his manner toward her. He was solicitous, but distant, nearly polite; he was affectionate, but without warmth, as if he was required to show more than he could feel. When they arrived at the small bustling restaurant he had chosen, he held her loosely by the elbow while he discussed the best table with the waiter, who seemed to know him. They took for granted, Lucy observed, that it was more desirable to sit outside, where the cloths flapped in the damp breeze and the motor scooters whined and sputtered, whipping up choking clouds of dirt as they whirled by, than at the quiet, largely empty tables in the pleasant interior rooms. When there was a pause, she tugged at Massimo's sleeve, gesturing away from the crowd. "I'd really prefer to be inside," she said.

He gave her a startled, incredulous look before he conveyed her inexplicable prejudice to the waiter, who, in turn, subjected her to a brief, fascinated perusal, then led them to a small table near the door.

"I hope you don't mind," she said when they had taken their seats. "It's so noisy outside."

"No, no," he said. "It doesn't matter." She noticed he had chosen a chair that allowed him to look out at the crowded, voluble diners on the sidewalk. His attention flickered among them, settling first here, then there, like a busy insect. So much for romance, Lucy thought. The waiter inquired about their wine and water. *"Bianco, non gassata,"* Massimo suggested, and she nodded her agreement. A bowl of bread appeared, a plate of crostini with chopped fresh tomatoes, then the big bottles of water and wine. The waiter engaged Massimo in a discussion of the food, which Lucy understood. She made appreciative noises at Massimo's choices, a dish of potatoes and porcini mushrooms, shrimp, the big ones, *mazzancolle,* grilled, followed by another of *cicoria,* which he knew Lucy favored, and perhaps, they would see, a mixed salad. Lucy sipped her wine and munched a crostino. She was ravenously hungry. The waiters passed in and out of the room, carrying plates of steaming, mouthwatering food, looking bored and exchanging terse comments with one another. But when they arrived on the sidewalk, they became animated, solicitous; they lowered their offerings with solemnity, passing them beneath the noses of the diners, many of whom stubbed out half-smoked cigarettes in tribute to the superior gustatory charm of the food.

"This is wonderful," Lucy said.

"It is a good place," Massimo confirmed.

"You eat here a lot?"

"When I am in this part of town," he said. He was looking

away from her, out at a couple who had just arrived. The woman was statuesque and dressed in a minuscule stretchy red dress that revealed every detail of her figure.

"Do you live near here?"

This got his attention. He turned to her and took her hand over the table. "Why do you want to know where I live, Lucy?" he said. His eyes searched her face with an intensity she thought inappropriate to the offhandedness of her question.

"I just wondered," she said.

"I think it would be better if you did not know this."

She shrugged, she acquiesced, but she thought, What does he think I'm going to do? Show up at dinnertime? Did he seriously imagine that she couldn't get this information if she really wanted it?

While the waiter filled their plates with fragrant mushrooms and potatoes from a heaping dish intended to serve eight or ten, Lucy had a moment to reflect that Massimo had seemed to like her better when she was unable to get out of bed. He had proposed this public venue himself; she had the impression that he thought it important that they be seen together. But he wasn't enjoying it. He seemed, in fact, to be having difficulty concentrating on it. Her past experience had led her to the observation that when a love affair starts out with some romanticized notion of us against them, disillusion is bound to set in, and the equation is rewritten then as us against each other. When Massimo was defending her from the jaws of death, or even from a threat as innocuous as the Italian medical bureaucracy, he had been full of quiet confidence and determination. Now that she was able to express contrary views, exhibit preferences, and ask for information, he was entirely ill at ease. She drank a little more wine, watching his handsome profile, which he was presenting to her at the moment, for his attention was given over to two young men who had arrived on motor scooters and were immediately engaged in a disagreement with the waiter. Studying his face in such an arrested pose made her think of their recent lovemaking—had it been only a few hours ago?—and of his mouth against her ear, saying softly, tenderly, with the perfect mixture of surprise and relief, "Ah, Lucy, I have missed you."

Gradually, he disengaged himself from his scrutiny of the young men and his attention drifted back to her. He saw the combination of affection and suspicion in her eyes—she made no effort to disguise it—and he said, "What is it, Lucy? Why are you looking in this way?"

There was an edge to this question that struck her as distinctly challenging, as if he expected her to lodge some preposterous grievance, one he would throw off disdainfully the moment she uttered it. And what could she say? You are different here? You are not paying enough attention to me? I think you are already bored with me? The substance of her impressions was unworthy of her, and she refused to give them utterance. She looked down at her plate, from which there arose such tantalizing aromas that, without her will, her hand grasped the fork and speared a section of succulent mushroom. She bit into it and opened her eyes wide. Massimo watched her as she chewed, waiting for her answer; he was not to be deflected with chatter about the food. She swallowed the mushroom. "I was thinking about how handsome you are," she said.

He gave a small huff of disbelief, but, she observed, he did believe it, and it was the best thing she could have said. The shallow pool of uncertainty between them evaporated and they were back on their proper footing—he was wonderful; she was appreciative. She tried a bite of the potato. "I think this is the best food I ever ate," she said.

He smiled. "The cooking here is the authentic Roman cooking. I prefer it to all others."

"Naturally," she said between bites.

Later, after she had eaten large portions of shrimp, *cicoria*, various bites the waiter insisted she must try—of breaded grilled sardines, of an odd sproutlike green called *puntarelle*, found, he assured her, only in Rome, of bright radicchio stuffed with seasoned meat—as well as salad, a rich panna cotta, and a glass of the special house *amaro*, Lucy declared herself good for nothing but a nap.

"And what will you do after that?" Massimo inquired.

"I will go to Santa Maria del Popolo in Piazza del Popolo to see the Caravaggios. My book says the church opens at four."

He shrugged. "It could be," he said.

"And then I'm going to look for Catherine Bultman in Via Margutta."

Massimo downed his inch of black espresso in one gulp. "What makes you think you will find her there?"

Lucy tried, without much success, to keep an edge of smug superiority from her reply. "Antonio Cini told me I would find her there," she said.

"I hope you did not acquaint him with your foolish suspicion that he is in love with this woman," he exclaimed.

"I didn't," she replied. "I merely said I wanted to find her, to find out why she left DV. And he said what he said before, that he thought she just got bored and left, and he pretended he knew nothing about it. Then, just when I was getting on the train, he told me I would find her in Via Margutta."

Massimo pulled down his upper lip, raising his eyebrows at

the same time in his "who can say" look. "So," he said. "He must have nothing to hide, where she is concerned."

"Maybe," Lucy agreed. "Or maybe he does and he wants her to cover for him."

"Shall I go with you?" he suggested.

"If you have time. But I thought this whole thing didn't interest you."

Massimo signaled for the waiter, who changed direction midstride to come to him. "It interests me a little," he said.

Chapter 15

L
UCY SAT BENEATH a gay umbrella, ignoring the
coffee cup on the bright tablecloth before her. She
looked out upon the Piazza del Popolo, where compet-
ing herds of tourists and locals milled ceaselessly, circling the
ancient obelisk and its honor guard of stately lions, whose
frozen marble jaws magically gushed four identical streams of
bright water into the basins beneath their paws. Beyond them
she could see the facade of the church of Santa Maria del
Popolo, where she had not seen the paintings of Caravaggio,
or the statues by Bernini that decorate the chapel designed
by Raphael for the great Renaissance banker Agostino Chigi.
Instead, she had seen a wedding, or the beginnings of a wedding, a remarkable assemblage in its own right.

She had arrived at the church just as the bride emerged
from a black limousine, attended not by giggling maids in pastel gowns but by several handsome young men, all impeccably
dressed, perfectly coiffed, tanned, flashing their dark eyes and

white teeth in charming boyish glee. They were engaged in shoving one another amiably in and out of the bride's path. The bride herself rose before them, one hand holding her veil, which was more like a small rigged ship of voile and lace set amid the perilous black seas of her lacquered coiffure. She wavered, looking back anxiously at her train, half of which was still in the car. Two of the intrepid young men dove in behind her and began carefully arranging the heavy satin folds around her ankles. Lucy wondered why, as economy was so clearly not a consideration in the skirt of the dress, a little more material hadn't been spared for the top. The bodice, stiffened by stays and covered over in tiny beads, was cut so low and laced so tightly that the bride's impressive breasts were forced up and out, so that they resembled two hard golden balls attached to her sternum. She chided the young men, who responded by raising the volume of their clowning. A small crowd of guests gathered at the entrance to the church, chatting and laughing, one or another turning from the conversation to smile down upon the bride. Lucy looked on from the side, near the bottom of the steps, invisible to the happy company, so much so that she thought she might slip in and have a quick look at the pictures before the ceremony properly began. But, on some signal she did not understand, the guests poured into the church, the car pulled away, and the bride began her progress up the wide stone steps. Her eyes fell briefly upon Lucy, without interest. She was still absorbed in the problems of equilibrium and motion presented by her dress. One of the young men, rushing up ahead, called back something that amused her. She laughed and raised one arm stiffly as if to brush him away. Lucy was close enough to see the cracks the laugh made in the thick lipstick on her mouth. She was wearing an enormous amount of makeup—crimson lip-

stick, ultramatte foundation, black eyeliner, thick mascara—
all applied lavishly and without much skill. The vision of this
garish face grinning above the absurd décolletage was so bla-
tantly in opposition to any idea of virginal innocence as to be
alarming, yet her Mamma had no doubt cried out when she
saw her daughter attired at last for the altar, *"Sei un angelo
bellissimo!"*

Lucy turned away, chuckling to herself as she wandered
into the piazza. She looked up and saw, above the fake rushing
waterfall, the tourists looking down from the Pincio. Ordinarily, she would have made the effort to join them, for she liked a
view, and this, she knew, was a celebrated one. But the exertions of the day had left her weary; after her nap, she had been
forced to wrap her ankle in an inelegant bandage and to ignore
Massimo's disapproval of the walking stick. She leaned gratefully upon it as she cast about for a way to pass the half hour
until he was scheduled to arrive. At length, she had decided to
pay whatever staggering price they were asking for the privi-
lege of sitting with a cappuccino at one of the cafés on the
perimeter of the piazza.

She saw him long before he saw her, and she took the
opportunity to watch him as if she had never seen him before.
He stood at the edge of the busy street ringing the piazza,
looking in the direction of the traffic. He waited, then darted
out to the safety of the pavement. He did this without appear-
ing at all rushed or awkward. He was wearing the usual casual
but elegant dark jacket—he seemed to have a closet full of
them—an even darker shirt, and black jeans. He had on sun-
glasses, so Lucy could not be sure he saw her, and he raised a
cigarette to his lips as he moved gracefully toward her through
the crowd. She swallowed a little throb of self-pity; she was
going to find it painful, their inevitable parting. A skeptical

inner voice inquired, Would you really want such a man? but she ignored it. The question was moot. She wasn't going to get the opportunity to make the choice. She could not doubt that he saw her now, for he made a sharp turn in her direction. She raised her hand to greet him, and when he was close, he bent over her and kissed her on each cheek, the standard greeting—she had seen it perhaps twenty times in her brief survey of the crowd—but it thrilled her nonetheless. "How did you find the Caravaggios?" he asked.

"I didn't. There was a wedding."

He opened his palm, lifting his chin slightly to punctuate the gesture. "You are not having much luck."

"It doesn't matter," she said. "The truth is, I have mixed feelings about Caravaggio." As the check was already paid and Massimo declined to sit, she got up, brandishing her stick. He made no comment but took her arm and led her off in the direction of Via del Babuino. They were immediately swallowed up in a stream of pedestrian traffic. "How is this possible?" he said.

"How is what possible?"

"The mixed feelings."

She laughed. "I've only seen the ones in the Uffizi," she explained. "Those awful simpering boys, that boring fruit."

"I didn't know you were a critic of art."

"I'm not," she said. "But I know a little. Like everyone, I'm full of opinions."

"And what is it that you like?"

"Bernini," she said. "Tomorrow morning, I'm going to the Galleria Borghese to see the *Apollo and Daphne.* I've wanted to see it forever, and the last time I was in Rome—"

"The gallery was closed," he finished.

"That's right."

They had arrived at the short alley that crosses from the bustling throng of Via del Babuino to the wide, quiet, sunny expanse of Via Margutta, a short street lined with art galleries and antique stores as well as gorgeous vine-clad villas belonging to important artists and film directors. Liberated from the oppressive choice between pushing or being pushed, Lucy came to a full stop, taking in the peaceful scene, so unexpected and serene and yet so close to the pulsing, blaring, exhaust-laden atmosphere of the piazza. "This is lovely," she said. She leaned on the stick and took a deep breath. Massimo stopped, too. "What is the address of your friend?" he inquired.

"I don't know," she said. "Antonio just said I would find her here."

"Does she live here, or does she work somewhere?"

"I have no idea," Lucy said. "She's an artist, so perhaps she works in one of the galleries."

"Well," he said. "We will walk along. It is not a long street."

They set out, stopping at the first gallery window and peering in hopefully. The walls were covered with the worst sort of tourist art, thick oil paintings of the Spanish Steps, the Pantheon, and the Castel Sant' Angelo, local gardens and villas, a few country scenes. Incongruously scattered among these were various ugly "surreal" fantasies, obviously the work of one painter, for they all featured women's heads and torsos coming out of clouds, walls, or furniture, all with melon-sized breasts and bared carnivorous teeth. "These are awful," Lucy said.

"They are not very nice," Massimo agreed. They moved on, past an antique store full of heavy and gilded bric-a-brac, to the next gallery window. This one was tamer; the artists were better trained and more inclined to please. Again the subject matter was largely Rome, but the medium was watercolor, gouache, or pen and ink. It was all very orderly and attractive, thoroughly dull. Massimo pointed to a small watercolor of the Bay of Naples; Vesuvius puffed a thin wash smoke into the background. "That is not bad," he suggested.

Lucy nodded, looking past the display to a desk where two young women sat chattering excitedly to each other. "Italians always talk at the same time," she said.

"So you are a critic of Italians, as well," Massimo said.

"No," she apologized. "Of course not. I haven't been here long enough to know anything about Italians."

They came to the next window. Here everything was non-representational, nonlinear, abstract at best. There were bad imitations of Jackson Pollock, smooth airbrushed acrylics with two colors in geometric opposition, and a few expressionist eruptions in swirling thick reds and yellows. "Now this is truly dreadful," Massimo declared. "I know this is not art."

Lucy stared numbly into the confusion before her. She knew it, too, though she couldn't say exactly how she knew. Presumably, people who did not know, or did not care, bought this stuff, all of it, and hung it up on walls somewhere because this street was famous for its galleries, for the quality of its offerings. On weekends in New York, she sometimes roamed the galleries in Chelsea and Soho, where one certainly could find much that was appalling and which, presumably, was bought. Was it better or worse than these? she wondered. It seemed to her that what she saw at home was more decadent, more aggressive, more desperate than anything in these windows. There was a touching naïveté here, a shameless paucity of imagination, and a brazen willingness to acknowledge sources, to broadcast the utter deficit of an original sensibility. Didn't the Romans notice the difference between what was in their churches, on their buildings, in their streets, and what was in these galleries?

They moved on, past another antique store and a shop that sold nothing but lamps, to a small gallery with a display window large enough to accommodate only one painting. This was an arresting work, an interior. It was an empty room; the walls and floor were various shades of gray. In the foreground, a man stood, his back to the viewer, looking across the room to a doorway that opened into a darker space. Another man was halfway through this doorway, nearly swallowed up by the darkness he was entering. The men were both dressed in nondescript suits. It was a moody, largely colorless, strangely disturbing scene; something about it gave Lucy a shiver of anticipation. "This is not bad," Massimo said.

The picture was mounted on a slim metal easel. Behind it they could see the walls of the gallery, where, carefully spaced, more paintings were displayed. Lucy stepped back to take in the doorway, which was to the side, under an overhang created by the roof adjoining the neighboring shop. There was no sign, only a brass plate with a bell. Engraved on the plate was BULT-MAN. "This is it," she said. Before Massimo had time to respond, she had pressed the buzzer. After a moment, they heard the automatic click as the lock released. Lucy looked up at Massimo, who had joined her under the eaves. "Go ahead," he said. "The door is open." She pushed it and they stepped inside.

From somewhere in the back, a woman's voice called out in rapid Italian, something Lucy didn't understand. "She says she will be with us soon," Massimo translated. "We are to make ourselves at home."

It was a long, narrow room, recently Sheetrocked and whitewashed, suggesting a large space divided. Most of the paintings on the walls recapitulated the mysterious gray room of the painting in the window. Beyond these were a few charcoal studies of a nude woman, seated at a table, standing in a doorway, sitting on a floor next to a bed. On the back wall, which was interrupted by an arch, were two landscapes in warm ochers and dark greens of hills that looked a lot like the ones around the farmhouse. Lucy thought these were oils until she got close to them; then she decided they must be pastels, for the surface was grainy. In the lower-right corner she noted the neat signature—Bultman. "These are hers," she said to Massimo, who was still inspecting the shadowy nudes. They both looked up to the sound of footsteps descending a staircase somewhere beyond the arch. Then, like the figure of a stained-glass saint illuminated by a sudden shaft of light, Catherine Bultman stood smiling in the frame.

What was it like, Lucy wondered, to know that whenever you entered a room the atmosphere would be decisively altered? Even though she had seen Catherine before and knew what to expect, she still experienced a hair-raising moment of surprise, as if some beautiful animal, a thoroughbred horse, or a lion, something sudden, dangerous, and bursting with health and life, had unexpectedly appeared. Catherine was all light—golden hair, hazel eyes, pale, creamy skin. Her features were well defined, perfect, but not insipid. She was tall without being angular, thin but not bony. She wore jeans, a gray flannel blouse, and expensive, certainly Italian, gray suede pumps. She spoke to Massimo, who stood in her line of vision. *"Buona sera,"* she said. Then, sensing someone else near her, she turned to Lucy.

Lucy watched her closely to see if there was a gleam of recognition. They had met briefly on a few occasions, and though Catherine had always been polite, Lucy wondered if she might not remember her at all. She observed a slight drawing together of the eyebrows indicative of a mental inventory.

Catherine's wide eyes pored over her, taking note of everything, her hair, her attire, the bandaged ankle, and, with a blink of surprise, the walking stick, but this inspection, though thorough, was so rapacious and quick, it was only a moment before she said, "It's Lucy, isn't it?"

"Hello, Catherine," Lucy said.

"But what are you doing here? Are you with DV?" She glanced out into the gallery, through the window to the street. "Is he here?"

Surely, Lucy thought, Antonio had told her. This was an act, and quite a convincing one, she had to admit. Massimo was gazing at Catherine with an expression of undisguised admiration, but he tore his eyes away long enough to send Lucy a cautionary frown—Don't be harsh with this angel, he seemed to say—which irked Lucy. In fact, the entire scene was suddenly intolerable. What was this game they were all playing? Was there some secret, something to hide, or was it just routine obfuscation? "DV is dead," she said flatly.

Catherine was startled, but not too much, which made it more likely that her reaction was genuine. "I didn't know," she said. "Was he in an accident?"

Massimo stepped forward. "Signora," he said. "Yes, an accident." He gave Lucy such a glare, she felt he had struck her. "I don't know what Lucy is thinking of, to tell you this unhappy news in such a way, such a blunt way."

Catherine answered him in Italian, something to the effect that she was not offended, Lucy gathered, for he made a small further protest. Then they turned to her, to give her the opportunity to explain her bad manners. Great, Lucy thought, now I'm the outsider. "Catherine," she said, "this is my friend Massimo Compitelli."

Catherine recovered quickly and for them all. She always

would, Lucy realized, she had that gift. She smiled upon Lucy, an open, generous smile. Wasn't she an amusing little thing, the smile allowed, so frank, it was refreshing. Then she held out her hand to have a proper American handshake with Massimo. "Caterina Bultman," she said. *"Piacere."*

"I'm sorry I was so blunt," Lucy said gloomily. "I thought you would have heard." This remark did not in any way explain her bluntness, but no one appeared to notice.

"I haven't heard anything from DV for months," Catherine said. "I thought he went back to the States."

"No," Lucy said. "He never left the farmhouse. And he never told anyone you weren't still there with him."

Catherine's expression clouded. Maybe she was telling the truth, Lucy thought. "How did you find me?" she asked.

Lucy gestured to the walking stick. "Antonio," she replied.

"Yes," Catherine said. "I recognized it." She glanced at Massimo, who had taken a few steps away, as if to absent himself from the conversation. "We should talk," she said to Lucy. "Do you have some time? Could I offer you"—in a gesture, she included Massimo in the invitation—"some coffee or maybe some wine?"

"I have time," Lucy said, looking to Massimo.

"You must stay, of course," he said; then, making something very near a bow to Catherine, he added, "Unfortunately, I cannot accept this kind invitation."

Lucy studied him with interest. Why did he look so uncomfortable and sound so stiff? Was it the thought of being with two women who were talking about another man? Was it because that man had been Catherine's lover, or because he was dead? "I'll stay a little while," she said, following Massimo, for he was already making for the door. Catherine joined them. "Perhaps another time," she said to Massimo.

He took her hand. "With much pleasure," he said. Then he bent over Lucy, kissing each cheek, but politely, as if they had never gotten past such proper, public embraces. "You will find your way back to the hotel?" he asked.

"Of course," she said.

"I'll call you there this evening." And with a nod to Catherine, he set off down the empty street.

"An attractive man," Catherine observed when he was out of earshot. "But then so many of them are."

"That's true," Lucy agreed. "The waiter who brought me coffee just now looked like Michelangelo's *David*."

Catherine contemplated Lucy momentarily, as if she found her an interesting specimen. "I hope you're not in love with him," she said.

Lucy smiled, looking past her down the street, but Massimo had disappeared. "No," she said. "I'm not in love."

"Good," Catherine declared. "That could be disastrous." Then she turned back to the gallery and Lucy followed, pulling the door shut behind her. "Let's go upstairs," Catherine said. "And have a talk."

Chapter 16

Y THE TIME Lucy held out her glass to receive a refill of the exceptional red wine Catherine was serving, she was entirely off her guard. The pleasure of conversation was as intoxicating as the wine, for it had been some time since she had spoken to another American and, more important, another woman. As she helped herself to an olive from the bowl on the table between them, her eyes wandered over the furnishings of Catherine's crowded atelier. There was a lot to look at. There was the big easel facing the window, flanked by two sturdy tables covered with all the paraphernalia of the artist—brushes, piles of paint tubes, stacks of tin pans for mixing colors, liter cans of thinner, smaller cans of spray fixatives, boxes of pastels and charcoal, all manner of knives, clamps, and tools for stretching canvas. Next to these was a folding screen painted over with a scene of two scantily clad figures, Adam and Eve perhaps, walking hand in hand through a dense thicket of leaves, too dark and forbidding to be paradise. The screen partially concealed the kitchen corner, deemed unfit for viewing. Lucy could make out a rusty two-burner stove and a half-size refrigerator. Beyond that, along the far wall, were paintings carefully stacked, all facing in, all sizes, five or six deep. An archway near the stairs opened into a small dining alcove with a round wooden table surrounded by old caned chairs. The back wall was a mural, cleverly painted to look like a window with a view of low hills dotted with cypress trees. The sitting area, where she and Catherine lounged in comfortable velvet armchairs, was set off from the rest of the room by its carpet, a venerable Oriental of deep winy hues. Lucy deposited the olive pit into the brass dish her hostess had provided for that purpose. She had told Catherine everything about DV's funeral, her own illness, and the affair with Massimo. She had made light of her fantasy that the Cinis had murdered DV and possibly Catherine herself, and that she was to be their next victim.

"It's not so far-fetched," Catherine said. "They are a sinister family."

"Do you really think so?"

"There's the ghost," she suggested.

"The dead partisan. But that wasn't sinister. He was killed by fascists during the war."

Catherine shrugged. "If every Italian who says he was a partisan really was one, Mussolini would have been the only fascist in Italy." She sipped her wine, then fished an olive out of the bowl. "But that's what DV thought." She raised her eyebrows suggestively. "That's the story the family puts out."

"But you don't believe it."

"That there's a ghost? No. I'm not superstitious." She chewed the olive thoughtfully. "Another story I heard is that the ghost was killed by his own brother."

"The old man!" Lucy exclaimed. "He certainly looks like he would be up to it."

"It was a quarrel over a woman. He found out his younger brother was sleeping with his fiancée."

"Wow," Lucy said. "How did you hear this?"

"Antonio told me," she said. "Just before I left."

"I see," Lucy said, though she didn't. Now was the time to bring up the letter, but she was disarmed by Catherine's frankness. Her lighthearted, confidential manner made Lucy feel as if she was a part of some warm, amusing, and dangerous female conspiracy. She didn't want to accuse Catherine of anything. "Why did you leave?" she asked, her eyes carefully averted.

Catherine took the olive pit from her pursed lips and dropped it into the bowl. She can even make that look appealing, Lucy thought. "DV and I didn't get along. I found him"— she shrugged—"oppressive."

"He was a difficult man," Lucy agreed.

"And then I read his novel."

"The ghost novel?"

Catherine nodded. "And that did it."

Lucy laughed, albeit guiltily; she thought it cruel to be merry at DV's expense. Catherine laughed, too, nodding and rolling her eyes heavenward with an exaggerated expression of pain and pleading that delighted Lucy; it so perfectly expressed what she felt when she read DV's prose. "Oh," she whimpered, struggling against a rising giddiness. She failed in this effort and succumbed to a gale of laughter, which started Catherine up, and then they both laughed until tears stood in their eyes.

"Oh, Lord," Catherine said at last, when they were too weak to go on and lay panting for breath in their armchairs.

She held out the wine bottle, which Lucy accepted, pouring her own this time. "You see," Catherine continued, "I'd never read anything of his before. I don't know why I hadn't. I don't read as much as I'd like. . . ." She gestured toward the wall of paintings—there was her reason. "I knew he was a popular writer, so I wasn't expecting Proust, but . . ."

"He really had no gift," Lucy suggested.

"Oh, it was worse than that," Catherine protested. "It was embarrassing. And so mawkish, so self-indulgent, all that stuff about how the Italians love this guy, this Max Manx—was that it?—my God, what a ridiculous name. Do people really buy that stuff?"

"Well," Lucy explained. "He had a good editor. But the answer to your question is yes, they do, by the millions. And not just in America, either."

"I don't understand it."

"No," Lucy agreed. "I don't, either." They fell silent for a moment, musing over this impenetrable mystery, the popularity of shabby work. DV wasn't really taking advantage of anyone, Lucy reflected. He gave his audience exactly what they wanted and he always did the best he could. He worked hard; he got excited about his work. When any criticism came his way, he fretted over it, but of course for the most part that didn't happen because he was protected from it by the combined efforts of his publisher, his editor, his agent, and Lucy herself. She had always understood it was part of her job not to discourage him, to allow him the carefully maintained illusion that he was, in every important sense, the real thing. "Did you tell him what you thought?" she asked.

"I did," Catherine said. "How could I not? I was appalled."

"What did you say?"

"I told him he should stop. I told him he was a hack, a prostitute, that he should do something else, sell real estate, or just something useful, like gardening."

"Jesus," Lucy said. "How did he take it?"

"He was furious. He said I was just a neurotic painter who didn't understand his work, which was really laughable. What was there to understand? I said, 'I understand it perfectly. You make up stories about how you wish your life was, about what a sensitive, interesting guy you are, and how much everyone likes you, how much Italians like you, for God's sake. Now that is really rich, because Italians can't stand you. Italians do not like drunks.'"

"Oh, Jesus," Lucy said again.

"So his response to that was to get drunk for several days and we had to go through all the scenes, the anger, the tears, the threats, the promises. I was really sick to death of him by the time I got out of there and I didn't care what happened to him—though I didn't want him to die, of course. I thought he would just go home and write another stupid book about how I was crazy and he was crucified on the altar of love."

Lucy smiled ruefully. "He never went home," she said.

"No," Catherine agreed. "He never went home."

"And he never finished the book. I've looked, but there's nothing."

Catherine's eyes flickered away, settling on the bowl of olive pits. "It doesn't seem a great loss," she said.

"No. I suppose not," Lucy agreed. "But his editor finds it odd, and I do, too, that there wasn't more. DV never had trouble writing. He usually wrote a thousand pages a year."

"Maybe if he'd written less, it would have been better."

"Doubtless," Lucy said. Catherine ate another olive. She

looked petulant; perhaps she was bored. Lucy decided it was time for a leading question. "So Antonio Cini helped you to get away," she said.

Catherine gave her a guarded look. "Yes, Antonio helped me. He knows people here who helped me to get set up. I would have preferred Florence, but there were various reasons not to go there. Too easy for DV to get to me, for one thing. All the interesting artists are in Florence. The show I have up now, the gray men in the doorways, he's a Florentine. Rome is really something of a backwater."

"Did DV know you were here?"

"Oh yes. I fully expected him to show up sooner or later, but he didn't. I was angry at first; later I didn't care. It certainly never occurred to me that he was dead."

"He knew you would leave," Lucy said. "He predicted it in the novel. Did you read that part?"

"Yes," Catherine said.

"I thought that part wasn't bad."

"He knew I would leave because he was suffocating me," Catherine protested, so hotly that Lucy assumed she felt guilty. "I wasn't working and he was always on me about it, though the truth was that he couldn't have cared less about my painting."

"I see," Lucy said.

"I had no choice, really," she concluded. "I could not survive as an artist in such an environment."

Lucy was silent for a moment, looking about the charming, comfortable, light-filled environment in which, it seemed, Catherine was able to survive. "So you'll stay here awhile?" she said.

"I think so. I'm working a lot, all the time, actually. I've never worked so well. That's the most important thing to me.

I'd live in hell if it meant I could work. It's really all that matters anymore."

"But you wouldn't be able to work if you were in hell," Lucy pointed out. "That would be how you would know it was hell."

Catherine gave her a puzzled look. "I guess so," she said. "Would you like to see some paintings?"

"*Volentieri*," Lucy replied. Catherine got up and began carefully sliding the last canvas from the stack against the wall. Lucy paused to refill her wineglass. "When I was packing up DV's things," she said, "I found a drawing you left behind."

Catherine looked up from the picture. "What drawing?" she asked.

"It was of DV. It was quite powerful, very scary, actually. He was—"

"Baring all." Catherine laughed. "I did that one night when he was going on about how much he needed me. He just would not let up."

"Oh," Lucy said. "Do you want it back?"

"No. You can keep it." As Catherine spoke, she turned a large canvas to face the room. It was a forest, very dark; what light there was seemed to be coming from the ground. In the shadows, two figures, a man and a woman—or was it two men?—lurked ominously. Was one in pursuit of the other?

"It makes me think of Adam and Eve, after they got kicked out of the Garden."

"It's Dante," Catherine replied, "lost in the wood." She pointed to the more shadowy figure in the background. "That's Virgil," she added, "about to offer him the guided tour."

Chapter 17

YOU WERE a long time with your friend, Lucy. Did you find out what you wanted to know?"

She had not been in the hotel room two minutes before the phone rang and Massimo's world-weary voice greeted her with this question. She threw her purse on the bed and collapsed in the room's only chair, which was an ugly tufted affair crammed into the tiny space between the phone and the door. "Why did you run off like that?" she said.

"I had some business to attend to."

There is no point in asking him such questions, Lucy thought. She tried another tack. "Where are you now?" She was, she realized, still giddy from the wine.

"I am in my office."

"Oh," she said. She kicked off her shoes and began unwrapping her ankle. "I wish you were here."

"You have been drinking," he observed.

"A little," she admitted. "Not that much. Can you come?"

He was silent for a moment, as if he was consulting some schedule, though Lucy suspected he was only checking the ever-fluctuating barometer of his whim at the moment. "Yes," he said. "I will be there in ten minutes. But I cannot stay very long."

"It shouldn't take too long," she replied coyly, for the sound of his voice saying her name, the timbre of it, the way he put the stress on the last syllable, had released a tide of desire that was nearly painful. She could feel her blood rushing around trying to accommodate it, gorging in her mouth and groin, draining from her fingertips. And Massimo had heard it, as well, for he said, "I think Rome is going to your head, *tesoro*."

"It's a very romantic city," she agreed.

When she hung up, she sat for a moment savoring the novelty of her situation. She recalled something Catherine had said, when she had confessed—how easily, almost eagerly she had confessed—to this affair: "Well, so you are having an adventure." It was true. She said it out loud into the empty hotel room: "I'm having an adventure."

Then, banishing every concern but the imminent arrival of her lover, she went into the bathroom to look at herself in the mirror. She looked fine, flushed from her walk, a little fatigued around the eyes. She made a few adjustments, lipstick, penciling of the eyebrows, then decided to change her blouse; it was too severe, too buttoned-up. She chose a thin black sweater with a scooped neck. When she removed the blouse, she caught sight of herself in the dresser mirror. Her bra was one of the three she usually wore for comfort, not unattractive, but rather plain. Rome, she had noticed on her walk, had a lingerie shop every hundred feet and the garments on display in their windows were uniformly expensive and seductive. Nothing practical was even considered. She went to the dresser and pulled out the black lace underwire bra she had purchased some time ago because it was both beautiful and on sale. She seldom wore it because it was killingly uncomfortable. It was designed to make her small breasts look larger, another feature she had found interesting in the fitting room but impossible on the street. She had worn it once to a party and spent the evening with the unsettling sensation that she was standing behind her breasts, as if she was presenting them for inspection. But this, this hotel room tryst, was the perfect occasion. With any luck, she wouldn't be wearing it long enough to become uncomfortable. She attached the band around her waist and lifted the stiff cups over her breasts. Why, she wondered, had she packed this thing? Had she had some intuition, or was it just a fantasy, a not entirely unconscious wish that somehow she would be transformed into the kind of woman who would routinely choose allure over comfort? Certainly she hadn't intended to wear it to DV's funeral.

She pulled the sweater on and went back into the bathroom to brush her hair. Had she been transformed? She studied her reflection. How glittery her eyes were, how unusually clear and delicate her skin looked, almost translucent. This was doubtless the result of her illness. And how full of appetites she was, how hungry for everything, for food, wine, art, but especially for Massimo. He had noticed her eagerness that morning and had attributed it to their brief separation. Though he was perfectly willing to join her in the rush to the bed, both of them throwing their clothes off in every direction, afterward he had teased her. "So you are no longer so shy with me?"

She lay on her stomach, her face turned away from him, which was good, she realized, for he couldn't see the flush that burned her cheeks. "Did I make a lot of noise?"

She could hear him fumbling on the nightstand for his cigarettes. "You were quite noisy, yes, I would say."

"God, I'm sorry," she said. "I guess I got carried away."

"Don't apologize," he said. "It is a compliment to me." She
heard the snap of his lighter, then the slow intake of his
breath. "Perhaps you will become insatiable."

"I don't think that's in my character." She felt his hand
drop across her shoulder, then move up, lazily riffling through
her hair. "Perhaps you do not know what is in your character,
Lucy," he said.

As she recalled this remark, Lucy gave her reflection a flir-
tatious smile and tossed her brush into her travel bag. Then
she rushed into the bedroom, for she heard his soft knock at
the door.

Chapter 18

HE PALAZZO THAT HOUSES the Galleria Borghese may have an impressive facade, or it may not. Doubtless there are living Romans who have seen it, but their children must rely on parental reminiscence if they want some idea of the exterior. Lucy came at it from the park, picking her way around the warren of scaffolding, catwalks, plastic sheeting, and corrugated tin that have, for so many years, hidden the venerable stone from view. It had turned chilly, the sky was overcast, and a damp, gusty wind made her hunch her shoulders and pull her shawl tight. She entered a rickety walkway that funneled her into a court piled high with lumber, steel, and rolls of plastic sheeting. Here she found the inauspicious door and the hand-lettered strip of cardboard that has for more than a decade now designated it as the *Entrata*. Beyond this, in a narrow chamber, a haughty public servant lounging behind a makeshift counter reluctantly exchanged five thousand lire for a generic museum ticket. Passing through another doorway, Lucy stepped into the high, wide expanse of the first salon.

She was absorbed in her thoughts, which were not particularly satisfying, and with the grumpy business of being physically miserable—she was chilled and her ankle throbbed from the long walk—but the scene before her canceled all preoccupations. Now this is something, she thought, this is grandeur. She was to see marvels in a marvelous setting. She leaned upon Antonio's stick, taking in the high vaulted ceiling, the gleam of marble and gilt, the spare furnishings supporting various busts of imperial Romans. The doorway to the next room was a wide one, and through it she could see two carefully positioned large works, the nearest of which she recognized with a gasp of delight. It was Bernini's *David*. Oh, she thought, this is here, too.

There were a few other people in the rooms, scattered in groups of two or three. Some studied the laminated informational cards they had discovered on a side table. The cards detailed, in various languages, the contents of the rooms. Though there was the buzz of conversation, it was subdued. The enormous proportions of the palazzo seemed to weigh upon the speakers, constraining them to hushed, even reverent, tones.

Lucy went through to the smaller salon, found a place before the intent coil of the figure of David, and gave herself over to the pleasure of encountering a famous work she had previously admired only in books.

He had been captured in stone at the exact moment when all fear gave way to the necessity for calculation. The polished rock, his weapon, was closed in the tight grip of his left hand. He held it down, flexing the strap of his slingshot back over his thigh with his right, his right knee slightly bent. He was taking

the measure of his opponent. Lucy experienced a shiver of
excitement as she felt the size of the giant at her back, for
David's burning gaze was fixed upon his enemy's temple,
where the stone must find its mark. She looked behind her at
the coffered ceiling—he was that big.

How did he do it? she thought. Her question did not refer
to the legendary subject, but to the sculptor, whose task, to
take up his chisel and hack from obdurate marble this startling
vision, had certainly been the equivalent of bringing down
Goliath with a slingshot. She glanced at the date on her card,
1623—this marble youth who appeared to be holding his
breath had been holding it for quite some time. Bernini himself
had been a youth when he made the *David,* and with youthful
exuberance he had used his own face for a model, scowling
into a mirror held for him, the story went, by his great patron,
Cardinal Borghese. For several minutes, Lucy took in the stone
a bit at a time, from the head down. "Wonderful," she said
before turning away.

She went out into the next room. Two children, a boy and
a girl, came running past her, shouting at one another in Italian, shouted at in turn by their father, who had just turned
away from the luscious seminude figure of Pauline Borghese,
Napoleon's sister, reclining on her marble couch. The man was
handsome. His black eyes flashed as he hurried out after his
children. Lucy approached Pauline, who smiled wryly at some
point across the room. She was smiling at the sculptor, Lucy
speculated, the great Canova. She remembered the exchange—
she'd read it in school—between Pauline and a friend who had
voiced dismay about the statue. "How could you model like
that, before that man, without your clothes?" the friend had
complained, to which Pauline had replied, "Why? His rooms
are heated."

She did look comfortable. The couch was richly cushioned; her smooth limbs left soft impressions upon it, at the elbow of the arm raised to her head, and beneath her lovely pampered right foot. She was the opposite of the athletic David, though, in her way, just as prepared for a contest. Her beauty was her weapon; her face was the challenge. Who would have the temerity to find her lacking?

Not Canova, Lucy concluded as her eyes wandered over the indolent marble woman. Her thoughts drifted, as well. The shouting father had reminded her of Massimo. Did he come here, now and then, with his children? Did he stand here before this voluptuous woman, admiring the full curves of her breasts echoed in the smaller but equally perfect globe of the apple she was holding? The apple was the prize Paris had given her, for she was not just Pauline but Venus, too, and she had never been in doubt that she would win it.

Wasn't this just the sort of woman Massimo would adore?

Lucy closed her eyes, leaning hard on Antonio's walking stick, as a precise recollection of a moment in her last meeting with her lover flared up in her memory, a burst of heat and brightness that threw everything apart from it into a deeper gloom. It was a string of tender kisses, she recalled, from the pulse at her ear to the inside of her elbow, accompanied by the pressure of his hands over her hips, sweeping her in close to him. The recollection was so complete and profound that she felt dizzy and panic swept over her. She opened her eyes, momentarily disoriented and confused, but Pauline as Venus, amused by everything, everything, but most especially by the flights and paroxysms of lovers, brought her back to her senses. She turned away from the smug, self-satisfied smile and wandered through the doorway that led back to the salon of imperial busts.

How could he know her so well in bed and so little outside of it? This was the substance of her ruminations. Why did he seem so eager to assume that she would make impossible demands, that she would try to keep him from his work or his family? He had created some obnoxious role for her, and now he was determined to have her fill it. A frank conversation might help. She could explain, I am simply not like that; I am like this, but he had a way of closing down all such protests with the assertion, obvious to him, that he knew more about her than she knew about herself.

Did he? Was that possible? Surely she had known from the start that it was a bad idea to enter an affair with a married man. She had never done so before and had always gazed with horror and amazement at the folly of those friends who did, but here she was, full of the inevitable bitterness that must come of such a liaison. She had entered it freely, and Massimo had known, from very early on—she had no doubt of that—that she would. And so he treated her like a woman who would—because she had. After all, wasn't he correct in all his assumptions?

No, her interior advocate cried out in her defense. There were extenuating circumstances. She had been so ill, so weak, it was a foreign country, he was so handsome and had cared for her so lovingly, it had all happened so easily and naturally, there had been no point when she had been faced with a decision that had not, almost magically, already been made.

She looked about herself bemusedly. A baroque villa filled with lavish statuary was no place for a moral crisis. The blank marble eyes of the emperors looked on indifferently; the marble flesh, which appeared so warm and supple but was, in fact, perfectly lifeless, cold, and dead, seemed to mock her inferior material. You won't last, the stone heads announced. You'll

grow old, stiff, wrinkled; you'll pass away, but we will still be here.

A living man, tall and fair, shabbily dressed, his shoulders hunched slightly beneath the weight of the backpack that declared his nationality, came into the room from a doorway Lucy had not tried. He was joined directly by a young woman, who looked back over her shoulder, obviously reluctant to leave. In the flat tones of the great American Midwest, she declared, "That was fantastic. Wasn't that just fantastic?" Lucy's eye traveled past her to the room of the fantastic experience. She could just make out the raised arm, the leafy outstretched fingers of Daphne. There it was, what she had come for. She approached the two Americans, who took no notice of her. "I'm tired of looking at statues," the young man complained as she passed by.

"But these are so good," the girl replied. "Don't you think these are really good?"

Lucy smiled as she entered the salon where the marvelous apparition of *Apollo and Daphne* burst upon the somber space of the eighteenth-century room with the fury of two wild horses. Again the contrapunto coil, again the climactic moment of a struggle, but this time nothing heroic or noble was about to happen. Daphne was exchanging one terror for another, and her face, mouth ajar, eyes rolled upward as consciousness both astounded and eluded her, made it clear that her father's idea of rescue was infinitely more horrible than anything Apollo had in mind for her. Her fingers and toes had begun the transformation to leaves and roots; tree bark encrusted her legs. Apollo, too, was frozen in a moment of revelation. He couldn't see what was happening, for he was behind her, in hot pursuit, and he had at last caught up with her. Everything he knew came to him through the hand he had slipped about her waist, which was still flesh, but altered. His expression was a mixture of triumph—he had captured her—shock—she was not what he thought—and something else—was it sympathy or just resignation? He was a god himself; this was a game for him, one he now knew he had lost. Her flesh beneath his fingers looked soft and impressionable still. Could he feel the blood thickening to sap, the convulsions racking her heart, the collapse of her lungs upon the last gasp of oxygen that would be of any use to her?

Lucy stepped closer to examine the thin roots forming from Daphne's delicate toes. Again the power of the story was matched, was eclipsed, by the supernatural artistry of the sculptor. How could stone express so clearly the distinction between flesh and bark? Lucy stepped back, taking in the whole figure of the terrified young woman rising before her suitor as if pulled up by some force from above. Apollo looked vapid and lazy; his body was no match for the lean, muscular, concentrated energy of the *David*. His legs were even a little thin and his stomach, above the decorous drape that covered his genitals, looked soft. His waist was thick. But he had a handsome face. His hair was plentiful and wavy; he had lovely, long, tapered feet that reminded Lucy of Massimo's feet. He took good care of them. She had never known a man to be fastidious about such things. And he was ticklish there; she could make him shout by running her thumbnail down the sole.

She let out a sigh of exasperation. She had not come here to moon over her lover, but to stand in awe of Bernini, about whose feet she knew nothing. The two children came careening and shouting through the room, in one door and out the other, oblivious of Daphne's horrific struggles, and after them, striding purposefully, his patience worn to a thread, their father. Lucy smiled at him as he went by. He shook his head, making some comment about *i bambini*, the impossibility of watching them—it was *un casino*—then disappeared.

She looked back at the statue, at Daphne's silent scream. The agony of her transformation never ended. There was something brutal in that. Bernini had created her in this way, brought her to this moment of extreme terror, and no further.

Though for him there had been a point when it was all over. He had labored over every strand of her hair, the perfect curve of her lower lip, the slight protrusion of her ribs visible below her small breasts. Over every inch of her body he had lavished his miraculous attention. No detail was too small; nothing escaped him. And then, one day, he was finished with her. He had stepped back, walked around her, felt—what, satisfaction, relief, eagerness for his fee or for his lunch, the pleasurable sadness of accomplishment, of a job done something more than well? He was still a young man, he had a lifetime of work ahead of him, and he was never to stop. He was working in the Vatican at eighty. Did he look back upon this young woman with the nostalgia of a lover, or was she simply of no further interest to him?

Lucy stood gazing up at *Apollo and Daphne*, mulling over these observations. A great sadness welled up, and all her excitement and pleasure at finally seeing the statue was dissolved. There was nothing marvelous in her appreciation of this work, she realized. One would have to be a stone oneself not to be moved by it; that was the whole point. She went out by the door she had entered, back to the first salon. There was much more to be seen, but she felt enervated, overstimulated, and moody. She decided to go out into the park, where she could sit on a bench, rest her ankle, and plan the rest of the day.

Chapter 19

*T*HE PARK BENCH PROVED cold, damp, and comfortless. Lucy had rested upon it only a few minutes before the claims of hunger overrode those of weariness and drove her farther into the park in search of food. She consulted her guidebook, which detailed a maze of possible walks, one of which led to the Spanish Steps. Though it looked a short distance on the map, the reality was a vast stretch of rolling terrain, scattered with bushes, rumpled and torn by tree roots.

She did not take in the view at Trinità dei Monti; she was too dispirited and hungry for tourism. Her plan was to find a bar on Via del Babuino, at the foot of the Spanish Steps. The steps themselves, littered with tourists and con artists, seemed impossibly steep and long, and the piazza at the base, with its barque fountain and tall palms, was so jammed with humanity that she had to push her way through to the opposite sidewalk. She heard half a dozen languages, all pouring into the air at high speed and top volume. Why is everyone always so excited here? she wondered. Is it something in the air, or is it the coffee?

The thought of coffee spurred her on. She spotted two bar signs ahead. The first turned out to be a chilly establishment with a few dry sandwiches and hard pastries stacked in a case near the register, a long bar, and no place to sit at all. The second was much bigger. There were tables in the back and the long glass case that ran beneath the bar was laden with hot trays full of steaming dishes, stacks of appetizing sandwiches and pastries of many varieties. Her heart lifted, though there was the nagging anxiety about procedure—did one order at the counter or the register, pay first or after, carry the food to the table, or sit at a table and wait to be served?

She looked about hesitantly. The place was busy. The barmen were in constant motion, taking new orders without looking up from the preparation of the previous ones. A harried, perspiring fellow lifted a tray heaped with plates and cups and carried it out into the crowd at the tables. There was no sign of menus; one evidently had to choose by looking at what was available and then describing it to the waiter. Lucy eyed a sandwich composed of thin sliced *prosciutto di Parma* and *rughetta* on flat seeded bread, and another of tuna and artichoke hearts on a thick roll. *"Dica,"* the barman said to her abruptly. She looked up into his serious, demanding eyes. She would have liked to examine the contents of the steam table, but the pressure was evidently on, so she pointed at the tuna sandwich. She knew the right words for that, and to the question, *"Da bere?"* she responded, *"Un cappuccino."* After a little more pointing and muttering of the simple phrases she knew for "May I sit?" and "Does one pay first or after?" the man, clearly aggravated beyond endurance by her ignorance and timidity, waved her into the seating area. She found a small table in the center of the room and sat down wearily amid the buzz of conversation, the clatter of dishes, the undercurrent of jaws chewing and throats swallowing. She propped Antonio's stick against the table leg; then, as it immediately fell over into the path of a waiter balancing a full tray, she leaned out over the floor to retrieve it. A man at an adjoining table addressed a remark to her. She didn't understand him, but he sounded sympathetic, so she looked up, offering him an apologetic smile. There was no need for her to say that she had not understood. He knew it at once, and it irritated him. He scowled and turned his attention to his plate. He had chosen meat and potatoes, Lucy observed, just like an American.

Her own food arrived and she set to it at once. After the first few bites, she paused, reminding herself to eat slowly. She sipped the hot coffee, so paradoxically stimulating and comforting, and she looked about at the lively company in whose midst she felt herself to be as invisible and insubstantial as a ghost. The room was warm, fragrant with the aromas of coffee, tomatoes, garlic, and fresh bread, smoky from the ubiquitous cigarettes. No one would hurry her now, or even notice her. When she wanted the check, she would have to ask for it.

Lucy chewed her sandwich. I could never live here, she thought. Even if she spoke perfect Italian, she would never be assertive enough to fit in; her diffidence would always enrage the barman and irritate the ticket taker. One had to be strong, confident, and preferably big to get along. One had to make an impression, like Catherine.

Against her better judgment, almost against her will, Lucy admitted that she admired Catherine. She had courage; some might call it "nerve." She had very odd taste in men and doubtless she took scandalous advantage of them, but she seemed curiously untouched by sex and independent in her thinking.

She had been hospitable and friendly to Lucy; she appeared to enjoy her company and had encouraged her to visit again before she returned to the States. Why not now? Lucy thought. The gallery was only a few blocks away. It would be her last chance. Perhaps she could draw Catherine out on the subject of her last days with DV.

She finished her sandwich and drained the sugary black liquid at the bottom of the cup. If she could get the check before hell froze over, she might easily reach the gallery before the afternoon closing.

As lucy made the turn into Via Margutta, the rain that had threatened all morning commenced in a sudden gush, like water overflowing from a bowl. She ducked in close to the shops, but there was little in the way of cover and what there was could be obtained only by diving through water curtains running off the eaves. She muttered her favorite Italian exclamation of despair, *porca miseria*—"pig misery"—and hurried along, poking the walking stick into the puddles and rivulets collecting already among the uneven stones. The street was not long, but long enough for her to become thoroughly soaked and chilled before she stepped up into the doorway with the brass plate marked BULTMAN. She wrung her hair out with one hand while she jabbed at the bell with the leopard head of the walking stick. She listened, but there was no click of the lock, no sound of footsteps from within. Was she too late? Was the gallery closed for the *pausa* already? Where would she take shelter if that was the case? It was a long walk to her hotel, and the rain showed no sign of letting up. She tried the bell again, this time holding it in for a good long ring; she could hear the loud buzz inside. "Please be here," she said, and, as if in answer to this request, the lock mechanism clicked and the door shifted perceptibly in the frame. She pushed it and stepped inside, pausing to shake the water from her shawl and stamp her feet. *"Vengo subito,"* Catherine called from the back, beyond the arch. But she did not, as announced, come at once. Instead, she continued a conversation she evidently intended to conclude before presenting herself to her prospective customer. Lucy could hear her deep voice, her clear, perfect Italian, and she recalled that Antonio Cini had grudgingly admired her good accent. She listened closely, trying to make out a word or two, and she smiled as she caught the final exclamation, *"Ma che imbroglio!"*

Then, as Catherine's visitor replied, her smile disappeared. He spoke rapidly, excitedly, as if he feared interruption. Though Lucy didn't understand a word of his conversation, she did receive an understanding, one that struck a sharp spear of light across her consciousness. She couldn't grasp the message, but she recognized the voice of the messenger: It was Massimo.

In the next moment, she was able to observe the same cataclysm of recognition and comprehension playing across the handsome features of her lover. He appeared in the archway, following Catherine, still addressing her with the careless animation Lucy seldom saw, for it was the ease of speaking his native tongue. He finished his sentence, evidently acquitting himself admirably in his own estimation, for his eyes, as they fell upon Lucy, were merry and complacent. In the next moment, this good humor vanished, his eyes widened, and his jaw tightened. Catherine looked from one visitor to the other with an expression of hearty amusement. Lucy felt, as she had before in Catherine's presence, small, uninteresting, plain. She was acutely aware of her wet, limp hair, the clamminess of her skin inside the damp cloth of her blouse, the homely smell of sheep emanating from her soggy shawl. For a long moment, the three stood encountering one another, their various emotions plainly to be read on their faces. Then Massimo, recovering control of himself, and thereby the women, the room, the world, let out an exasperated sigh and advanced upon Lucy. "But Lucy, look, you are completely wet. You should not be out in this weather. You will die of cold. You must get back to the hotel and go to bed. You are not yet fully recovered." As he delivered these directions and dire predictions, he put his hands on her shoulders and held her at arm's length, careful, she observed, not to get his suit wet.

"I'm fine," she said. "You're being ridiculous."

He looked back at Catherine, enlisting her as a witness to this folly. "I can feel how chilled she is through this cloth," he exclaimed; then, turning back to Lucy, he chided, "What possessed you to come out in this weather?"

"I thought you had to work today," she said dryly. She shrugged, trying to free herself from his grasp, but he held her fast, looking down into her face, his mask of deep concern tightly in place. He would not be distracted; this was his tactic—she had been naughty, but he had come to her rescue.

An awkward moment followed in which Lucy fairly writhed in her lover's grip, but Catherine intervened, rescuing them all. "Let Lucy come upstairs with me," she advised. "I'll give her a towel."

Massimo released her. "Of course," he agreed. "She must be made dry as soon as possible." While Lucy followed Catherine obediently, Massimo clucked nervously after them, his warnings tempered now with excuses: He could not stay much longer. Really, he was just leaving, having only stopped by on his way back from the bar where he had taken a hurried *panino,* but he would wait, of course, and see Lucy into a taxi.

"That's really not necessary," she said. Catherine turned at the staircase, adding, "Lucy came to visit me. She should at least have a nice cup of tea before she goes back. Then I'll call her a taxi." To Lucy, she added, "They come in two minutes, literally. Taxis are the only thing in Rome that work properly."

"Well, you are right," Massimo said. "This is a better plan. I will return to my work and you ladies may have a pleasant visit. Lucy, I will come for you at the hotel at seven-thirty."

She cast him a look heavy with skepticism, which he countered by raising his eyebrows and opening his hands in a gesture of exasperated pleading so entirely spontaneous and inappropriate that she could only smile. "I'll see you then," she said.

He called a farewell to Catherine, who sent back a cheerful "Ciao, Massimo" from the landing. Lucy watched him—he had his back to her—as he took up his stylish raincoat and umbrella from the chair next to Catherine's cluttered desk. He hadn't come out unprepared for anything. He ran his hand over one side of his hair, an unnecessary gesture, for his hair was always perfect, pulled on the coat, and, without looking back, went out through the archway. Lucy labored up the stairs to Catherine's studio. By the time she got there, Catherine had draped a towel across the banister and put the kettle on to boil. "How long was he here?" Lucy asked as she applied the towel gently to her face and then roughly to her hair. It was plush and smelled faintly of lavender.

"About an hour," Catherine replied from behind the kitchen screen. "Have you eaten?"

"I had a sandwich." She rested Antonio's stick against a table and collapsed into the nearest armchair. "Jesus, I'm exhausted," she murmured. Catherine came out from behind her screen and stood cross-armed, smiling at her guest. "What did he want?" Lucy asked.

"Oh, I think he wanted to further our acquaintance."

Lucy frowned. "How much further?"

"He's an Italian. He wants to go as far as he can, though, oddly enough, they are often satisfied with very little."

"He could have waited until I got out of town. I'm leaving tomorrow afternoon."

"He said you were annoyed with him for going off so suddenly yesterday, and he feared he had made a bad impression. He was in the neighborhood, so he stopped in."

"Do you believe that?"

"No."

"What did he talk about for an hour?"

"It was just gossip. His family knows my landlord's family. He told me a few scandalous stories about them."

The teakettle shrieked and Catherine disappeared behind the screen. "What kind of tea do you want?" she asked.

"Anything," Lucy said. She folded the towel and placed it over the arm of the chair. She felt a cloud of gloom and consternation settling upon her, and no resistance rising to meet it. She gazed longingly into the shadows of Catherine's forest screen. How pleasant it would be to lie down in some such peaceful place and drift off to sleep. *Whose woods these are I think I know,* she thought.

Catherine appeared bearing two steaming cups, smiling and solicitous like some ministering angel. The artist's life didn't seem to be causing her any anxiety or discomfort, Lucy thought. She leaned forward to take the cup, murmuring her thanks. The aroma that rose from the tea had a familiar sharpness, and she sniffed it appreciatively.

"Ginger," Catherine said. "Very restorative."

"Wonderful," Lucy replied. "I could use a restoration."

Catherine took the chair across from her, cradling her cup

between her palms. "I suppose *you* really were in the neighborhood."

"I was," Lucy protested. "I went to the Galleria Borghese and then I walked all the way through the park, and then I had lunch on Via del Babuino."

"That's a long walk," Catherine observed.

Lucy nodded, rubbing her ankle. She hadn't worn the bandage and the bruise showed through her stocking. "It would have been nice, but it's so cold, and my ankle slows me down. Then it started raining."

"And then you came here and found Massimo."

"Really." Lucy shook her head disconsolately. "Perfect."

Catherine sipped her tea thoughtfully. "But you're not in love with him?"

"I can't figure out why he was so eager for me to come to Rome. *He* invited *me,* but now he acts like I'm pursuing him."

"But you're not." Catherine's tone was teasing and provocative.

"He's married. I'm going back to New York in a few days. This is supposed to be a fling. It's supposed to be free of recrimination, no expectations, nothing but fun, and then *ciao, basta.* Why is he trying to turn it into a contest?"

"You really are a romantic, Lucy," Catherine observed. "Of course it's a contest. And if there are no expectations and no recriminations, how can he come out the winner? There has to be the danger of exposure; you have to be a threat. Otherwise, what's the point of having an affair?"

Lucy listened glumly. "I know you're right," she admitted. "I shouldn't have come here. But he took care of me when I was sick, and I imprinted on him, like a duck."

"He does seem concerned about your health," Catherine said.

Lucy took a swallow of tea, recalling the absurd scene

downstairs. She looked up at Catherine, who was holding her own cup to her lips, her eyes frank and interested above the rim.

"That was pretty transparent, wasn't it?" Lucy replied.

Catherine nodded.

"Fortunately, I'm not in love,"

"You are sure about that?" Catherine said.

"I think so," Lucy said. Then, because Catherine looked so arch and so interested, she added, "I don't know, really. How could I? Is there some simple test?"

Catherine set her cup on the side table and flipped off her shoes. Then, with surprising grace, she drew her long legs up under her on the chair. "I wouldn't know," she said. "I've never been in love."

"Never? Not with DV?"

Catherine laughed. "No. Certainly not. Not for a minute."

And not with Antonio Cini, either, I'll wager, Lucy thought.

"Sex can be very powerful," Catherine mused. "Very persuasive. Once, when I was a student in Florence, there was a man. He was my teacher."

"An Italian?"

"No. He was an American. He was a brilliant painter himself. I was naïve. I thought he cared about my painting, but it turned out he didn't understand it at all."

"So you broke up because he didn't understand your painting?"

"An artist can't really care about anything but the work. The work comes first."

Lucy sat in silence, considering the implications of this sweeping and grandiose statement. She was ready to admit that art must be a powerful calling, a vocation, like the religious life, but did it really release its disciples from the ordinary obligations of affection and trust? It was true that artists were often cads. Bernini was famous for his irritability and bad temper, though he was not as vicious as Caravaggio, who had murdered a man in a quarrel over a tennis match. Catherine, Lucy recalled, was a fan of Caravaggio.

This was what had troubled her when she stood gazing up at the beauty and terror so inextricably commingled on the face of Bernini's Daphne. She had half-framed the thought that it didn't matter what Bernini was like, whether he was a saint or a monster—the agonized cry that filled the still and chilly air around the marble face of Daphne proved he knew what it was to be betrayed. In that moment, Lucy had peered tremulously into a world where only art has value and no moral laws apply. "What would you do for it?" she asked Catherine abruptly. "Would you murder for it?"

"For what?"

"For the work, as you say." She gave Catherine a penetrating look. "For art."

Catherine pursed her mouth, pretending to entertain the question. But she wasn't serious, Lucy realized. Her declaration had had its origin in pique and stubbornness rather than in conviction; it was the rote response she applied to any and all opposition, anything that restricted her personal liberty, which she equated with her integrity as an artist. She had applied it to a man she both loved and admired, and dismissed him when he was bold enough to criticize her painting.

And, of course, she had applied it to DV. Catherine gazed off dreamily into space, her mouth slightly open, pulling a curl slowly between her thumb and forefinger. Then her eyes shifted to Lucy's. She had arrived at her answer, she was entirely satisfied, and she leaned forward in her chair to deliver herself of it. "I haven't had to so far," she said, and she gave Lucy her most radiant smile.

Chapter 20

WHEN JEALOUSY AND ANGER ignite the flame of desire, the result can be an all-consuming blaze. As Lucy raised her wineglass to her lips and gazed into the calm pools of Massimo's eyes, she knew herself to be in danger of a conflagration.

She didn't mind; in fact, the elevation in her emotional temperature suited her perfectly. She would need to be hot to do what she intended, which was to burn her image ineradicably into the landscape of Massimo's memory, a scene she knew to be an alien thicket of impenetrable lore, but she had stumbled in, she was about to exit forever, and she wanted to leave behind a small, charred, blackened clearing that wouldn't be overgrown too quickly with the dull flora of everyday life.

He had arrived at the hotel in a good humor, forestalling any inquiry into the awkward meeting at Catherine's gallery with the happy news that he would stay the night, their last night, in the hotel. After a brief absence in the early morning, he would return in time for lunch, after which they would set out for Ugolino. Lucy accepted this information as the fabulous gift it was meant to be. They cleared a space for his suitcase; he laid out his toothbrush and razor on the narrow bathroom shelf with her own.

Now he reached across the table and touched her cheek with the back of his hand. He was complacent, as always, but he was playing the part of the lover saddened by the cruel twists of fate. After he left her in Ugolino, he was going on to Milan, where his business would detain him for several days, well past the date of her departure. "I wish you were not going," he said.

"Me, too," she agreed.

"We will not speak of it."

And indeed they could not speak of it, for the waiter arrived with a bowl of snowy mozzarella, which he served out carefully while engaging Massimo in a lively discussion of its freshness and perfection. Lucy nodded, smiled, and made appreciative noises, though she was generally bored by cheese and thought it a heavy way to start a meal. When the waiter had gone, Massimo stabbed a little sphere with his fork and informed her, as he cut it into neat quarters, that she would enjoy these because they were very fresh.

"So I gathered," she said, following his example. "They milk the cow right there in the kitchen."

Massimo chewed his bite worriedly. Irony was largely lost on him, and he disliked having his enthusiasms contradicted. Lucy concentrated on her cheese, which was, to her surprise, unlike anything she had ever tasted, succulent and light, with a delicate, slightly salty flavor that poured out over the tongue. "You're right," she said. "This is wonderful."

He nodded, but her remark had silenced him. He ate the

rest of the cheese without comment and pushed the plate aside. "I am afraid you are having a bad influence on me, Lucy," he said.

"In what way?"

"I am behaving in a way that is not entirely proper."

"It's a little late to worry about that."

He gave her a sharp look. Clearly he was not speaking of their relationship, and it annoyed him that she should suggest that he was. She held his eyes, irritated herself now at the game he was playing. "What are you talking about?" she asked.

"I am becoming like you," he said, "full of suspicions. You will be pleased to hear that I have today accomplished some useful detective work for you."

Here it comes, Lucy thought. The lie about why he went to see Catherine. "What did you do?" she said.

"When we found your friend yesterday, I asked myself how she could afford to have such a gallery."

"She rents it," Lucy said. "That's no mystery."

He laughed and refilled his wineglass. "Lucy, you are naïve," he said. "Have you any idea what rents are on Via Margutta? It is one of the most expensive streets in the Centro. No one could afford to rent a closet on this street only with the sale of pictures."

Lucy nodded. He was right again. She had made the assumption that Catherine's gallery supported itself.

"I went there today to see what I could find out by making conversation."

Lucy smiled, but not from pleasure. She had asked for no excuse and did not want or believe this one. "So you asked her and she told you?"

"No, Lucy. That is what is interesting. She did not tell me. I did not even ask her; I am not a fool. But she was so reluctant to speak on this subject at all that I became even more suspicious. Then she was called to see a customer and I was left alone in the room near her desk. There is a book of checks there, such as are used in business, with the name of the account printed on it. And this is where I behaved poorly, in a way I can hardly explain. I lifted the cover of the book and read the name."

The waiter appeared, bearing two bowls of minestrone, which he set before them with elaborate concern. Lucy had a moment to conjure up a picture of Massimo in a Sherlock Holmes hat leaning surreptitiously over Catherine's papers, gingerly lifting the cover of a large leather-bound book, and dropping it back again, his eyes agleam with gratified conjecture. The waiter cleared away the cheese plates and refilled their water glasses before hurrying off to a table of chain-smoking businessmen nearby.

Massimo had pressed his upper teeth into his lower lip, holding back the crucial information until the moment of maximum dramatic effect. "You were right, Lucy," he said.

She lifted her spoon. "About what?"

"The name was Cini. The account is in the names Cini and Bultman."

She put the spoon down. "Antonio Cini is supporting Catherine?"

"But this is what you thought all along."

She had thought it, she admitted, but she had changed her mind. She found this irrefutable proof unsettling. What a smooth liar Antonio was, with his air of disinterest and dismissal, his haughty assurance that he knew very little about Catherine, that he had only seen her about, driving DV's car or sketching in the fields. He had almost persuaded her, though the evidence of the letter contradicted everything he said.

When Catherine showed so little interest in speaking of him—he was apparently little more than a helpful acquaintance who had referred her to the right people in Rome—Lucy had concluded the letter might, as Massimo had suggested, have been sent by some other Antonio, some former lover, perhaps this Florentine whose paintings Catherine hung in her gallery. In truth, her conversation with Antonio on the drive to the train had persuaded her that he was too lifeless and certainly too aloof to entangle himself in such a liaison, and her two interviews with Catherine had led her to conclude that she was too willful and too fond of her liberty to submit to a sex-for-cash arrangement with such a man. But if Antonio Cini was paying her bills, what else could it be?

"Why did he tell me where to find her?" Lucy wondered aloud.

"She is a beautiful woman," Massimo said. "Why should he be ashamed?"

"But if he wanted me to know, he could have just told me."

Massimo leapt to the defense of their aristocratic connection. "He leaves it to Catherine to tell you, Lucy. He is a gentleman."

Lucy sputtered, "Oh, for God's sake." Next, she thought, he will tell me I don't understand because I'm an American.

"This is perhaps not something you can understand," Massimo said.

"Because I'm an American?"

"Because you are not Italian."

I understand perfectly, Lucy thought, her pulse pounding in her ears. Lie about everything all the time, that's the policy. But she said nothing. Instead, she took up her spoon again and tasted her soup. Minestrone was another choice she'd thought uninspired, but the first mouthful changed her mind about that, too—simple ingredients in perfect proportion, almost no salt. Minestrone was another secret beyond the comprehension of the foreigner. "This is delicious," she said grudgingly.

Massimo nodded sagely. The waiter appeared, carrying a tray laden with glittering fishes, all sizes, shapes, and a few colors. Massimo studied them seriously, discussing his choice with the waiter, who appeared fascinated and excited by the process. They settled on a large sea bass whose round flat eye gazed up attentively at the two men. Even the fish is interested, Lucy thought. They were to have it grilled whole, with just a touch of olive oil and salt. No parsley, they agreed. This was sometimes done, but it was unnecessary, for it added nothing to the perfection of a good fresh fish.

To the delight of the two men, Lucy concurred. *"Prezzemolo, no,"* she said. As the waiter hefted the tray up to his shoulder and strode away proudly through the noise and smoke of the narrow dining room, Massimo beamed at Lucy. Her Italian, he informed her, was really coming along.

LUCY ROLLED OVER and looked at the clock: 7:00 a.m. Next to her, the sheets were thrown back; that side of the bed was empty. She could hear the shower running in the bathroom. They had hardly slept an hour.

She pulled the covers up around her chin and stretched out languorously, noting with pleasure and very little surprise the soreness in her hip sockets and across her shoulders. "I've been rearranged," she said dreamily.

On their return from the restaurant, Massimo had pressed his palm to her cheek and forehead. She had a fever, he maintained; it was the result of walking about in the rain. She had made herself ill again. Lucy laughed, shaking off his hands;

she felt fine, full of energy. She was hot, it was true, but this was no ordinary fever. She told him a few stories of saints who evidenced unnaturally high temperatures: of one who, when she drank water, was reported to emit a sound like sizzling coals while steam issued from her mouth and nostrils, and another, an Italian, whose temperature could not be recorded because he routinely burst thermometers. "It's called," she said, throwing her sweater over a chair and following it with her blouse, "*'incendium amoris.'*"

"You are making me anxious, Lucy," he said. "I am afraid I will be burned."

"You're perfectly safe," she assured him.

"But I am not a god." He unbuttoned his shirt, slipped it off, and sat next to her on the edge of the bed. She kissed his cheek, bit his ear, wrapped her arms around his bare shoulders.

"That's okay," she said. "Because I am not a saint."

Later, she had the thought that she had been right: He was safe, but she was in mortal danger. By then, she was far too excited to care. As the hours slipped by, Massimo was always willing, never tired; he did not, as she did, burst out in a sweat or pause to gulp down whole glasses of water. His eyes did not roll back beneath the lids; he was not even breathless. He was with her every moment, encouraging her, occasionally expressing admiration for her stamina or complimenting her on some adroit maneuver. He seemed blissfully unaware that she was up to something, that his self-possession drove her on and she would not give in until she broke through it somehow and left him gasping, as she was, somewhere outside the world he knew so well.

At last she did give up, though it was her body and not her desire that failed her. She was forced to take the measure of the challenge she had set herself. Massimo was not, perhaps, a god, but he was a fortress, and she did not constitute a serious threat to his defenses. She was like some absurd swashbuckling mouse flailing away at the great iron gates with her toothpick sword. This image accosted her as she was on top of Massimo, holding him down by the shoulders, her arms rigid, ramming herself maniacally against him, and it struck her as so ridiculous that she collapsed against his chest in helpless laughter.

He held her, bemused and interested. "What is it?" he said. "Lucy, what is funny?"

"It's nothing," she said. "I'm just knocking myself out here."

"You are," he said. "This is true. You will be worn out completely."

"But I don't care," she said. Then her amusement turned to chagrin and bitterness, because it was a cruel fate to be a brave mouse with no hope of success.

Massimo sensed the change in her mood and drew her face up to his, kissing her so tenderly that, for a moment, she thought he was touched by her. "My poor Lucy," he said. "You do care for me." Then he rolled her smoothly beneath him and, while with her last remaining strength she held on tight, he brought the matter to a tumultuous close.

He had turned the shower off now. She could hear him moving around in the narrow bathroom. The door opened and he stood before her, wrapped in a nonabsorbent hotel towel, his hair still dripping onto his shoulders.

"Good morning," she said.

"How do you feel?" he asked.

"I'm fine."

He came to sit beside her on the bed and laid his hand upon her forehead. "No. You do not have a fever," he said.

"I'm fine," she repeated. "I sweated it all out last night, whatever it was."

"You didn't get much rest, Lucy."

"I didn't come here to rest," she said.

He flinched at this indelicate remark and she felt the withdrawal of his approval. "What will you do while I am gone this morning?" he asked. He got up and busied himself over his suitcase, giving half his attention to her answer, the other half to the correct choice of socks.

Lucy stretched and yawned. A great weariness came over her; she was not, she realized, up for the battering racket of the streets outside. "I think I'm just going to stay in this bed," she said.

"This is a wise decision," he said. "Shall I have them bring you some coffee?"

"No. I'll go out later and get breakfast at a bar."

He pulled on his shirt and shorts. "I will come back at eleven-thirty," he said. "We will have lunch at a *fattoria* outside the city, a beautiful place. I think you will like it."

"Great," she said. And that will be it, she thought. The arrangements were all made. He would leave her in Ugolino; tomorrow the mail service would pick up DV's boxes and Antonio Cini would take her to Sansepolcro to return the car. The next day, a new driver would come down from Milan to drive her to the airport.

Massimo had finished dressing. He was bent over his suitcase, making sure everything was folded properly, that he had left nothing behind. Lucy turned away from him, toward the heavily curtained window, where a slender thread of light escaped in a thin white line across the carpet. She closed her eyes as she heard the double snap of the suitcase lock.

Be very strong about this, she told herself, or you will regret it. No tears. He clearly isn't going to be shedding any, so why should you?

But at the order—no tears—as if in protest, hot, bitter tears gathered in her eyes, overflowed, and rushed down her face into her hair. She lay there helplessly, trying to blink them away. Massimo came to the bed and leaned over her, kissed her cheek, her neck, her shoulder. She stayed still, though her impulse was to reach out and drag him back into the bed. "Why are you weeping, Lucy?" he said. "You should not be so sad."

"I shouldn't have come to Rome," she said; then her voice broke. So much for being strong, she thought. But what was the point? Strong people never got to say what they really thought.

"What are you saying, Lucy? Why should you not have come here? Has it been so disagreeable to you?" This last question had an edge of impatience to it. Could she be so ungrateful as to complain of his treatment of her?

"No. It's just that I don't want to know all the things I know now."

He sat down on the bed beside her and rested his hand against her cheek, for all the world, she thought, like a mother comforting an unhappy, fretting child. "What things, Lucy?" he asked.

She turned onto her side, facing away from him, sniffing and rubbing her eyes. "I need a handkerchief," she said. He produced a clean one from his coat pocket, which she snatched greedily without looking at him. As she pressed it to her nose, she thought, I'm keeping this handkerchief. I am not giving it back.

"What things?" Massimo said again.

"Oh, everything," she whined, dabbing at her eyes. "I don't

want to know that Catherine left DV for Antonio, and I don't want to know that DV fell into a septic tank. . . ."

"A septic tank?" Massimo said. "What is this? What are you talking about?"

"Antonio told me," she said, turning onto her other side to face him, her tears allayed by the pleasurable urgency of giving information. "It wasn't a well; it was a septic tank. A *pozzo nero,* you say."

Massimo's brow furrowed in deep lines of disbelief. "A *pozzo nero?*" he said. "How is this possible?"

"Some neighbor had opened it because the tank was cracked."

"Please," Massimo said. "This is too unpleasant."

"It is," Lucy agreed. "It's too unpleasant. It's all too unpleasant."

"You must not think about such things, Lucy. Especially when you are overtired. You are still not well, you know. You should sleep a little now, and then when you wake up, you will see that everything is not so terrible."

"Whenever I try to tell you how I feel, you tell me I'm sick," she complained.

"Please, Lucy," he said.

"I think you like me better when I'm sick."

His eyes made a quick survey of the distance to the door and back again. "Let us not have a stupid quarrel," he entreated. "We have so little time left. Why should we argue pointlessly?"

"Why not?" she replied sharply. She succumbed to an urge to recklessness she recognized as both dangerous and irresistible. "We've nothing to lose."

He shrugged. It was a game he didn't much care for, but if she insisted, he would play. "Perhaps it is more true to say you like *me* better when you are sick, Lucy," he said. "I am always the same. It is you who changes."

This stopped her momentarily. Was it true? "That's another thing I don't want to know," she replied, turning away from him again.

He said nothing, only stroked her arm and patted her shoulder gently. He *is* trying to help me through this, she thought as another flood of tears blurred her vision and she pulled her knees up to her chest, weeping as quietly as she could into the handkerchief.

"My poor Lucy," he said.

"I *am* changed," she sobbed. "And it's all your fault. Do you think I ever spent a night like last night in my life? And what do you think the odds are that I'll ever have another, Massimo? Well, I'll tell you, the same odds as that Jesus Christ is about to knock on that door."

His hand rested on her shoulder and he looked momentarily at the door. "You are saying that you will not enjoy lovemaking so much with someone else."

Lucy rolled onto her back and looked up at him mournfully. "Yes," she said. "That's what I'm saying."

He took her hand in his own, smiling ruefully. "How can I wish that you will?" he said.

"This is not a compliment, Massimo," she said. "It's an accusation."

"Who would not be flattered to be accused of such a crime?"

"It is a crime," she observed.

"What do you want to say, Lucy? That you wish you never met me? That I have harmed you in some way?"

"No," she admitted. "I can't say that."

"Do you imagine that I am not sad, too, that you are going back to America?"

"Yes," she said. "That is what I imagine. I think your life is so full, you'll be relieved to have me out of it."

"My life is very full, that is true," he said. "But this time I have spent with you has made me wish sometimes it was not so."

"Is that really true?"

He gave her his most serious attention. "Yes, Lucy. That is really true."

The paltriness of this cold comfort amused her. It was the closest to a profession of strong feeling she would ever get, she realized. On cold nights in Brooklyn, she would warm herself with the memory of it; she had made him wish he was not too busy for her. "Okay," she said. "I believe it. You can go now. But I want to keep the handkerchief."

He gave a weak laugh of assent and stood up next to the bed, repeating the time of his return. When he looked back at the door, she said, "I'll be ready." Then he was gone.

She pulled the pillow under her head and stretched her arms and legs wide apart, taking up as much space as possible. It was one of the feeble pleasures of the single life, this position. There were others, which she toted up, saving the best for last, which was never having to answer to anyone about where you were. "Why does this hurt so much?" she said, for now, on top of physical weariness, came misery, followed by jealousy. It was ridiculous, she knew, to be jealous of a married man, especially as she was not jealous of his wife, but of a woman he had just met and with whom he could not possibly be having an affair. But she didn't believe his story about Catherine Bultman; at least she didn't believe he'd gone to see her because he wanted to help solve a mystery. Lucy was leaving, but Catherine was here, and certainly available and safe, what with her aristocratic lover tucked away in the country and her ready access to his fortune. She wasn't likely to give that arrangement up, but how often could Antonio be in Rome? Massimo had sniffed out the truth in his own interests; he was, as he had pointed out himself, no fool. Why would he not take advantage of what was clearly a very attractive situation?

Lucy's only consolation was her conviction that Catherine was more than a match for Massimo. If he could get her attention, it would only be long enough for her to make him suffer.

Lucy disliked knowing what Massimo had discovered about Catherine, though it certainly made sense. It meant Antonio Cini had another face, one she hadn't even been able to glimpse, and that Catherine herself, as she freely admitted, actually was willing to do anything for her art. Did that make her less or more sincere as an artist? There was no way of knowing. Artists needed money, like everyone else, and patrons were always insistent upon their right to exercise some kind of control. DV had believed in Catherine's ambitions, had certainly done what he could to enable her to pursue them, but she'd found him oppressive, or so she said. Perhaps she'd only found out how much money was going out in child support every month. He certainly had not been willing to set her up on her own in a city he rarely visited. No, Antonio's was the better offer.

How devastated DV must have been, for in spite of his bluster, he was never confident. He worked hard, doggedly, because he believed that with diligence and determination he could somehow win the prize. To have Catherine, his goddess, the woman he wanted for his muse, tell him he would be better off gardening, and then leave him for the foreign fop next door, well, Lucy could understand why he had closed himself up in the farmhouse and applied himself entirely to the steady consumption of alcohol.

But why had Catherine felt the need to destroy DV with ridicule before she left? Had she actually persuaded herself that she was leaving not because she had received a better offer, but because she had discovered he was a mediocre hack? DV was not an artist—that was his tragedy—but did that mean he had no right to love beauty?

So Lucy came through jealousy and self-pity to a state of sympathetic identification with her dead employer, a man she had not known well in life, nor had what she did know inspired her admiration. Their situations were not dissimilar; they had both fallen in love with beauty, and beauty had briefly toyed with them. But beauty was inviolable, like great art; it both excited and resisted the passion for possession. That was why she always had the sensation that she could not break through Massimo's self-possession, and it was exactly that sense of exclusion that made their lovemaking so constantly tantalizing. Beauty is a cruel mother, Lucy thought sleepily. She draws us in and then rejects us. Irresistible, unobtainable.

Amid these esoteric musings, Lucy slipped into a deep sleep, from which she woke feeling refreshed and cheerful. There would be no further scenes, no protestations of regret, or expressions of anxiety about the future. When Massimo arrived, she greeted him with warm affection. She had slept so long, she confessed, she had failed to have breakfast, and now she was famished. He was surprised by her good humor. Certainly he had no wish for a gloomy parting, but wasn't it a little insulting, how eager she was to leave the hotel and hurry on to the next meal?

Chapter 21

"ESUS," LUCY EXCLAIMED as she rammed both feet down hard on the brake and clutch, narrowly escaping collision with the dented rear fender of Antonio Cini's car. It was impossible, she thought. Catherine Bultman could not have submitted to the embraces of a man who drove this poorly. Whenever he got up to a decent cruising speed, Antonio seemed to panic and reverted to this spasmodic braking. Fortunately, there was very little traffic on the autostrada.

She both dreaded and welcomed the day ahead, for the plan, as usual, had been changed at the last minute. Antonio had called to say that the shippers would not be coming, as planned, this morning, but early the next afternoon. As this gave Lucy the entire day free, he proposed that after they dropped off DV's car, he might take her to lunch in Sansepolcro. It would be too bad if she were to leave Italy without seeing something of this ancient town.

She accepted the invitation willingly. At least it meant she wouldn't have to sit through another dinner at the villa. And she was determined to wring some sort of confession out of Antonio. She wanted to make him drop his pose of indifference on the subject of Catherine and admit the truth, that he had lured her away from DV and that he had an emotional as well as a financial stake in her affairs.

How she would accomplish this, she didn't know. She had proved so far a very poor detective, and she disliked the sensation of harping on a subject once it was clear the person she addressed wished to change it. She had been a perfect dupe with Catherine, as disarmed by her frankness and beauty as, she felt sure, Catherine had intended she should be. Even Massimo, who had succumbed to Catherine's spell on sight, had been more observant and certainly more secretive than she had been.

The thought of Massimo stung her, as it was, she knew, only the thought of him she would have from now on. They had parted at the farmhouse without bitterness and without any specific plan for a reunion. Someday perhaps he would travel to America; surely she would return to Italy. She wrote her Brooklyn address and phone number on the back of a postcard she had purchased but never mailed; it was a photograph of a cat sitting on the head of a great stone lion, and he gave her a card with his business address in Milan. She thanked him for saving her life. "It was my pleasure," he said. "Anytime you are dying, you must call me."

She looked up from the business card. He was smiling down at her, his habitual, indulgent, patronizing smile, but as her eyes met his, the smile disappeared, replaced by an expression of genuine sadness. "I will miss you, Lucy," he said. He took her hand, kissed the back of it, then the palm, released her, and strode off to the car.

She stood on the drive, watching him turn the car around. But instead of waving and driving off, he stopped the car, got out, and came back to her with the easy feline grace that had always charmed her. "I want to kiss you once more," he said. The kiss that followed was so full of heat and longing that she decided to believe it. She pressed her body against his; she clung to his neck. She would never know what his real feelings were, as they were submerged in his bravura performance, but her own condition was crystal clear.

Now Antonio had put on his turn signal, though there was no crossroad in sight. He braked again next to a sunflower field and Lucy had a vision of him plunging into the dense ranks of dark, dry stalks. He crept along for half a mile; then the road he was searching for appeared and he accelerated triumphantly into the oncoming lane.

Lucy followed, the memory of Massimo's kiss, which it was better not to dwell upon, dislodged by her irritation at Antonio Cini. The new road was rutted and twisty, so he increased his speed. His antique car lurched and shuddered before her in the bright morning sun. As she swerved to avoid a pothole, she saw his rear tire disappearing into the next one. "Where did this man learn to drive?" she said.

In this manner, they traversed several miles of back roads where the only sign of life was the occasional eruption of raucous crows over a field. Then they passed a few low farm buildings, a dirt lot crowded with farm machinery, and another, smaller lot in which several new cars were clustered about a concrete building barely wide enough to accommodate its single window and door. As Lucy followed Antonio into a parking space, she noticed a small sign in the dusty window. EURAUTO was stenciled in faded red, white, and green letters.

She turned off the engine and joined Antonio on the pavement. "How did you ever find this place?" she said.

"It is not difficult," he replied.

"Right," she said, falling into step behind him. They went into the office, where a nervous young man equipped with a computer he knew nothing about tried for several minutes to generate some vital information about the paid contract Lucy presented. He studied the screen hopefully. *"Niente,"* he said.

Antonio was patient but clearly bored. "These machines make nothing better," he confided to Lucy. Again the boy's fingers raced across the keyboard; then he stood blinking nervously at the shiny screen. *"No, niente,"* he said again. He discussed the problem with Antonio, who conveyed their conclusion to Lucy. It had been decided that the clerk would take an imprint of Lucy's credit card and the charge would be added later, when someone who knew something about the system could figure out what it was.

"But there shouldn't be any charge," Lucy complained. "It was all paid in advance. It says so on the contract."

Antonio looked perplexed. "Then what are we wanting here?"

"A receipt," she said. "Just ask him to give me a copy of the contract."

Antonio made this request. Another long conversation ensued. The contract was produced, examined; Lucy pointed to the line that showed it was paid. It was a single sheet, and there was no copy machine in the place. "How was it paid?" she asked Antonio, though she hardly expected him to know. She had found no receipt for it, and DV was careful about such things.

"They do not take credit cards for such a large amount,"

Antonio explained. "Your friend paid in cash. I know this because I took him to the bank to get the money and then I brought him here to take the car."

"So you know it was paid!" Lucy exclaimed. "So why would I give this guy a blank credit card now? It makes no sense. Can't you tell him I want only a piece of paper that says it was paid?"

Antonio was losing patience as well, but he endeavored to remain in control. "The credit card is only for the event of small additional charges," he explained calmly, "or in case the car has been damaged."

"Damaged!" Lucy felt her blood pressure shooting up. "We can walk outside and look at it and see that it isn't damaged. Anyway, it's insured. That's on the contract, too."

"Please, Lucia," Antonio pleaded. He was deeply uncomfortable with the developing scene, Lucy realized. The dull clerk, the boorish American tourist—it was the stuff of his nightmares. He was so miserable, his eyes rolled back under the lids and for a moment Lucy thought he might faint, or simply bolt from the room. But he mastered his emotions and forged on. "This is a stupid boy, but he is not dishonest. It is the way it is done here. I believe if you will consent to give him this credit card, I will persuade him to write out a receipt for you, and that will be the end of the matter. If some charge should appear on your bill, you will please send it to me and I will take care of it, but I assure you, such a thing will not happen."

"So that's what people do here?" Lucy said. She opened her purse and dug out the requisite card. "They just hand over huge sums of money and leave blank credit-card vouchers lying around and no one keeps track of anything?"

"I am sure everything is much better in America," Antonio

murmured. He subjected the clerk, who took the card with alacrity, to a long harangue, complete, Lucy noted, with several references to his own family name. The poor young man was so rattled that, when he handed Lucy the card and the half sheet of paper on which he had written the amount DV had paid, a number so rich in zeros that it ran halfway across the page, he forgot to ask Lucy to sign the credit-card form. The receipt, Lucy noticed, was undated, but the insignia *Eurauto* was printed in the bottom margin. Antonio noticed nothing; he was so eager to be out of the place, he had gone to stand at the door like a dog waiting to be let out. *"Grazie,"* Lucy said to the clerk, who puffed himself up as he replied, *"Prego, signora."* He had completed the business to his own satisfaction. Lucy stuffed the papers into her purse and followed Antonio out into the parking lot. How long, she wondered, before the poor fellow discovered his mistake?

Antonio started the car and they continued on the dirt road without speaking. There was plenty of noise and excitement, however; the engine creaked and complained, the tires thudded in the holes, and the brakes squeaked. He needs a brake job immediately, Lucy thought, but she knew this was not the time to offer mechanical advice. The road joined up with the smooth two-lane highway to Sansepolcro, and the car settled down to its habitual low whine. "Thank you," Lucy said, "for helping me with that. I couldn't have done it without you."

He smiled without looking at her; the road ahead engaged him. He's annoyed with me, she thought, because I was annoyed by the clerk, though he thought the clerk was an idiot, too. She resolved to say no more about the business. She certainly wasn't going to tell him she had not signed the credit-card form. They had entered the ugly strip of warehouse stores, and Lucy looked out the window in gloomy silence.

And she would remain silent all through lunch, she promised herself, before she would offer a new topic of conversation.

"You must tell me, Lucia," Antonio said, "how did you find Roma?"

"Noisy," she replied.

"You did not enjoy your visit?"

She relented. She wanted to say a good deal about her visit. "Actually, I enjoyed it very much. I went to the museum in the Villa Borghese and saw *Apollo and Daphne*. That was worth the whole trip."

"Ah. You are an admirer of Bernini."

"Oh, yes," she said. "Aren't you?"

"Of course," he agreed. "Everyone is. He gives one no choice."

"I had an odd experience there," she said. "Shall I tell you about it?"

He nodded again.

"Well, I've wanted to see that statue for years. I'd only seen it in pictures, and there it was. And of course, you know, pictures can't really do it justice. . . ."

Antonio made a circular motion with one hand, signifying his entire agreement with this opinion. His eyes left the road for a millisecond, taking her in with guarded interest.

"So it was infinitely more wonderful than I'd imagined. At first, I just wanted to look and look at it, and I had the sensation—I think most people feel this in some way—that this statue was speaking somehow to me. To me personally."

Antonio raised his eyebrows, his eyes still on the road.

"But then I realized what a crass reaction that is. How dull and vain it is to think that I have anything to do with Bernini, or he with me."

Antonio looked at her again, frankly curious, as if she had

really said something unexpected. "After all," she continued, "here I am, an American, for God's sake, I can't even speak the same language he spoke, and I live in this world"—she gestured out the window at a garden-furniture outlet—"where people build things like that, and nothing lasts. . . ." She paused. Was this what she had felt? It was difficult to remember, and she wanted to get it right. Antonio was silent, but she could feel the force of his listening. "So I began to think about Bernini, and how hard he worked, and how he did it for himself, not for anyone else, certainly not for me, and how he couldn't see into the future but that, because of him, I can see a little, just a little, into the past, and I felt grateful to him, just for having lived, and that gratitude was so big, it was so strong, it made me sad. It brought tears to my eyes."

"You were weeping in the Galleria Borghese?" Antonio asked.

"Well, only a little. No one noticed, I'm sure."

Antonio drove on without speaking, and Lucy was left to go over her explanation. She had not mentioned, of course, how vulnerable she had been to any and all intrusions of feeling because of her general anxiety about Massimo. But that was a precondition, she thought, of no interest to anyone but her. She looked out the window as Antonio executed a turn onto a wide tree-shaded street lined with double- and triple-parked cars. There were small shops along the pavement and several bars with tables set out in the sun.

"Why is it, Lucia, that people so often believe what you have described, that a work of art has some personal message for them?" Antonio asked.

Lucy looked at him closely; there was no archness, no mocking in the tone of this, the first outright question he had ever asked her. She wanted to give a thoughtful answer. "It's a wish, I think," she said. "Because when we see something that stops us"—she paused, not liking the conclusion that beckoned at the end of her conjecture—"something that really holds us still, it reminds us of how empty and short our own lives are, and that is truly unbearable."

The walls of Sansepolcro loomed up ahead of them. Antonio was dodging traffic now and could not respond. To her surprise, he ignored the generous public parking lots on either side and drove straight through the narrow opening in the wall. The world on the inside was entirely different from the one outside. The streets were cobbled and narrow, the shops pressed together on either side in a continuous line of stone, their windows clean and bright in the sun. Antonio veered into a side street, an alley, actually, designed with nothing wider than a horse in mind. He pulled the car half up on the sidewalk and turned off the engine. "Are you very hungry?" he asked.

She shrugged. So her remarks had meant nothing to him. "A little," she said. "I'm always hungry, actually."

"Would you mind if I took you to see something before we eat?"

"Of course I wouldn't mind."

"It is a fresco," he said. "Do you know the work of Piero della Francesca?"

She nodded.

"He was born in this town." Antonio reached over the seat for his jacket and opened the door of the car. "It is here," he said, pointing to the building opposite.

Lucy got out and followed him along the high bare wall, for he had parked behind the building, to the wide steps and heavy double doors at the front. There was a sign on one door that read MUSEO CIVICO and gave the opening hours. It would be closing, she noticed, in the next thirty minutes.

While Antonio purchased tickets at the counter, Lucy wandered out into the first room. The ceiling was high; the walls were white. Two massive doorways framed in wide oak boards opened into the other rooms. There were a few large pictures on the walls, religious scenes; nothing, Lucy thought, unusual or interesting. Antonio joined her and ushered her through the nearer doorway. "We have not much time," he said. "But it will be enough for you to see the *Resurrection*."

As Lucy followed him through several rooms, past various paintings, a display of reliquaries, a section of a fresco so ravaged by time that she could barely make out the subject, she ran through a mental catalog of famous Resurrection paintings. It was not so thick as the file on the Annunciation, nor was she able to visualize even one that stood out from all the others.

"Here we are," Antonio said, pausing in the doorway to the next room. Lucy joined him, conscious of an effort to present an eager expression, though she had a faint trepidation that the picture would be of scant interest to her. They entered a small, spare room, a kind of chapel, in which the vaulted ceiling curved down all around, like a white parachute settling over the cool terra-cotta of the floor. They had come in alongside the fresco. Lucy followed Antonio to a wooden bench that faced the niche in which the scene of the Resurrection glowed with an eerie, subaqueous light, like a window open upon another world. Antonio took a seat on the bench while Lucy approached the fresco.

The figure of Christ seemed to come forward to meet her. He was both perfectly still and in motion, one foot raised on the edge of his marble tomb, one hand grasping the staff of his simple flag. In the next moment, he would complete the action of climbing out of his grave, step down among the four stolid soldiers asleep at his feet, and astound the world. He was clothed only in a sheet of a pellucid, diaphanous pink, which was wrapped about his waist loosely, one end draping his shoulder, toga-style. His flesh was startlingly pale; he was thin, but his chest was strong and muscular, the bicep of his raised arm thick enough to throw a shadow in the declivity at his shoulder. His face was not extraordinary: He was plain-featured, his beard was short, but his expression was such a wonder, it spoke of so many emotions, of shock, anger, extreme fatigue, and determination, that Lucy felt she could read in it the whole process of his waking in the terrifying blackness of the grave, pushing back the stone, gathering up the winding-sheet, remembering all the while who he was, why he was here, who had betrayed him, what he must do now. As he pulled himself to his feet, he would have seen the slumbering guards gathered around his tomb. It was some hour of early dawn, and though two of the men had rested their heads against the tomb, they were sleeping soundly; they had heard nothing. He would have to wake them to get them out of his path. So he had paused, resting his pierced hand on his raised knee, to look again at the world he loved so well. Behind him the low hills, the gray trees just coming to life after a long winter, the thin racks of clouds drifting in a sky the color of a robin's egg; all nature was still and calm. He alone was awake; he alone knew he had kept his promise and come back.

Lucy stood transfixed before the painting for some minutes. The double perspective was both impossible and magical, for the soldiers were foreshortened, as though seen from below, while the figure of Christ was presented dead-on to the viewer. The colors, too, were the stuff of legends: a deep blue-green, like weathered bronze, repeated in the stockings and helmets of the guards, a shield and hat of burnt sienna. There weren't very many colors, and they had been laid in next to one another with loving precision. The composition moved the eye around and around inside the painted marble columns that framed the whole, so that the process of looking at the fresco was entirely absorbing. It made one feel busy just to stand and look.

At last, she turned away and joined Antonio on the bench. "Thank you for bringing me here," she said.

He nodded, his eyes fixed dreamily on the fresco.

"He looks startled, as if he just woke up," Lucy said.

"He's been in hell," Antonio said.

Lucy looked back at the picture. "What?"

"He went down to hell after he died. To release the souls of those who had not had the opportunity to know him."

"Of course," Lucy said. "I'd forgotten. The Harrowing of Hell."

Antonio looked puzzled.

"That's what it's called," Lucy explained. "In poetry. The Harrowing of Hell. It's good, isn't it?"

"Yes," he agreed.

Then they sat for a few minutes in silence, side by side, looking at the painting.

"When I was a young man," Antonio said, "I had before this painting a sensation such as the one you have described. I believed the artist was speaking to me alone."

Lucy regarded him with interest. He was about to tell her something personal, and it didn't come easily to him. She said nothing, allowing him the time to gather his thoughts.

"There was not for me this barrier of the language," he

continued. "Perhaps I would have been better off if there had been. It seemed to me there was nothing between myself and this artist. We were from the same town, I was baptized here, probably in the same church he was, and I was young enough to think that the centuries made little difference. First I began to study his life, which takes not too long, because very little is known about him, and I made excursions to see all the paintings I could find. There are not so many, and what has survived is often badly damaged. Many of his frescoes have been lost. We have only accounts by people who saw them."

"What a pity," Lucy said.

"Yes, it is. Very sad. He was a most influential painter, but his life was like so many; he went from town to town following commissions. At the end, he stopped painting. His eyesight failed gradually. By the time of his death, he was blind."

Lucy looked back at the startled, dark eyes of the Christ figure. Was he blinded by the light of day? Was that what made him look so vulnerable?

"Then I began to paint myself," Antonio said. "I set up a studio in my house. My family approved my ambition, and I had various teachers come to me. I studied mathematics, as well, because *he* studied mathematics. . . ." Antonio lifted his chin to the painting as if the artist himself were standing before it. "He wrote a long treatise on this subject, very dull reading, which I studied."

He paused. His story was not over, but he was considering how best to tell it. Now comes the bad part, Lucy thought. She could see it in the set of his jaw and the rueful inwardness of his eyes.

"Often I came here to look at this painting. It never failed to inspire me, but I began to lose my sense that it spoke to me. No, that is not right. It continued to speak to me, but it did not speak in a friendly way." He smiled at this observation. Lucy understood that it represented a vast understatement. "This went on for several years. My struggles were great, my intentions were . . . noble. My teachers encouraged me. At last they told me they had nothing more to teach me. I had completed many paintings, but none of them pleased me at all. They were competent. Ignorant people praised them. But they had no life. Everything that came from me was already dead." He examined his hands moodily, as if he held them responsible for his failure. Then he looked up at the painting. "As surely dead," he said, "as that dead man is surely still alive."

He fell silent while Lucy considered the question of which dead man he referred to—the figure of the risen Christ or the artist who had created him. Antonio was slumped forward at her side, dangling his hands between his knees. "So you gave up painting?" she asked.

"Yes. I gave it up. All the inferior pictures are locked away. I do not come here very often anymore. This picture has become a reproach to me. But because of what you told me, Lucia, I saw that you are wiser than I am, and I knew you could appreciate this great painting without your life being destroyed."

Lucy laughed. "I do appreciate it," she said. "But it isn't wisdom that keeps me safe. I can't draw a box."

He accepted this, nodding his head with his habitual air of bored resignation. "Now we will go and have something to eat," he said. "The restaurant is nearby."

Outside the museum the day was warm and sunny, and the streets were thronged with shoppers, their arms laden with packages, for the closing hour was near. Lucy walked beside Antonio, enjoying the scene as well as her ability to stroll through it without external support. Her ankle had survived the treacherous streets of Rome and seemed, in fact, strengthened by the ordeal. Antonio walked so slowly, she was in no danger of stumbling or falling behind. His confession had surprised and pleased her, and she viewed him now in an entirely different light.

His attraction to Catherine had surely been something more complex and esoteric than the crude lust she had imagined. Perhaps, she speculated, he really was Catherine's patron and nothing more. She chided herself for having been so small-minded as to think the only reason a wealthy man would invest in a beautiful woman was to gratify some base desire for possession. No, Antonio had recognized in Catherine the full blaze of the spark he had tended so diligently and hopefully in himself. He had observed how things stood with DV, how incapable he was of giving Catherine the one thing she required, which was liberty. So he had stepped in where he saw the opportunity. He was not an artist, but he had served on that altar, he had participated in the sacred rites, and he had seen in Catherine a fellow initiate, one who could, if she were only given the chance, ascend into the blessed company of the saints.

Lucy was restored to earth from this rhetorical flight by their arrival at the trattoria Antonio had chosen. It was a simple room with exposed beams, stone floors, and good linen cloths on the scattering of tables. Antonio was evidently well known and much respected here, for no sooner were they seated than two waiters, followed by the chef himself, descended upon them to discuss the refinements of the meal. It was noted that Antonio's guest was an American who was leaving for her own country on the morrow, and it was determined that she should not be allowed to go without tasting the true Tuscan cuisine. Lucy owned herself willing to eat whatever was set in front of her, and, almost immediately, the procession of dishes began. Antonio examined, tasted, and approved each one, but Lucy noticed the only thing he actually ate was a quail. He lives on little birds, she thought, stabbing a piece of sausage on the platter of roasted meats. The wine was a hearty local red, and Antonio pressed it upon her, filling her glass twice as often as he filled his own. It doesn't matter, she thought. She could have a nap when she got back to the farmhouse. Wine did not flow this freely in Brooklyn.

Their conversation rambled, interrupted by the enthusiastic waiters and Lucy's exclamations of pleasure at each new dish. Antonio was more at ease in this atmosphere, Lucy noticed, than he was in his own home. He was even capable of a certain dry humor, though no one would ever call him gay. They talked of the food, the town, her plans for her return to the States, the perfect weather. At last, the plates were cleared away and the waiter brought two cups of black espresso, and, at Lucy's request, a pitcher of hot milk, followed by two narrow flutes of a rosy strawberry dessert wine made, he confided, by his family and not available for sale.

The subject had drifted back to Rome; Lucy wasn't sure which of them had brought it up. She was careful not to mention Massimo, and the studied omission of his name felt like a shadow cast over the conversation. Antonio expressed regret that she had not seen more art there, and she was not able to explain that this was partly because she had spent so much time in bed with Massimo. "I tried," she said. "But everything always seemed to be closing just when I arrived."

"And of course you had your business affairs to carry out."

"Right," she agreed, studying her cup so that he wouldn't see her guilty confusion. He had noted it, had, in fact, brought up the transparent excuse they both knew was a lie, just for the pleasure of seeing it. She decided it was then perfectly fair for her to introduce a subject she knew would make him equally uncomfortable. "I did see Catherine Bultman," she said.

"Oh, yes," he said. "So you found her there in her little shop?"

"I did," Lucy said. "I had two long conversations with her. She was shocked to learn that DV was dead."

Antonio lifted his cup to his lips and tossed back the contents in a motion so sudden, it had an air of desperation about it, like a condemned man downing an emergency dose of cyanide. Then he rested his chin in his palm and gave Lucy a searching, anxious, but not unfriendly look. "No doubt," he said, "in these conversations, she told you something of her"—the choice of the next word seemed to pain him—"connection to my family."

"Actually," Lucy said, "she was discreet. But I had already guessed something of it. And after what you've told me today, I think I understand it."

"There is no understanding it." He sighed. "There is no excuse for it. But I will show you something that will, perhaps, explain a little." As he spoke, he drew an old leather wallet from inside his jacket and extracted a small faded photograph, which he passed across the table to Lucy.

The woman who looked out from the photograph leaned against a stone arch Lucy recognized as part of the Cini loggia. She was smiling; her eyes were bright with confidence and gaiety. She had pinned her fair hair back at the nape, but it was so thick and wavy that some short curls had strayed, framing her face in an airy halo. Her nose was aquiline, her strong jaw suggested a tendency to stubbornness, and the large, even, white teeth exposed by her wide smile made her look fierce and merciless, like a cat whose playfulness is both charming and dangerous. She was dressed in a suit with thick shoulder pads and dark trim at the cuffs and collar, tucked in at the waist and flaring at the hips, forties-style. "She looks like Catherine," Lucy said.

"So I am told," Antonio agreed, taking the picture back and restoring it to his wallet. "I do not see it myself. But then my mother died when I was very young. Her name was Elena. I have no memory of her. I have heard from those who did know her that the resemblance is striking and more than physical. It is in the voice, they say, even the gestures. I cannot believe this."

"How did she die?"

"An automobile accident. She was, by all accounts, a reckless driver."

Lucy nodded sympathetically. Did the mother's untimely death explain the son's infuriating caution behind the wheel? She poured half the pitcher of milk into her espresso and took a sip. Antonio watched her, his hands folded in his lap. He looked different. His aloofness, his air of boredom and contempt had been replaced by an expression that was almost wistful. Was he thinking of his dead mother, or of Catherine? How overwhelming it must have been for him to find a woman who was both the artist he knew he could never be and the image of the beloved mother he had lost so long ago. No, Lucy decided. He wasn't just Catherine's patron. He was a man consumed by an irresistible obsession; how could he be otherwise? She recalled the passionate language of the letter, *"Carissima, amatissima,"* and her heart swelled with pity. "I must tell you," she confessed. "I saw a letter you sent to Catherine. When I was going through DV's things, I found it in a drawer. Catherine must have left it." A new possibility occurred to her. "Or perhaps DV took it and hid it from her."

Antonio's response was to rub his eyes with one hand in

what Lucy took to be chagrin and dismay. "What letter could you be talking about, Lucia?" he said.

She paused. Surely he wouldn't persist in denying his attachment to Catherine after revealing these two strong motives for his complete surrender—his love of art and her resemblance to his mother. "I didn't read it," she added. "I couldn't. I only saw that it was a love letter and that it was signed 'Antonio.'"

His hand dropped to his mouth and he blinked at her with the unfocused eagerness to comprehend of a man who has just awakened from a deep slumber. Then, gradually, something came clear for him. *"Dio,"* he said softly. "So you think . . ." Whatever it was he thought she thought struck him as outrageously funny. She had not seen him laugh before. It was not an agreeable thing to see. His mouth stretched wide in something more like a grimace of pain than an expression of pleasure and his dark eyes over the rictus of his grin were full of wild, unwonted merriment. "Oh Lucia," he said, rubbing his long face against his palm as if to release an involuntary clenching of his jaw. "What must you think of me?"

"I think I understand," Lucy said defensively. "I think I can see why—"

"No, no," he said. "Please stop or I will die of laughing."

Lucy looked about the restaurant, feeling exasperated. The place was nearly empty; no one had noticed that she was the source of great amusement to her dining companion. When she looked back, Antonio had calmed down. In fact, he regarded her with something very like affection. "Lucia," he said. "Please forgive me. I must explain. You are again the victim of a great misunderstanding."

"I don't really see how," she said.

"You will see as soon as I tell you one small detail. I think it has escaped you."

"Which is what?" she asked testily, for she had grown impatient with his superior delight.

"You see, Lucia, I am not the only Antonio in my family."

She looked at him steadily, trying to process this salient tip, but for a moment she made no sense of it.

"I am named after my father," Antonio said. "He is Giuseppe, but in the war, when he was with the partisans, he took the name Antonio. He still uses this name in the family, and with his friends who know him from that time."

Lucy saw again the bold signature at the bottom of the letter: *"ti abbraccio, Antonio."* "Your father?" she said, as all the little pieces fell into place. "It was your father who wrote that letter?"

"I am afraid this must be true, though, of course, I did not know of it until now."

"And it's your father who owns Catherine's gallery, who supports Catherine."

"This, unhappily, I know too well."

"And he stole Catherine from DV?"

"This was not a difficult feat," Antonio pointed out in his father's defense. "As soon as Caterina arrived, it was clear that she did not intend to stay very long with your friend. We invited them to dinner only once. They argued the entire evening. I thought her pretentious, without manners, and also very conceited, but my father was enchanted. Caterina had never one moment of interest in me. I have no money, you see; also I am not an admirer of her painting."

"I think she's a pretty good painter," Lucy said.

"Please, Lucia." He held his palm out and pulled his chin in as if to ward off a disagreeable odor. "She paints as she was taught. Her teachers may have had some ability, and she has learned to imitate them."

"Does your father think she's good?"

"My father is a fool," he exclaimed. "I do not want to believe this, but he has given me no choice. He has no ideas about her painting, however."

"I see," Lucy said. She finished off her coffee, hoping to clear out the last clinging webs of her confusion with the jolt of it. He was right: There was something academic about Catherine's painting. It was skillful, even facile. Lucy had been persuaded of its value and originality by Catherine herself, not by anything she had actually seen on the canvas. Antonio interrupted this reappraisal. "But listen, Lucia," he said. "Did you really imagine that I sent a love letter to this woman?" He looked serious, appalled, yet not entirely displeased by the proposition.

"I must admit," she said, "I did find that part hard to picture. But what else could I think?"

"And in these conversations with her she said nothing that made you think you were mistaken?"

"No. She acted as if she was independent. I assumed the gallery was hers. But Massimo figured it out because he happened to see your family name on a checkbook."

Antonio's good humor dissipated at this information and something of his habitual impatience surfaced. He pushed his coffee cup aside as if it, too, was annoying him. "Of course," he said. "Signor Compitelli. He has also been investigating my family?"

"I'm sorry," Lucy said. "He didn't want to do it. I put him up to it. He told me he thought it was improper."

"I wonder how he would know." His eyes engaged hers with a sudden cool effrontery that she could not meet. She examined the tablecloth, a pattern of swans swimming placidly under puffy clouds. "Please don't say anything awful about Massimo," she said.

"There is nothing awful to say, that I know of," he replied. "He is insignificant, a *noioso,* a type, I think that is correct."

Lucy kept her eyes on the swan. She was conscious of a burning desire to speak of Massimo, just to hear his name, to conjure him up for a few moments with someone who had actually seen him. This would be her last opportunity to do so. Yet she was hesitant in the face of Antonio's evident disapproval. Antonio had disabused her of several mistaken notions—of the actual and awful manner of DV's death, of Catherine's motives and ability, of his own involvement—and she had been willing, even eager, to grasp at whatever enlightenment he had to offer. He was alert and observant—she understood this now—nothing slipped by him. Any judgment he passed upon Massimo would be an informed one.

But Massimo is gone, she thought. There was no need to know anything more about him. Wouldn't she be better off embroidering the memory of him in silver thread, untarnished by the skeptical observations of an outsider? She followed the swan's gracefully curving neck with a speculative fingertip. "What type is that?" she said at last.

"A man of no property, and no breeding."

"His family is very old," she protested. "They've lived in Rome a thousand years."

"This is what he told you." Lucy made no reply, as this remark was not, as far as she could tell, a question. She regarded him anxiously. After a moment, he shrugged. "Well, it may be true. His cousin's family is very old."

"You know his cousin?"

"I know the family," he said. "The Tacchino. Their house is

not far from here, near the supermarket at Granagno. As Signor Compitelli was so eager to inform us, they can no longer maintain the property. They have sold off the farmhouse and much of the vineyard. Your friend is involved in an unpleasant lawsuit against his cousin. He hopes to profit in some way from the sale of the land, at the same time he discourages his cousin from parting with the house because he likes to stay there. He has no claim to anything, of course. His cousin tolerates him because their fathers were very close, and because Signor Compitelli is so enamored of the house. His great passion is to have a fine villa, though he has no hope of owning even an *appartmento*."

Lucy sipped the sweet wine, considering this new characterization of Massimo: the poor relation, house-poor, blood-proud. He had opened Catherine's checkbook because he wanted to see what she was worth; this struck her as entirely credible. His great passion, she thought.

"I don't like to think that such a person has made you unhappy," Antonio said.

Lucy looked up at last. His eyes rested upon her mildly now, with sympathetic interest. "It was my own foolishness," she said. "I knew what I was doing. And I am not unhappy."

"How extraordinary you are, Lucia," he exclaimed. "I thought so the first time I saw you, at your poor friend's funeral. You were so calm and thoughtful; you spoke to me of Santa Lucia, do you remember? Every time I have seen you, you have said something to surprise me. Today when you confided to me your feelings upon seeing the Bernini in Roma, I thought, She is speaking directly to my own suffering and showing me how to bear it."

Lucy listened openmouthed to this unexpected praise. "I thought you were contemptuous of me," she said.

"No, you must not think that," he assured her. "It is because I so rarely see anyone I admire that I am confused and cannot show my feelings. For this reason, I have few friends. But it would please me very much to count you among them, Lucia. It would be an honor to me."

How ironic, Lucy thought, that the only friend I have made on my trip is this plain man with his crippling family, his failed ambitions, and his ruined life. And he had been her friend from the start, steadfastly standing on the sidelines and wishing her well. He watched her now, his face set in an expression of hopeful expectancy, waiting for her answer to his modest request.

"For me, too," she said. "It would be an honor for me, too."

Chapter 22

HE EVENING WAS CLEAR and mild, and when she finished the dinner Signora Panatella had left her, which was like her first meal—cold meat, cheese, spinach, bread, and fruit—Lucy took the pitcher of wine and her glass out onto the terrace, where she sat for some time listening to the night birds and watching the stars grow bright against the blackening sky. Solitude and stillness suited her; she had had little of either since her arrival in Italy, and she welcomed the opportunity for reflection. Scattered impressions, snatches of conversation, half-formed observations and opinions flitted across her thoughts, and a sense of tranquil well-being settled upon her. She was returned to herself, and she had a heightened consciousness of the pleasure of her own company. She leaned back in the iron chair and sipped the wine unhurriedly. What a peaceful, quiet place this is, she thought. She heard Massimo's skeptical reply, "Quiet? The grave is quiet." She had recorded his voice, she noted, with astounding accuracy; the pitch, timbre, inflection, it was all there, stored in her memory, capable of intruding into her thoughts without being summoned. He would not, she reckoned, in some future colloquy with himself (indeed, it was unlikely that such a meeting might ever occur) call up willingly or not her own intonations or opinions. It requires a lively curiosity to identify and incorporate other voices than one's own, and Massimo was in short supply of that. He had, she knew, hardly listened to her voice at all.

Perhaps at some point in the future she would look upon their brief affair as a charming interlude, but now she was keenly aware of how disappointing it had been. She could not, she would not, magnify it into a grand passion, but neither could she take it lightly. She was conscious of a wish to do it justice. He had not been changed, but she had; there was something humiliating in that confession. She knew more about herself now, and what she knew, she did not admire.

She had proved an abysmally poor judge of character, that much was clear. In fact, she had gotten just about everything wrong. Antonio Cini was not a liar, but Massimo was. Catherine Bultman was not an artist struggling to maintain her integrity, but a self-centered opportunist. DV was not a victim of anything beyond his own drunkenness and a hopeless infatuation.

And Lucy Stark was not a practical, principled woman who was perfectly content to look on the folly of others with distant sympathy, but a foolish, impressionable creature, as much a prey to longings and cravings, as eager to justify her own impulsive behavior with an appeal to the sovereignty of passion over reason, as anyone else. She had not, as Massimo observed, really known all that much about what was "in" her character. And now she did. She sat under the stars on a perfect night, alone in a romantic setting, struggling to come to terms with this new view of herself, which allowed her, among other unthought-of liberties, to admit that she still longed for the embraces of a man she did not particularly like. Such wisdom as this led directly to cynicism; she recognized this possibility and set herself against it. She knew that when we prove small to ourselves, it is an easy matter to assume the world is smaller still.

And so she sat, far into the night, absorbed in the tiresome task of turning inward a searching and critical eye. When at last she gathered up the glass and empty pitcher, she was exhausted from the rigors of a profound introspection, but she had made peace with herself. She washed her few dishes and fell into the narrow bed gratefully.

But she slept poorly. Again and again she woke, confused and dislocated, with shreds of unsettling dreams, and the impression of speaking or of hearing someone speak lingering in the dark air of the room. She had only just drifted into a deep and peaceful sleep when she was awakened by the racket of a car toiling up the driveway. The shippers, she thought, though a glance at the clock assured her that it was much too early; they were not scheduled to arrive until noon. She threw on a T-shirt and jeans, brushed her hair with her hands, and rushed out the door to the terrace where she was met by Signora Panatella, her apron askew, patches of flour dotting her arms and her hair, thrusting out, with an expression of great urgency, a brown paper parcel. *"Buon giorno, signora,"* Lucy said, taking the package. Signora Panatella revolved in her tracks, muttering a brusque *"Buon giorno"* as she disappeared down the steps. An unwilling messenger, Lucy thought. *"Grazie, signora,"* she called after her. *"Grazie tante e arrivederla,"* but there was no reply. She never liked me, Lucy thought as she went back into the kitchen. She inspected the package sleepily. There was no label, only the word "Lucia," scrawled across the paper in an unusual purple ink. "Antonio," Lucy said. Was it a parting gift?

She went to the counter, cut the string with a knife, then, pulling away the paper, she sat down at the table. Inside she found a hand-written letter and a typed manuscript, not large, perhaps a hundred pages. She recognized the typeface—DV's old Royal. This is it, she thought. The rest of the ghost novel. The pages were unusually clean for DV; only the occasional typo had been corrected neatly with a blue pen. She turned to the letter and read:

Cara Lucia,

I hope you will forgive me for not giving you this manuscript sooner, and also for certain misleading statements I made to you about what happened before you came here.

When Signor Vandam died, I went to the farmhouse with Signora Panatella to help her find the name of someone to notify in America. I found this manuscript on the writing table. Your friend was evidently at work on it when he died. I took only a casual look before I realized that it concerned my family. Signor Vandam had not even bothered to change the names. I took it away with me that day.

When you came to our house that first night, you spoke of an unfinished manuscript. I thought you might mean this one, but when you described it, I knew it was not so. You were looking for a ghost story. This, as you will see, is a story of the war.

I did not like your friend, Lucia, but I did see him more than I led you to believe. After Caterina left, he became something of a problem here. In the mornings, he often took long walks, all the way to the town. To pass the time, and to keep an eye on him, I joined him on several occasions. From the beginning he expressed a great interest in the story of my uncle's death, and then in all the stories about the war in this neighborhood. I know a great many. It is a time my grandmother has always enjoyed talking about, though only when my father is away. He cannot bear to hear of it. I thought it might be good for your friend to find out something of the region. Though I knew he was a writer, it did not occur to me that his interest, which was often intense, was because he was using my stories, sometimes even my exact words, for his own purposes.

In the evenings, he drank a great deal, too much, and then he became difficult, full of anger and self-pity. He was a stranger to himself. At such times, he was convinced that my family was plotting against him. More than once I was waked very late at night to hear him shouting outside the house for my father to come down and fight with him. The next day, when he was sober, he appeared to have no recollections of these behaviors.

Often I encouraged him to return to his own country. He repeated that he could not go until he convinced Caterina to come back. One day he persuaded me to tell him where she was, and the next morning he took the car and tried to drive to Roma. But he could not find his way, and in the evening he returned, much dispirited. He did not take the car out again.

Obviously, I would prefer that these stories never be published, but after you and I parted today, I knew that to have a good conscience, I must send them to you, and trust to your discretion. You have spoken of Signor Vandam's books as very poor and full of lies about himself. Of course, I am no judge of such things, but this writing does not seem so bad to me. The story is melodrama, but it is not lies, and Signor Vandam is not in it.

Cara Lucia, I so much wish you would stay longer, and that we could pass again together an afternoon as delightful as this one was for me. I have been going over the conversations all this evening. In the morning, I will have Signora Panatella bring this package and this letter to you. I hope you will write to me, and when you have next the opportunity, you will return to stay in my house. There are many pictures and places I would want to show you. Until that time, I wish your trip to America without incidents.

> I send to you my most warm salutations,
> your friend,
> ANTONIO CINI

Lucy put the letter aside and looked at the top page of the manuscript. A stranger to himself, she thought. Antonio's description was an apt one. She pictured DV and Antonio walking together along the dusty road to Ugolino. Two more mismatched companions had probably never been seen in these parts. She glanced at the clock. There wasn't time to read it all, but she could look into it now and finish it on the plane. She got a glass of water from the tap and sat down to DV's manuscript, feeling, for the first time ever, a sense of keen anticipation for what she was about to read.

The manuscript was untitled. It began with a description of the scene—the villa, the farmhouse, the piazza in Ugolino—as it looked during the last war. There was a brief sketch of the Cini family. The mother, a stern, devout matriarch, whose husband had died shortly after the birth of her second son. As he was many years older than his wife, the father's death, though sudden, was not unnatural. The two fatherless boys, Gian Carlo and Giuseppe, shared a warm affection for each other, though they were different in every way. Gian Carlo, the heir, was a bookish, artistic boy, given to sketching architecture and researching the family history in dusty volumes he brought down from the attic. He was tall, dreamy, and his health was poor. Giuseppe was athletic, he liked hunting and preferred to be outdoors. He took an interest in the property, especially the vineyards, and at an early age began plans for their improvement and expansion.

DV told all this in a straightforward summary. Clearly he'd gotten the details from Antonio and filled in the rest with his own observations on their walks together.

Then the story jumped ahead. It was near the end of the war. The Italians had surrendered to the Allies who had landed in Sicily and were steadily pushing north. The German army, once Italy's partner in the Axis, was now an occupying force, furious with the Italians for having betrayed them. The Cini brothers had been enthusiastic supporters of Mussolini at the start, but as the war dragged on, Giuseppe became disillusioned, defied his mother and his older brother, and joined the partisans in the hills. The Americans landed in Sicily and began steadily pushing north. There were skirmishes all over Tuscany. After one such engagement, a German contingent passing near the villa learned from their informants that the capo of the local partisan unit was from the Cini family. They saw Gian Carlo on the drive near the farmhouse, mistook him for his brother, and shot him.

"Quite a story," Lucy said. She flipped through the pages to the scene of Gian Carlo's funeral.

They set out in the afternoon under a threatening sky. It was cold and damp. When the wind whipped up, the leaves made scurrying circles in the dirt. There were six of them, Giuseppe at the front of the coffin, his comrades ranged around it. In the night, they had made the coffin out of boards ripped from rifle crates. It was a poor box, but Giuseppe's cousin Lorenzo Pica from Spello was a fine carpenter and he showed them how to plane the boards smooth and groove the edges and how to fit it all together so that it would be watertight, better than most in this war. The women, Signora Cini, their neighbor Elena Caravita, and her mother, stayed up all night with Gian Carlo's body. They washed and dressed him and then they washed him again with their tears. They brushed his thick hair and buffed his nails and his mother slipped his father's wedding ring onto his finger and her own gold cross into his hand. In the morning, the women came down and lined the coffin, first with blankets and then with a bolt of dark blue silk that Elena had brought from her chest. She had been saving it until the spring, in the hope that the war would be over and she could make a new dress for the celebrations. They laid Gian Carlo in the silk and left the box open on the big dining table. The women made coffee and they all went into the kitchen to drink the coffee and to eat hard bread. The men went out to their posts to find out whether it would be safe to bury Gian Carlo that day. That was when they got the news that the Allies were advancing on Rome and that, in reprisal for a partisan attack in Via Rasella, the Germans had rounded up three hundred and thirty-five Roman civilians, driven them in trucks to the Ardeatine caves on the outskirts of the city, lined them up, and shot them.

With bitter hearts they met again at the villa and sat down to a bitter, joyless meal in the kitchen. When they told the women the news from the south, there were no tears, only bitterness closing them each in a circle of silence. They ate in silence, swallowed the wine in silence, and when the meal was over the only sound was their chairs scraping the stone floor as they pushed back from the table. They went out to the dining room where Gian Carlo lay in his poor coffin. They nailed on the lid, took their places on either side, lifted the box onto their shoulders, and set off down the long avenue of cypresses to the villa gate.

The wind whipped their clothes and chilled their skin as they pushed on, carrying their heavy load, their leaden hearts heavy in their chests. They jockeyed the coffin over the deep ruts left by the trucks and tanks and caravans of supplies, past the abandoned tires, the mounds of spent shells, shards of broken radio equipment, empty ration tins, and the endless trail of cigarette butts. Giuseppe's shoulder ached from the weight of the coffin. The edge wore a groove into his trapezius muscle and each step drove it in deeper. He welcomed the pain; he didn't want it to stop. Elena and his mother walked ahead, holding hands. Now and then Elena raised a hand to push back a strand of her hair. She'd tied it all back tightly with a black ribbon, but the golden strands came loose in the wind. The skirt of her black dress pressed against her legs and she bent her head down to keep the wind from her face. Giuseppe let his cheek rest against the coffin and fixed his eyes on Elena's back. He and Gian Carlo and Elena had played together as children, but now they were no longer children. The war had made them grow up all at once and cruelly; now Gian Carlo was gone, though he had been hardly more than a boy, and Elena Caravita—the wild, carefree girl they had shouted and sung with all the long, idle summers of their youth—was a bitter young woman leading a funeral procession. Giuseppe had known for some time that he loved Elena more than anything else in his life, except, perhaps, for Gian Carlo.

As they turned into the cemetery gate it began to rain, all at once and very hard. The sky is weeping for Gian Carlo, Giuseppe thought. They carried their burden across the graves to the new hole that was black and deep. The men shifted the coffin down to their hands. Giuseppe was facing his mother, but she didn't look at him. Elena was weeping into her shoulder and she was stroking Elena's hair. As the men lowered the coffin, Elena sank to her knees, clutching his mother's skirt. She turned toward the men. Her face was raised to Giuseppe's but she was not looking at him. She was blinded by the rain, and her tears, and her grief. As he watched, her mouth opened and she let out an animal howl of grief. She fell forward, face down in the mud, and didn't move, didn't even turn her face aside. His mother knelt beside her, stroking her back and shoulders. Giuseppe felt his heart turn into something cold and dead. He looked down at the coffin. She was in love with

Gian Carlo, they had been lovers; he knew that now. As far as
Elena was concerned the wrong brother had been killed. It
should have been Giuseppe. She would never change her mind
about that.

"Sad," Lucy said. It was ironic as well, devilishly so. Antonio was right. DV's style was melodramatic, but it suited the
story. She looked through the pages to the end. The war was
nearly over. The partisans in the north had ambushed Mussolini and his mistress as they tried to escape to Austria,
executed them, and strung their bodies up by their heels in
Piazzale Loreto in Milan. The Americans had arrived in Tuscany and set up headquarters in the police station in Ugolino.
They were in the bar giving out tins of Spam and chocolate.
Elena and Giuseppe were there in the piazza, celebrating with
their neighbors.

And that was it; he'd gotten no further. Lucy looked back
through the pages. They were hand-numbered to seventy, then
ten more without numbers. Eighty pages, she thought, a perfectly unpublishable length. And it had taken him five months
to get them, less than a page a day. Once Catherine left and he
had abandoned the ghost novel, he was thrown entirely upon
the unexercised resources of his own imagination. He was like
a man rushing headlong and oblivious through a forest, who is
suddenly struck blind and must feel his way forward, listening,
stumbling, attentive, wary, his progress slowed to a crawl. She
added to her picture of the floundering DV the appearance of
a pale hand, reaching out to him in the dark wood, helping
him to his feet, brushing him off, leading him out into the
open. Gradually, with Antonio as his guide, DV had begun to
imagine a world he knew nothing about. He was imagining
himself into the past, into the war, into the alien mind of his

rival. This was how he intended to get Catherine back. He was drinking, he was driving Antonio crazy, but he was working, too—slowly, to be sure, but at least he was working. Lucy got up and put the kettle on the stove, then took down the tea bags and a cup. He was certainly not the American writer endearing himself to the locals, but perhaps he wasn't entirely unhappy. Though he must have felt trapped, especially after he got Catherine's address from Antonio, then tried, and failed, to get to Rome.

DV always got lost, Lucy thought. Even when he had a good map. Sometimes he had called her to say he couldn't find the bookstore where he was due to give a reading in five minutes. "I don't know where I am," he would complain, and she would say, "Is there a bank with a name of the town on it, can you see a street sign?" Then she would call the bookstore and say, "He's coming. He got lost," and there would be a little banter about how writers always got lost because they were wandering around in a fantasy world. The kettle boiled and she filled her tea cup. He got lost, she thought. He got lost in Italy forever.

She would do as Antonio requested, though not solely because he wanted the manuscript repressed. She was certain no one, not even Stanton Cutler, would be willing to publish it. It was too short, unfinished; even if it had been finished, DV's readers would not tolerate a book about dead Italians in which the popular American writer didn't make an appearance.

Later, Lucy put the manuscript in her carry-on suitcase, showered, and dressed for her trip. When the shippers arrived at noon, she was ready for them. They turned out to be two handsome men, one tall, one short, who knew only a few words of English between them. Lucy led them to DV's apartment and pointed out the boxes, which they immediately attacked, taping and numbering each one with speed and efficiency; Lucy remarked to herself that Italy was indeed a land of contrasts. The boxes began to disappear one by one into a bright new van they had pulled up flush to the bougainvillea arbor. The taller one gave Lucy a form in four languages, which she filled out with Jean McKay's address and phone number, the information that the boxes contained books, papers, and personal effects, and the promise that the shipping costs would be paid on arrival in the States. The whole process was finished in under an hour. Lucy received one of the many copies of the lading bill, there was a brief exchange of thanks and farewells, and they drove away.

She stood in the doorway, jangling the house keys until the truck was out of sight. Then she turned back into the apartment. There was one small item of DV's Italian business left to attend to.

She had not packed the love letter with the rest of DV's papers. Her reasoning was simple: She did not believe it belonged to him. She had left it where she'd found it, in the drawer next to his bed. But she knew if she didn't move the letter now, it would fall into the hands of Signora Panatella, who would, Antonio had warned her, start preparing the apartment for Lucy's successors the minute she was out of the driveway. In one sense, she thought, it would serve the elder Cini right to have the evidence of his current folly fall into the hands of the Panatellas, his former tenants. They would not be, as she had been, confused by the signature, for they had undoubtedly seen examples of the handwriting of all three generations of Cinis presently residing in the villa. But Lucy disliked providing her landlords with such fuel for gossip and sneering. Though it was unlikely that he would ever learn of it, she knew it would wound Antonio sorely if he ever did find out. Lucy was in the odd position of wanting to protect Antonio from a humiliation he might never actively feel. But he would feel it, she thought. He was sensitive about his family; his father's connection with Catherine was a thorn in the side of his highly developed amour propre and it vibrated painfully with the slightest breath of scandal.

No, she concluded, it was none of the Panatellas' business, nor anyone else's, for that matter. Her options were clear. The letter should be returned to its sender, sent on to Catherine, or destroyed. As she slipped the key into the door beneath the bougainvillea arbor, another possibility presented itself. She could send the letter to Antonio and let him decide what should be done.

Yesterday, on parting, she had exchanged addresses with Antonio. He had written his carefully into her notebook in small neat handwriting, completely unlike his father's bold magisterial style. "Do you think you might ever come to America?" Lucy asked as she tore out a deposit slip from her checkbook to give him in return.

"I think that is very unlikely," he said. "I am always here, you see." He opened his hands, indicating the hills, the trees, the dome of the sky. The corners of his mouth lifted slightly in an expression Lucy might once have characterized as sardonic, though now it struck her as self-mocking, a form of modesty. He was, in the oddest way she could ever have imagined, an unassuming man. "But if you come to Italy again, Lucia," he said, "you will not forget to visit me, I hope. And you will not stay in this. . . ." He dragged his eyes contemptuously over the farmhouse. "There are so many rooms in my house. If you would be interested, I will take you to see the frescoes of Piero in Arezzo and the *Madonna del Parto*, as well. That is not to be missed."

"I'd like that," she said. "I'd like that very much."

If I survive the car ride, Lucy thought now as she opened

the door. Perhaps she could persuade him to let her do the driving. She crossed the chilly sitting room to the stairs, shivering involuntarily. This apartment was always colder than the smaller one. When she and Massimo had stayed here, he brought over all the blankets and piled them up on the big bed upstairs, the only one in the house that could accommodate two people comfortably. Massimo couldn't stand being cold. Lucy looked up the wide staircase, recalling how laboriously she had climbed it then, how she had leaned on his arm while he paused on each step, how excited she had been at the prospect of passing the whole long night by his side. She hurried up the stairs, away from this memory, which seemed to come from a much deeper past than that indicated by its actual distance in time. On the landing, she stopped and stared into DV's study, bothered by an even nearer recollection, that of closing the door behind her as she followed the intrepid moving men down the stairs. She had not done it for any reason, but she knew she had done it, had felt the latch slip into place as she released the heavy glass knob, but now the door stood wide open. "This house has a mind of its own," she said. She stepped into the room and looked about. The shutters were closed, the light was dim, but she could see that everything was orderly and as she had left it, the bed neatly made, the table cleared, the chair drawn up against it. She pulled the door nearly closed and stepped back to see if it would drift open in response to some imperceptible slant in the floor. It stayed just as she had placed it.

"My mind is going," she said, turning away. She must have been mistaken about closing the door. She went into the bedroom, opened the drawer in the bedside table, and took out the letter. The sounds of wood rubbing against wood as the drawer slid open and the whisper of the paper as she lifted the envelope out of the drawer made sudden intrusive explosions in the ponderous stillness of the house. She could feel it brooding over her like some heavy, muffling feathered creature settling down upon the smooth, hard shells of its own future. Though she had no need to open the letter and had taken it with no intention of doing so, something in the eerie silence of the place made her want to rupture it, and the rustling of the paper seemed as good a way as any.

Again she read the elaborate address: *Carissima, amatissima,* but this time she pictured not the bland, world-weary countenance of the younger Cini, but the fierce-eyed hawklike visage of his father. The old man had courted Catherine with all the passionate abandon of the old, dead world in which he had come of age; it was the only way he knew, and Catherine had thought so little of his effort, she hadn't bothered even to keep track of it. Or perhaps she had left the letter here on purpose to enrage DV, who would have had to spend some time over a dictionary figuring out what was going on right under his nose. Lucy imagined herself into the scene of her dead employer's unhappiness. As mysteriously as Catherine had come into his life—for the entrance of the one who can totally destroy our happiness is always a cloak-and-dagger affair—Catherine was gone out of it, and he was left in a foreign country with no one to contradict the ringing of her harsh judgment against him. DV had been a man of few resources, with the interior life of a brick. He had believed Catherine was the real thing, the very thing he needed, and that she would open the way for him into the sacred grove of art, where inspiration and wisdom flow eternally in twin streams from the same mythic fount. Instead, Catherine had thrown him out, slammed the gate in his face, and adjured him to take up gardening.

This last image made Lucy smile; it was so like that of the

first expulsion, the one she had thought she saw echoed in Catherine's paintings: DV, expelled from paradise, condemned to Tuscany.

The silence of the room was pierced by the harsh cry of a crow near the window, and then another, farther off, in response.

They had all just wanted to get rid of him, Lucy thought. Catherine, the old man, Antonio, the Panatellas, but he had refused to go. And after he was dead, everyone wanted to forget him, get him buried, distribute the proceeds, close the books. She recalled the night she was burning with fever and DV had visited her in a fury, shaking her until she thought her neck would snap. The old man had stolen his love, Antonio had stolen his manuscript, he had died ignominiously, confused and drunk, wandering alone in the dark. No wonder he was in a rage.

Lucy felt a pang of sadness and another of guilt. She had intended to visit his grave to make sure the stone was suitable and to plant something that would grow without care, but she had been so caught up in her foolish love affair that she had failed to do it and now it was too late. "I'll do it when I come back," she said, though she had no idea when that might be. She folded the letter and slipped it into its envelope. She would destroy this letter. It had done enough damage already. She reached out to close the drawer, but her hand stopped just short of its destination, for in this motion she had turned toward the doorway, where her eyes were assaulted by a sight that froze her from head to foot as thoroughly as if she had been plunged into a glacial pool. The door to DV's study was open.

Lucy's eyes strained forward in their sockets, and she was dimly aware that for some moments now there had been a barely audible sound; she could make it out with difficulty through the roar of her own heart, a steady, scratching sound, like fingernails on smooth wood. She gave herself several moments of counsel before she could move even her eyelids. It was impossible for anyone to be in the room she had just vacated; the only entrance was from the landing. The scratching sound was not new; she had heard it before in this house, and it was probably attributable to mice or insects gnawing between the walls. The open door was obviously . . . well, it was obviously just one of those doors. This last rationalization was so feeble, it gave her more trouble than comfort. She could not recall ever encountering one of those doors before. But her fevered reasoning had sufficed to bring her heart down to a dull pounding, like a distant pile driver, and she was able to raise her hand to wipe away the moisture that bathed her forehead and upper lip. Except for the scratching sound, which was intermittent now, the quiet around her was intense. She took one, then another, step toward the landing, moving stealthily, in exaggerated slow motion, as if she really did expect to surprise some intruder, though the truth, she realized, was that she was actually moving as quickly as she could. In this way, she crossed the landing. If only all the shutters weren't closed, she thought. How absurd this trepidation and caution would be if there were a flood of sunshine to light the way. She would stride into the room, look about boldly, and stride right out again.

At the threshold of the door, she stopped and looked wistfully down the staircase. Was there really any need to investigate further this nagging mystery of the open door? She had the letter; it was all she had come for. She could simply descend the stairs, lock the door, and walk away. Surely she would have no reason ever to enter this house again. As she had the thought that the scratching sound had stopped, it started up again. Then she heard something else, something small, but so clear and recognizable, her heart took off before it like a spooked horse and she felt her ears pulling away from her head. It was the delicate whoosh of a piece of paper sliding off a table onto the floor. She was close enough now to see into the room by leaning forward. She would then have a clear view of everything but the bed. Just lean forward, she told herself. Just look in quickly and then go on down the stairs. Another moment of perfect silence passed, no scratching, no breathing; then Lucy rested one hand on the doorsill, stretched out her neck, and peered into the room.

There was a man sitting at the table, his back to the door, hunched over a sheet of paper, holding a pen poised above the page in one hand, his cheek resting in the open palm of the other. Though there was everything in the picture to excite Lucy's terror—the sheer impossibility of it was enough to unhinge her reason—there was nothing of threat or danger in the aspect of the man. He did not appear to sense her presence, or if he did, it was of no interest to him. As Lucy watched, her brain awash in conflicting assertions about the exact nature of reality, the pen came down and scratched out several words across the page, then lifted, poised again for action. The man stretched his fingers from his cheek to his eyes and rubbed them hard, then readjusted his position so that his chin rested on the ledge of a loose fist. Lucy had not moved a hair; indeed, she had hardly breathed since the moment her astounded eyes had found him. He studied his page and she studied him, both of them motionless and absorbed by their contemplations. Everything about him was familiar, though it was difficult in the gloom of the shuttered room to make out much in the way of particulars. And there seemed to be a deeper gloom, a gathered gloom, about the entire figure of the man, as if he absorbed what little light there was, so that he was outlined by a nimbus of darkness. How could he even see what he was writing? she thought uselessly. But evidently he could see, for the pen came down again, this time in a series of quick strokes, striking out the words he had just written. He threw the pen down on the page and buried his face in his hands. His shoulders shuddered; was he weeping?

Lucy relaxed her grip on the sill, but her knees were much too weak and her brain much too startled to attempt anything as demanding as speech or motion. She was condemned to stand in this tense, attenuated posture, watching an unbelievable tableau. The pen began to roll toward the edge of the table, claiming the attention of its owner, who lifted his face from his hands and looked down upon it. He stopped its progress, took it up again, and, as he did so, something caught his attention. He turned his head slightly. Lucy could see a little of his profile. There was a piece of paper near his foot; this was what he had noticed. He stared at it for several long moments, as if he was not sure what was to be done about it. Then, slowly, with an effort that seemed enormous and completely disproportionate to the task, he pushed back his chair and reached down through the dark air to retrieve the page that had strayed from him. Lucy drew in her breath and held it. Her mouth stayed open, her throat contracted over a sound she could not utter, and her heart bucked in her chest. As the man leaned over the floor, he turned toward the doorway and Lucy saw his face. It was DV.

Her head whirled; the world whirled about her head. She was fainting; she would fall into the room. He remained as he was, one arm stretched out to reach the paper, his face lifted over his shoulder to take her in, for he saw her, too; she had no doubt of that. His face was ravaged almost past recognition. The gray webbed skin stretched taut against the bones, his dark lips looked more like a black smear than a mouth, and his eyes, red-rimmed and hollow, were wide with a speechless horror, as if he were ever in the presence of his own reflection. And yet those eyes burned into the space between them, burned into Lucy's consciousness with such force, they seemed to hold her up. What agony was this, what unthinkable depths of suffering had he endured? He held her in his gaze for a moment with an expression of such mute and eloquent pleading that her fear evaporated and she understood he was incapable of harm. He was incapable of everything but suffering. And when she had understood this, he released her. Giving a sigh so deep that it seemed to come from the bottom of the world, he turned away, back to the problem of picking up the page, which he accomplished. Then he took up his pen again, bent over the table, and resumed the eternal labor of his composition.

"Oh Lord," Lucy said. She let herself fall back against the wall and slid down to the floor, where she sat with her legs splayed out before her, unable and unwilling to move. Her breathing was rapid and deep, as if she had been running. She closed her eyes and rolled her head back against the wall. It was impossible. That was all she knew. DV was certainly dead. He was not still sitting in this damned farmhouse trying to write a decent sentence. People had hallucinations; she had had one—that was possible. She opened her eyes. She was still holding the letter; she had, in fact, been gripping it so furiously, it was creased and damp. "I'm burning this," she said. "First opportunity." She pressed her palm against her chest. Her heart was still beating away in there, pumping ordinary blood in the ordinary way. She edged along the floor toward the stairs. She wasn't looking into the room again. She didn't need to. She could tell he had gone; she could feel it in the air, which had perceptibly lightened and grown warmer. She could see a slab of light across the floor at the foot of the staircase pouring in from the window near the door. Just get down there, she advised herself, any way you can. She negotiated the first few steps sitting down, like a baby. Then she stuck the letter in the waistband of her pants and hauled herself up by the rail, holding on to it with both hands while she made her way down to the sitting room. Her heart rate had slowed, but her thoughts raced out of all control, leaping and raging, colliding with one another, crashing up against the solid walls of reason and sanity, which she was now heartily grateful she had spent so many years constructing. She had never imagined they would have to stand against such an assault as this, but stand they did. "I'm not mad," she said. She crossed the sitting room and threw open the door upon the fresh, welcome light of day. It was behind her now, this thing, this horror, whatever it was; it was gone and she would never speak of it to anyone as long as she lived. She breathed in and out slowly, counting a few breaths, and then she concentrated for a moment on the reassuring beauty of the bougainvillea flowers, still blooming, though it was certainly late in the year. She heard the sound of a car in the distance, approaching rapidly along the road at the bottom of the hill. She lifted her head, listening closely. Yes, it was making the turn into the drive. It was the driver, coming to take her away from here, to the airport and then to Brooklyn. Back to Brooklyn! she thought with a thrill of pure joy. She stepped out into the drive. She could see the car now whirling up the hill, and as she watched its steady progress, she was overcome by a powerful exultation. DV would be here forever, but she did not have to stay. *"Andiamo,"* she said, striding purposefully away from the house and down the drive to welcome her deliverer.

ACKNOWLEDGMENTS

ROME, "the eternal city," has perhaps earned its sobriquet for the never-ending restoration work that has occupied its industrious citizens for centuries. Since Lucy Stark's visit, the scaffolding that for so many years hid the Galleria Borghese from view has come down, revealing an impressive facade of beautiful proportions and nearly blinding whiteness. The visitor now enters via a grand staircase, there are modern bathrooms, a souvenir shop, and long, long lines of eager art lovers waiting to get inside.

I would like to thank Stefano and Anna Rizzo, Roberto Chiappini, Mavi Cini, Alice Falconi, and Walter Falconi for their hospitality and patient interest in my questions about all matters Italian, from property law to plumbing.

Thanks also to my agent, Nikki Smith, for her tireless defense of my interests; to my editor, Robin Desser, for her energy and enthusiasm; to John Cullen, for reading and correcting this manuscript repeatedly, intelligently, and generously; and to my daughter, Adrienne, as always, for inspiration.

A Note About the Author

Valerie Martin is the author of six novels, including *The Great Divorce* and *Mary Reilly,* as well as two collections of stories. She lives in upstate New York.

A Note on the Type

The text of this book is set in Sabon, a typeface designed by Jan Tschichold (1902–1974), the well-known German typographer. Based loosely on the original designs by Claude Garamond (c. 1480–1561), Sabon is unique in that it was explicitly designed for hot-metal composition on both the Monotype and Linotype machines as well as for filmsetting. Designed in 1966 in Frankfurt, Sabon was named for the famous Lyons punch cutter Jacques Sabon, who is thought to have brought some of Garamond's matrices to Frankfurt.

Composed by NK Graphics,
Keene, New Hampshire

Printed and bound by R.R. Donnelley & Sons,
Harrisonburg, Virginia

Designed by Cassandra J. Pappas